The People Factory

Iain M Grant

Pigeon Park Press

Paperback ISBN: 978-0-9933149-6-4
Ebook ISBN: 978-0-9933149-7-1

Cover artwork and design copyright © John Bowen 2016

Published by Pigeon Park Press

www.pigeonparkpress.com
info@pigeonparkpress.com

- The Death of Hartagga of the Lukka Tribes 5
- St Quiricus and St Julietta 11
- The Ballad 15
- The Sultan's Dream 23
- Eustachius Martingale 29
- A Feast of Bats 49
- Osloff and the Turk 55
- And children love kittens 98
- Blaubart 117
- Appropriate Thunder 125
- Three Birds of Saint-Cyr 133
- Numbers 137
- Sanders 146
- Blalk 156
- Eulogy 162
- The Land of Take-What-You-Want 168
- Hrönir Malin 177
- The Token 185
- The People Factory 189

- The Mumblies 205
- Made To Love 213
- The Town...227
- The Train...234
- Smooshy Girl, Smooshy Boy 243
- The Final Vindication of Hartagga of the Lukka Tribes .253

The Death of Hartagga of the Lukka Tribes

They dragged him into the courtyard of the king and threw him down at the feet of the usurper who had brought not only bloodshed to the once-proud city of Tarsa but also the foetid stink of his army of freebooters, of unperfumed men in badly cured leather.

Arkamijala rolled painfully on his bloodied knees and gasped as his broken fingers touched the sand of the courtyard floor. He raised his head as best he could. He had been inside the palace on more than one occasion and was dismayed at the changes Hartagga of the Lukka tribes had worked on the place. The white sand was stained with wine and clumps of horse dung. The pool that had once held dozens of tiny gold and silver fish in its clear depths was now clouded and dead. The fine curtains of Damascus cloth had been artlessly ripped down and used to cover figures that lay in the shadows of the colonnade (though whether as bed sheets or death shrouds, Arkamijala could not tell).

The bandit chief, Hartagga, gripped the arms of the dead king's summer throne and leaned forward to peer at the broken storyteller.

"And what is this?" he asked, as though regarding something he had found under the sole of his sandal.

One of the men who had dragged Arkamijala in prodded the broken man with his bronzed sword. The other spat on the sands and said, "A storyteller, Hartagga."

Hartagga grunted with laughter.

"Do you not know I have banned stories in my kingdom?" he asked.

"You have been our king for two nights," said Arkamijala. "I did not know, sire."

"Then you shall be the example that teaches others the danger of foolish words," said Hartagga.

Arkamijala coughed, feeling each of his ribs as a splintered rod of hot iron.

"And does my king fear words? Fear them more than the armies of Shalmaneser?"

Hartagga stood then.

"The Assyrians might come to reclaim their city. They might come tomorrow; they might come after the rains. Let them dash themselves against our walls – my walls. If the gods choose it, let the walls crumble and the Assyrians take us and strangle us and display our bodies for the sun and wind to eat. But words... words sneak upon us, stab us with their meanings, and bind us to their own truth."

"Words are nothing but words," said Arkamijala. "Sounds in the air and lines in the sand."

But Hartagga was shaking his head.

"When I was married, my wife and I spoke vows of love and fidelity to one another. Only afterwards did I see that my Warsa, my dew of the morning, had tied me up in those vows and bound me to herself. I could not forgive this crime, but even as I had her buried in the salt plains, she cried out to me, declaring her love."

Hartagga stepped forward.

"And I felt my love for her too. Ellel, he who lives in the thunder and the lightning and does not die, makes vows and oaths unbreakable and had forged chains from my wife's words. But I was strong enough to resist, to see the trap into which she was pulling me. I fought against those bonds, and I myself threw the last fistfuls of dry earth down on her mewling mouth. What story?"

"Sire?" asked Arkamijala.

"The story you were telling when my men took you."

Arkamijala, who had once played lyre and cymbal for the old king, stared bow-headed at the bloodied and swollen ruin of his hands.

"A children's tale, to entertain my sister's children."

"What tale?"

"A fiction of my own devising." Arkamijala hesitated a moment. "A tale of a boy and a girl, both with hair the colour of honey, who visit three caves, each inhabited by a fearsome bear who is out hunting. They eat his food, sleep in the empty beds, and when the bear returns -"

"Enough!" said Hartagga.

There was a smile on his lips. He clicked his finger for a boy to bring him wine. And he drank.

"My father named me Hartagga, the bear. Perhaps your story is about me."

"No, sire."

"Perhaps I have pillaged your city, taken your finest youths as my slaves and put men to the sword because of the name my father gave me: Hartagga, the bear, the wild slayer. Perhaps if he had named me Wukali, the goat, I would have lived as a shepherd on the shores of the Middle Sea."

The bandit chief's men laughed dutifully.

"Or maybe I should have been named Susil, the squid."

Hartagga flipped aside his leather skirts and relieved himself in the fish pool.

"The nomadic tribes of Israel hold that Ellal, who has many names, has one true name of four sounds, and that he formed the lands and the seas through the utterance of that one name. Words make our world and shape it."

"But I am not a god," pleaded Arkamijala.

"But you speak words. Sounds on the air and lines in the sand. Whispers in the world. Who knows, maybe you have conjured into existence caves and bears that now await me. You spin horrors with your lying tongue."

"Sire," said Arkamijala, "I implore your forgiveness. I will tell no more stories."

"Indeed," said Hartagga, and waved forward a man with tongs and a pair of shears.

Arkamijala cried and made to stand but Hartagga's warriors held him.

Arkamijala screamed and pleaded to the gods and offered bargains to Hartagga that he had no power to deliver. And then, only when the shears were before his face, the stink of goat hair still on them, did Arkamijala threaten the bandit chief.

"Three words!" he yelled. "The gods will kill you with three words! If -"

But he could say no more for the man had seized his tongue, pulled, and with two snips of the shears, cut it out of the storyteller's mouth. Arkamijala fell to the floor, blood spilling from his mouth like vomit, screaming wordlessly, forever wordlessly.

Hartagga had the storyteller thrown out into the street and his offensive tongue nailed to the door of the king's palace as a warning to all.

The following morning, Hartagga of the Lukka tribes was woken and called to the city walls by the captain of his guard. The captain pointed out over the scrubby plain. Hartagga peered out and saw a rock on which a carving had appeared in the night.

Hartagga could not read and was glad of the fact, but knew writing when he saw it. Hartagga and three of his men saddled up and, taking one of the captive scribes of the old king with them, rode out to the rock. It was as high as three men, and a curving ideogram had been hewed by hand from the sandy stone. There were cuts, sharp and rounded, in the surface, and bloody fingerprints across the whole – as though the writer had worked his fingers to the bloody bone to create a single word.

"Hartagga," said the scribe. "Bear."

"So it is for me," said the bandit chief, already scouting around for tracking signs.

They were not difficult to spot. The writer of the word had left on foot, heading east towards the mountains.

The men rode east until the tracks grew faint among hard stones and featureless lands. Before the tracks became unreadable, they found another word by the bed of a dried-up river. It was not as clear a sign as the previous word, made up as it was from light rocks placed as a mosaic over a darker flat rock, corners and lines found among carefully selected stones that bore droplets of the writer's still-glistening blood.

"Jakrim," said the scribe. "Cave."

Hartagga wheeled his horse and scoured the slopes about him. The tracks that had led them here went no further, petering out on the unimpressionable stone.

"Is he taunting us?" cried the bandit king.

"There are caves to the east," said one of his men. "Less than a half day's ride."

And so the five of them made further eastward, the sun no longer ahead of them but above them, and in time they came to a high place not far from the road to Hattusha. Beneath a sharp escarpment, Hartagga saw deep overhangs and the dark mouths of caves. He ran up, his sandalled feet slipping on loose earth, and found a third word.

The scribe scrambled awkwardly to reach his new king.

The scribe looked at the single symbol, painted on the rock in blood. It glistened darkly, still wet.

"Lalissa," said the scribe. "Thunder."

Hartagga automatically looked to the skies, expecting against all expectation to see clouds forming, but it was a fine day. The cold high wind dragged faint wisps of cloud across the heavens but that was all.

He touched the bloody paint and felt its tackiness between his fingertips.

"So," he said to himself and, drawing his bronzed sword, stepped into the nearest cave.

Hartagga was no fool and did not rush into the darkness. If there were bears, conjured by the storyteller's unnatural stories, then Hartagga would see them before they saw him. But there was no bear, only a man, in the farthest corner of the shallow cave. Hartagga's men drew close, in case the man attacked, but the figure in the shadows remained still. Hartagga recognised the orange and brown weave of the storyteller's robes.

"You have brought the bear to your cave but where is your thunder?"

The storyteller Arkamijala did not respond and Hartagga knew that he was dead. He stepped forward. Arkamijala's mouth and chin were black with dried blood, but his flesh was otherwise pale and lifeless. Hartagga lifted one of the man's hands and saw that it was a ruin, like the chewed end of a knuckle bone, the dusty blood with which the storyteller had painted his final word dried in that mess of broken fingers and scoured flesh.

"Words," said the bandit king wearily. "Words and madness."

He then became aware of a sound, very faint at first but rapidly growing in volume and timbre. It growled like a gathering storm, rumbling with the force of an oncoming tide.

Hartagga and his men rushed to the cave entrance. An endless column of chariots approached at speed, passing the base of the escarpment, already cutting off Hartagga and his men from their horses. The bandit king looked at the studded wheels and white horses, the high helmets and the swords gleaming in the sun, and recognised that this was the army of Shalmaneser the Assyrian, on their way to besiege Tarsa.

The lead charioteers had already seen them and wheeled their way. The captive scribe was already running away, pointing violently and shouting in a language that Hartagga did not understand.

Words. Sounds in the air.

Hartagga of the Lukka tribes held his sword high and charged at his enemies.

Some said that Hartagga was slain by an archer before he reached the Assyrians. Others asserted that he was taken alive, strangled before the throne of Shalmaneser, and his body displayed for the sun and wind to eat. But only the god Ellel, he who lives in the thunder and the lightning and does not die, knows all.

• St Quiricus and St Julietta

Here, we see Julietta and her infant son, Quiricus, hand in hand. Here, we see Quiricus, improbably sat astride a wild boar. Here, alone, Julietta is seen variously holding a cross, a palm leaf and the reins of an oxen. Now, in a darker representation, we see Quiricus's death, the boy dashed to the ground (or, otherwise, a flight of stairs); a fountain of blood gushes from his head. And here, Julietta's own death, perhaps bleeding from multiple wounds or in silent agony as she is burned at the stake. Roman Catholic iconography gives us these two saints in their formal poses, imposing and impossible snapshots of ancient lives.

Quiricus and Julietta also find representation in an eighth century fresco in the Santa Maria Antiqua in Rome. Scenes from their lives are similarly enacted upon a twelfth century altar frontal, now housed in the Museum of Barcelona, and in stained-glass windows in Issoudun. They appear as statues in the church of St Quiricus and St Julietta in Tickenham, North Somerset: Quiricus' moment of martyrdom in the south parapet; Julietta, holding a sword, in the east parapet. Three similarly dedicated churches can be found in Cornwall, at Luxulyan, St Veep and Calstock. The infant saint's name is variously given as St Cyriac, St Ciricus and St Cyriacus, and it is after him that the Caribbean island of Saint-Cyr is named.

The story of Quiricus and Julietta begins in fourth century Lycaonia, that high, cold land of sheep and wild asses, hemmed in by Galatia to the north, Cappadocia to the east, Mount Tarsus to the south, and Phrygia and Pisidia to the west. Lycaonia's salty and drought-struck plains nourished naught but hardy grasses, discontent, and a desperate, amateurish lawlessness. However, the city of Iconium, which straddled the trade route from Ephesus to the Cilician gates at the very point where it passed through Lycaonia's most fertile lands, was the one place of consistent prosperity – not a beacon of civilisation, but a poorly expressed suggestion of what the Lycaonians might have been capable of had the fates ever smiled on them.

Julietta and her son lived in Iconium. She was a widow. We know nothing of her husband save that, having left her with a young son and a handsome pension, he had been neither old nor poor. Julietta was also a Christian. Again, sources do not furnish us with the details. When had she converted to the Christian faith? Was this a point of disagreement between her and her husband or had he too been a convert? Was his death somehow linked to his piety or possibly his lack of it? There is only conjecture on this point.

During the Maximinian persecution, Julietta was compelled to flee Iconium, taking with her two loyal maidservants and her son, Quiricus. Some sources say they travelled first to Seleucia Sidera, a city famed for its iron-works. Others say they went to wild and rebellious Isauria. Whichever was the case, there they found a Roman governor, Alexander, whose anti-Christian zeal far outshone that of the rulers of Iconium; and Julietta's small party was forced to move on once more.

Finally, they came to Tarsus in Cilicia. Since the time of Paul, there had been a Christian community at Tarsus and, for a while at least, Julietta and Quiricus would have been among friends. It is likely that they knew the man who would become St Boniface. Unfortunately, Tarsus was not to be a sanctuary for long. Whilst paying a visit to the city, Governor Alexander saw and recognised Julietta and she was arrested and placed on trial.

Quiricus was with Julietta in the courtroom. His age is given as either three months or three years. The number three is not insignificant in Christian folklore. Julietta stoically refused to answer the questions put to her by Alexander, except to acknowledge her name and that she was a Christian. Faced with such a response, the court was quick to pronounce its sentence: she was to be stretched upon the rack and then beaten.

The guards, making to take Julietta away, tore the crying Quiricus from his mother's arms. Alexander, perhaps in an attempt to calm the terrified toddler, perhaps to speed the woman's exit from the court, took Quiricus and danced him on his lap. Quiricus kicked out at Alexander and scratched his face. In one account, it is said that he then declared his own undying Christian faith, although it is hard to imagine these words coming from the mouth of a three year old, let alone a three month old babe. Wounded and enraged, Alexander hoisted up Quiricus by his ankle and hurled him down the steps of the platform on which his magisterial throne sat. Dashing his head against the stone stair fractured Quiricus' skull and he died instantly.

To comprehend what happened next requires an understanding of the mentality of the early Christians, for Julietta rejoiced at her son's death. There may have been tears but they were tears of joy. Quiricus had died for the Christian faith and so his crown of martyrdom was assured. At that moment, Alexander must have looked on Julietta as a woman deranged, a woman infected by an impenetrable belief system that, despite all efforts to suppress it, was devouring the empire he served. He looked on Julietta and found only rage in his heart. The rack was suddenly too good for her. Some say he decreed her sides be ripped open with hooks. Others say she was drowned in burning pitch. Others say she was beheaded. Whatever the case, Julietta went to her death with a glad heart and a prayer of thanks on her lips.

The bodies of Quiricus and Julietta were flung from the city walls onto a heap made up of the corpses of foreigners, criminals and the nameless. Julietta's loyal maidservants searched the pile, retrieved the pair and buried them in a field some distance from the city.

Two years after their death, the man they had known as Boniface was killed for protesting against the persecution of Christians. This was the era of martyrs and no Christian could hope for a greater honour.

The Golden Legend tells that Charlemagne once dreamt of meeting St Quiricus and the boy appeared to him naked and riding upon a wild boar. Throughout France, where his cultus was once strong, he is referred to as Saint Cyr.

In the *Decretum Gelasianum*, a sixth century papal text, the acts of Saints Cyricus and Julitta were declared non-canonical and of apocryphal origin.

Many modern scholars argue the point further and say the holy mother and child never existed at all.

The Ballad

Stamford's spear bent like a bow as the bear's weight sank upon it but, against all credence, it did not break and the spear passed through the bear's thick hide and rode up into the creature's heart. The bear growled mournfully, spitting a cloud of condensation into the air, and then collapsed onto its side.

Stamford, wiping a trickling raindrop from the end of his nose, got painfully to his feet. He looked down at his boots, now filled with mud, and cursed.

The bear was not yet dead. As it fought for breath its dirty great flank rose and fell like a newlywed couple's bed linen.

"Your sword, my lord," said Stamford.

Henry de Valence gave the grizzled soldier a questioning look.

"The coup de grace," said Stamford.

Henry nodded in understanding and stepped forward. The young knight raised his sword and brought it down in an executioner's chop, ripping open the bear's throat and partially severing its neck. Hot blood gurgled onto the soil.

The news that John of Rensey's only daughter, Matilde, had been killed by a bear had spread across the county with unholy speed. Her not entirely undeserved reputation as one of the most beautiful young women in Henry of Winchester's England gave legs to the bad news. As always, each retelling brought new embellishments to the tale and some truly outrageous stories were passed on as God's own truth, but certain facts were a matter of record or witnessed by persons of impeccable character.

She had met her doom whilst out riding with Henry De Valence, the third son of the Earl of Pembroke. With Matilde's cousin, Mary, as chaperone, they had ridden north from her father's manor, along the brook and into the lighter part of the Wychwood. Bears and English wolves were known to habit that area (it was even said there were wild men in those woods who still offered inhuman sacrifices to Wotan, Thor and older gods) but Henry de Valence was young, strong and a gifted swordsman. Two hours after setting out, Mary returned to the manor at Shipton and raised the alarm. The reeve and three of John's men immediately rode north to where Henry held vigilant guard over the corpse.

There was no doubting that it was a wild animal that had killed her. Her body had been brutally savaged. One of her arms had been torn off and was never recovered, presumably consumed by the monstrous animal.

The corpse was wrapped in cloth, laid over the back of the reeve's horse and taken back to Shipton Manor. At the manor house, Henry threw himself on the floor before John of Rensey, lord of Shipton-under-Wychwood, and wept. John did nothing for a great while and then got up and embraced Henry with some muttered words of prayer. John then took himself away to grieve in private. Matilde was entombed in the family chapel the following day.

Though there was much mourning to be done, there were also practical and political matters to be attended to.

A great injustice had been done, and God himself would look unkindly upon all if no attempts at restoration were made. It was clear to all that the bear must be sought out and killed and that Henry, acting as Matilde's protector on the day she died, was the man to do the job.

However, things were not so simple. Henry had no intention of being diverted by a quest for the bear's hide. He was only visiting John of Rensey in passing, being on his way to his father's castle at Bampton. The notion of spending days or even weeks, tramping through the dank wet Wychwood, in search of an indifferent, mindless killer, did not appeal to him at all. Furthermore it was quite clear to him that, although he had been Matilde's travelling companion that day, ultimate responsibility for Matilde and the goings-on in the Wychwood lay with John himself.

John could have ordered Henry to take up the mission but the issue of signeurity, of authority, was a complex one. John of Rensey was the lord of the surrounding lands and Henry, as a mere guest and landless knight, was subject to his command. And yet, John, in addition to his own lands, held a fiefdom near Oxford, given to him by the Earl of Pembroke, Henry's father, and thus John owed fealty to Pembroke. To complicate matters further, part of the fiefdom's revenue was payable to Pembroke as a knight's fee, moneys which paid for the equipment, upkeep and expenses incurred by Henry de Valence, amongst others.

In short, Henry, living off the profits of John of Rensey's lands and subject to his rule, had a clear moral duty to John but, at the same time, Henry was Pembroke's knight. John could hardly demand satisfaction from the son of the man to whom he owed fealty.

In the days that followed, the two men circled each other warily. John of Rensey dropped hints, subtle and not subtle, about Henry de Valence's moral obligation. Henry ignored the hints, to the point of rudeness, but remained a guest at Shipton Manor, feeling unable to leave until John publicly absolved Henry of any responsibility for Matilde's death.

The deadlock seemed unbreakable.

****

The bear twitched convulsively and was still.

Stamford spat on the dead animal, wiped his nose on his sleeve again and leaned heavily against a sodden beech tree.

"You are hurt?" asked Henry.

Stamford shook his head. In truth, he had wrenched his knee in the fight and every second he stood on it was agony. He knew he was too old for such daftness as a bear hunt, too old to be running around the Wychwood in the rain. Today's would be his last kill, his last favour to John of Rensey.

"But it is done now," said Henry.

"Just about," said Stamford.

"The beast is dead."

"As good as."

****

Henry de Valence had brought a balladeer with him to Shipton Manor, a lad of thirteen with a remarkable gift for the lyre. Henry had the lad play at every meal, even in the days following the funeral. Some might have argued that music was improper for a house in mourning but Henry, sensitive to such thoughts, had the boy perform a repertoire of sombre and tragic songs that he felt were not inappropriate.

One evening, so completely transported by the boy and his lyre, Henry failed to notice that a stranger had joined them at the dining table. Only when the lad took a break to grab a drink and adjust his strings did Henry look round and see a gnarled, wiry old man sat by John's side. The man caught Henry's eye and raised a goblet in a silent toast.

Henry frowned. The man wore the ragged uniform of a soldier, his soiled tabard bearing a boar's head crest that Henry did not recognise. He may not have been a menial but nor was he a noble and Henry did not appreciate being toasted as an equal by a base commoner.

"Who are you?" asked Henry.

"This is Stamford. My man," said John of Rensey.

"Yes?"

"He is going to kill the beast that took my Matilde."

"Oh!" Henry's mood lightened enormously. "You are a hunter, Stamford?"

"Of a sort, my lord," said Stamford humbly. "I'm a soldier by profession."

Henry judged him to be at least fifty years old and found it hard to imagine such a man being up to the task at hand.

"And you will find this demonic bear for us, will you, Stamford?" he asked with a smirk.

"Within three days," Stamford agreed.

"I find that hard to believe," said Henry.

John of Rensey raised an eyebrow.

"Do you?" he asked. "Maybe you should accompany Stamford and see it for yourself."

"And if your man's quest takes more than three days?" asked Henry.

"Then you can be on your way to Bampton, your obligation to me fulfilled," said John.

Henry mulled upon it for a minute.

"Very well," he agreed.

"And when we do find this bear of yours," said Stamford, "perhaps you will be the one to deliver that fateful vengeful blow, my lord."

"Perhaps."

"It would be the makings of a good ballad, that would," said John, and there was a tone in his voice that Henry could not comprehend.

****

"Here. Let me clean that sword for you, my lord."

Henry passed his bloodied and muddy blade to Stamford. Henry looked up at the green canopy above them and then in a circle about himself.

"Which way is it back to Shipton?" he asked.

"This *will* make a good ballad, my lord," said Stamford, seeming to not hear him. "Henry De Valence and the Great Bear of the Wychwood."

Henry smiled and prodded the dead bear with his boot.

"You played no small part in this, man."

"Ach!" Stamford waved his comments away. "We little people have no place in song and legend. The songsters erase what they do not like. But your story has all the ingredients of a fine song. A beautiful maiden. A handsome knight. The consummation of your love."

"Hang on, Stamford. Matilde and I were not -"

"Oh, don't be coy, my lord," grinned the old soldier. "We're men of the world and chaperone or not, we both know why you and Matilde were in the Wychwood."

"Well..."

"You've got all them ingredients for a superb song. Her. You. A bit of rumpy-pumpy. A savage creature and, of course, the essential tragic ending?"

Henry frowned.

"Tragic ending?"

****

19

The Wychwood did not welcome visitors. Henry and Stamford's journey into the heart of the woodland was slow, laborious and predominantly characterised by brambles, concealed bogs and a great deal of cursing on Stamford's part. The woodland was too dense for horses. Also, it rained heavily. They spent the first night, cold and shivering in the lee of an oak while Stamford tried and failed to start a fire.

The second day, they walked more than two dozen miles, looking for bear spoor. Stamford found some signs that he declared to be promising but no actual bear was sighted. He did, however, snare two rabbits and they ate well that night. It rained again before sunrise.

On the third day, they found a bear. Stamford's principal plan of attack was to enrage the bear with arrow-fire and then spear the creature as it charged him. Dubious of such a plan, Henry held back and expressed considerable surprise when it worked. Stamford allowed Henry to deliver the finishing blow.

Stamford offered to clean Henry's blade and leaned against a beech tree to do so. He had hurt his leg in the fray and vaguely worried that he had seriously damaged his knee.

"You are a fine fighter," said Henry. "You have seen battle?"

"I fought in the Fourth Crusade," said Stamford, wiping down the sword with the edge of his tabard. "In Boniface's army."

"A just war."

Stamford spat venomously on the blade and rubbed it with his thumb.

"Hmmm. I was there at the sack of Constantinople. We burned what was possibly the most beautiful city in all Christendom. We put a harlot on the throne and put half the population to the sword."

Henry was silent for a while.

"So, how do you come to work for John of Rensey?" he asked.

"I have talents he occasionally has uses for. He calls for me when he wants something killing."

"So, you are his huntsman?"

Stamford shook his head.

"He found justice for me, many years ago, when there was none to be had. I have spent my later years paying back that favour."

Stamford pushed himself away from the tree.

"John of Rensey commanded me to kill the one responsible for his daughter's death."

He held the sword up to the light. The cloud cover was clearing a little.

"It's a good blade," he said.

"I'll have it back now," said Henry.

Stamford let the blade drop so it was pointing directly at the handsome knight.

"I will tell them what happened, my lord."

"What are you doing, man?" said Henry hotly.

"I will tell them that you slew the bear, that just retribution was exacted from this creature. And I will tell them of how, with its dying breath, the bear laid a fatal blow on you, my lord."

"Give me the sword, now!" demanded Henry.

Stamford breathed with some difficulty. The sword was heavy. His leg was agony. He could feel the winter in his bones.

"I have seen slaughter. I think I know something about death. And beasts. I know more than I did once about the nature of responsibility."

"Yes!" exclaimed Henry. "There! There lies the beast responsible."

"No. That is merely a bear, my lord. There are many bears in this wood and, in truth, there are many fair maidens in this world. But John of Rensey had only one daughter and only one beast took her from him."

Stamford raised the sword to strike.

"Don't do this!" Henry pleaded and began to weep.

"Shush, my lord," said Stamford gently. "Be brave. Think of the ballad."

The Sultan's Dream

One morning, the sultan awoke from a dream of such stunning vividness that, even before morning prayers, he summoned his grand vizier, Mehmed Koprulu, so that they might discuss it.

"I dreamt I was a tiger," said the sultan and then shook his head to contradict himself. He had not merely dreamed that he was a tiger but he had actually become a tiger in his dream. He had possessed a body of unimaginable power, a sleek thing of muscle and sinew, of teeth and claws. He had felt the cool mountain air ruffle his golden fur. He had tasted the air with his fat tongue and caught the scent of deer and zebra on the plains of Asia below. On paws as wide and round as dinner plates, he had travelled the breadth of the land that was his kingdom, proud and fierce and feared.

"It was so real," the sultan breathed dreamily. "I wish I knew what it meant."

"You dreamt of yourself," said the vizier plainly. "Allah has blessed you with an image of your true self. You are proud and fierce. You are master of all the lands on which you tread. It is a good dream."

Koprulu believed none of what he said but nor was he an idle flatterer. He simply knew which words would put the sultan's mind at rest most swiftly. With the dream brought out into the light and explained, the vizier went about the business of running the empire and assumed the dream would be quickly forgotten.

However, the dream was not forgotten. The sultan became obsessed by it and, when he heard that a travelling menagerie had come to his capital with a caged tiger, he sent the vizier down into the city to purchase it. Koprulu, though bored by the sultan's infantile fascination with tigers, was at least pleased to discover that the beast he was sent to purchase was not the half-starved and mangy creature he had expected. The tiger in question was broad-shouldered, straight-backed and with a whiskered jaw that could encompass a man's head.

The sultan was similarly impressed and had a cage constructed in his throne room so that the tiger might be by his side throughout the day. The cage had gold and jewels worked around its iron bars.

"A gilded cage, like my own," said the sultan to visiting dignitaries with a sly wink.

Visitors were certainly suitably taken by the sultan's new pet and made loud and favourable comments about the beast's lustrous coat, his beautiful head and his fearsome teeth. None was bold enough to mention the foetid earthy stink that the tiger had brought into the palace with him. The sultan appeared not to notice it and indeed seemed to prefer the tiger's company to that of other people, even his wives and concubines.

More than once, Koprulu came upon the sultan late at night in his throne room, staring enraptured at the caged tiger. The vizier, naturally, asked the sultan if everything was as it should be.

"It is like staring into a mirror," replied the sultan. "I see myself in him. It is as if there are two sultans in this room."

The vizier was alarmed to discover later that the sultan was not speaking figuratively. The rightful ruler of the great Ottoman Empire began to refer to the tiger as 'The Sultan' and, tacitly, made it clear that everyone else should do the same. To highlight their apparent kinship and double the confusion, the sultan (the man, that is) would speak about one, both or either of them in the third person singular. So, seeing the tiger lain beside his untouched bowl of meat, the man would sadly exclaim, "The Sultan is off his food today." And when the man was bored he might ask a courtesan to "sing for the sultan," and the unfortunate individual would not know where to address their music making.

And while the sultan thought there was nothing wrong in his manner or actions, the courtiers dithered in sycophantic bewilderment, and the grand vizier worried deeply about what had become of his master. Koprulu had many fears of all types about the sultan's deterioration, but he did not yet comprehend how bad things would get.

Nine months after the tiger's installation in the palace and, coincidentally, while the vizier was visiting a distant province, the sultan decided to release the giant cat from its cage. Though some courtiers were brave enough to suggest that the sultan should reconsider, the man brushed their arguments aside. Could they not understand that, since man and beast were one, the people of the sultan's court had no more to fear from the animal than it did from the human being?

It was said that the vizier heard the resultant screams from a hundred leagues away, although, when all was said and done, the tiger only killed two members of the court that day. The vizier rushed back to the capital, furious, not at the sultan and his lunacy, but at his own lack of foresight. He returned to a palace filled with fear and strangeness and an almost euphoric delirium. Many court officials were unwilling to stray from their private quarters. Some vanished on what they declared to be urgent business. Several of the sultan's army chiefs resigned their commissions.

The throne room was deserted and, with lamps unlit, in near darkness. The stink of the tiger dung and the beast's raw musk filled the air. The sultan was upon his throne. The tiger lay curled at his feet, asleep. Once more, the vizier, naturally, asked the sultan if everything was as it should be.

"Of course," said the sultan, surprised.

Koprulu, speaking softly so as not to waken the tiger, pointed out that the creature had recently eaten two courtiers.

"Does the sultan strike you as an unjust or capricious man?" the sultan asked.

"No, my lord," said the vizier.

"Then logic dictates that those whom the sultan struck down must have been deserving in some way."

"What was their crime?" asked Koprulu.

The grubby figure on the throne tapped a finger against the side of his blood-smeared nose.

"The sultan keeps his own counsel, vizier," he said.

The vizier bowed low and retreated from the room in horror. He took to his rooms, considered his next course of action and came to what he saw as the only possible solution. Koprulu wrote a long letter to the sultan's cousin, Suleiman, in Edirne inviting him to raise an army with which to take the sultan's throne by force, thereby saving the empire from the sultan's madness and saving the sultan from himself. Koprulu might have been a practical soul but he was also a man of honour and so, once the letter had been dispatched, he returned to his master's throne room to reveal what he had just done.

It was night and the vizier confessed his crime to the eyes that glinted in the darkness. Two eyes at first and then four. His final cries were heard by all who remained in the palace, but none went to investigate. To the contrary, those who had locked themselves away double-checked the locks on their doors and windows. The sultan's most senior wife ordered the eunuchs to place additional barricades against the door to the women's quarters.

Two months later, Prince Suleiman arrived at the capital with an army of two thousand men. They met no resistance. The sultan's generals greeted the prince at the gates and formally offered their swords up in surrender. Suleiman swept in, through the city streets and on to the palace. Brushing aside obsequious courtiers who had come down from their rooms to prostrate themselves at his feet, Suleiman made directly for the throne room.

His men flung the doors wide and Suleiman strode in. He was moderately surprised by what he saw. He had expected to find a dribbling imbecile on the throne or, at least, a pale wretched man, squatting in his own filth and taking fright at every shadow, but the sultan wrapped in white finery upon the throne was none of these. His back was ramrod straight. The ruddy cheeks above his white beard positively glowed with good health. His eyes, sharp and incisive, were windows into a mind that burned with intelligence and passion.

Seeing that bold and noble figure, Suleiman was momentarily robbed of his voice and stumbled over his words. The sultan waited patiently for him and, when Suleiman hesitated, gestured for the man to speak his mind. Suleiman, uncertain, began to explain, in a voice much humbler than he had imagined himself using, that he had come to take the reins of government from his cousin, to make himself sultan and to steer the empire away from its imminent collapse.

Throughout Suleiman's speech, the sultan listened attentively, nodding now and then. At his own mention of the tiger, Suleiman recalled that the beast was supposedly allowed to roam freely within this room and immediately looked round for it. He espied the gilded cage and peered inside. On the floor was a fat bundle of rags, snoring softly, with a small slippered human foot poking out.

At that, Suleiman realised his mistake and turned back to the throne with renewed awe. The sultan yawned widely and stepped down to greet his usurper on feet as wide and round as dinner plates.

• Eustachius Martingale

Eustachius Martingale cannot be honestly described as an important historical figure. He only appears at the periphery of other noteworthy lives, a shadow momentarily glimpsed from the corner of the eye. This conspicuous obscurity can be attributed to his amateurish dabbling in academia, the frustrating opaqueness of his mind and motives, and a wealth of contradictory biographical detail, much of it given to us by Martingale himself. Nonetheless, he leaves us many items of interest; and it these that pin him to the pages of history, preventing an otherwise inexorable slide into anonymity.

Eustachius lends his name to the binomials of a number of birds including Martingale's Barbet (*Lybius Martingalus*) and the Saint-Cyr Lizard Cuckoo (*Saurathera Martingalus*)[1]. Popular history also cites him as the unwanted patriarch of the island kingdom of Saint-Cyr, where his supposed great great great grandson sits upon the throne today. Furthermore, he is credited with the design of numerous automata. Several were inferior copies of Vaucanson's work, others probably never existed at all and, of the three we have reliable accounts of, the birds were destroyed in a house fire in Paris, the card-player disappeared sometime during the dissolution of the Holy Roman Empire and the angel is reported as currently in the possession of the Caledonian scientist Alexander Graham Bell (although he has refuted this claim on more than one occasion).

However, Martingale's final and most lasting legacy must surely be the mystery that surrounds his disappearance, the ingredients of which are an inescapable house, an impossibly high window, a decapitated stranger, the automaton angel and a large white feather.

---

[1] The notion that Martingale also gives his name to the gambling system in which the player doubles his stake with each loss is a work of erroneous etymology, though he was an incorrigible gambler and amateur probability mathematician. The Martingale system predates Eustachius' birth by several years and has no links to his family.

At the feet of Angels

On 3rd November 1752, the five day old Eustachius was abandoned on the steps of the Saint Eustachius de Paris church. Eustachius Martingale was the illegitimate child of the Chevalier Louis-Camus Martingale and the writer Marie-Jean Le Cat. The Chevalier Martingale had been in Egypt for six months at the time of the boy's birth and was entirely unaware of his son's existence until his return to France in early 1753. By that time Le Cat was dead, driven to suicide we might presume by the potential scandal of having borne a child outside of wedlock. It is clear that Le Cat, who was well-known for her mental delicacy, had become almost hysterically irrational following the birth[2], for over the next few days she sent out to the basket makers of Paris for a "reed basket, such as would be suitable for the infant Moses," and proceeded to reject every sample that was brought to her bedside, dismissing each on the most spurious of grounds. Only after inspecting more than fifty baskets did she settle upon one that she felt met her peculiar needs. At once, Le Cat wrapped the boy in swaddling clothes, delivered him to the church, positioning his basket beneath the stone angels whose bodies and curved wings form the outer arch of the south door, and then walked to a village just outside the city where she drowned herself in a millpond.

Infinitesimal and ineffable cogs

Named after the protecting saint of the church outside which he was found, Eustachius Martingale was placed in an orphanage but was soon adopted by the family of a local watchmaker. Raised by such folk, he grew up amidst finials, bushings, bobs, arbors, verges, pinions, pallets, springs and wheels, in an atmosphere of strict piety, earnest labour, and that specialised form of near poverty that skulks at the edges of everything and of which no one dares speak lest it ceases its skulking and manifests itself fully. As well as working and learning a trade in his adoptive father's workshop, the young Martingale supplemented his personal

---

[2] The woman's flightiness and jejunity can also be witnessed in the sentimental characterisation within her final novel, *La Comtesse de Tencin*, which was published posthumously in 1758.

income by capturing and selling birds. Greedy pigeons, snared in Martingale's glue traps, were sold by the half-dozen to poulterers and pie makers. Starlings, blackbirds and thrushes could be sold as pets but their live capture without harm took considerable skill and time. Martingale later remarked to Maria Theresa, the wife of the Holy Roman Emperor Francis II, that a "healthy song thrush, enclosed in a wooden cage of my own manufacture, could be sold for a whole silver écu," although, as this would have been more than the average Parisian at the time would have earned in a month, we should not attach too much credence to this claim.

The Chevalier Martingale was aware of Eustachius' existence but never formally acknowledged him as his son. However, upon his death in 1761, he left Martingale the sum of 1200 livres, a trust fund to pay for his education and to start him up in business. The trust fund was managed by the Chevalier Martingale's cruelly parsimonious nephew, Claude Martingale, who placed stringent conditions upon Eustachius' access to the money. In 1764, under the instruction of his cousin, Eustachius Martingale took his father's surname, left his adoptive family and began his studies at the Collège Mazarin in central Paris. The Collège Mazarin (or Collège de Quatre-Nations as it was formally known) presented a fine institute of learning but it is likely that Claude was more interested in the college's religious ethos for, although Eustachius was a devout Catholic, Claude regarded the bastard offspring of a philanderer and a suicide as essentially damned and in need of firm moral guidance. In the mid-eighteenth century, the Collège Mazarin was a focus for Jansenist thought. Jansenism, with its emphasis on original sin, the fundamental depravity of mankind and the need for divine grace, must have appealed to Claude Martingale who saw all these attributes at work in the life of his cousin.

Martingale studied philosophy, law and the arts but excelled in the natural sciences. He was a voracious reader and it was possibly at this time he came across the works of Heron of Alexandria and Agostini Ramelli, which he cited as the inspirations for his later work on automata. The link between Martingale's love of clockwork automata and the Jansenist adherence to a belief in predestination is not merely a metaphorical one. We might easily imagine that, through a childhood spent in his adoptive father's workshop, Martingale developed an almost unthinking belief in the ordered and preordained nature of the universe. Indeed, he had assisted his father in the repairs of the orrery at the Paris Observatory (now at the Chateau-Neuf, Meudon) and so saw the movements of the planets translated into the rigid language of gears and cogs. Perhaps, even before the Jansenists laid their hands on him, Martingale sensed those infinitesimal and ineffable cogs that, but for the grace of God, wind us all towards damnation.

It is curious though logical that Martingale's love of birds and musings on determinism should lead him to a study of ornithomancy. The most enlightening account of ornithomancy comes to us through the writings of Galen, who sought to explain this peculiar form of fortune-telling through his investigations into the mechanics of flight and it is probable that Martingale's studies of Galen endeared him to his tutor and mentor, Jean Nicolas Massillon, a man who Martingale claimed "consciously modelled himself on the great Galen of Pergamum."

Martingale worked as Massillon's laboratory assistant during his latter days at the Collège Mazarin. His experience and skill with handling animals, particularly birds, made Martingale a skilled vivisectionist and Massillon acknowledges his apprentice's contributions in the preface to his major work, On the Usefulness of Parts of the Body[3] (1770). Massillon's published work reveals a man obsessed with death and its causes. In a career spanning five decades, Massillon dissected nearly a thousand human corpses, mostly victims of disease, and meticulously recorded the state of the internal organs and tissues. He would often try to replicate the symptoms in his live subjects (mostly pigs, but also a number of primates) and record the results. Many of Massillon's contemporaries disapproved of his methods, not on moral but on scientific grounds, but his contributions to the science of disease pathology are clear. Without Massillon, it is quite possible that Jakob Heine's work on identifying the poliovirus sixty years later, for example, might never have taken place. Martingale's respect and

---

[3] Massillon unashamedly took the name of his book from Galen's seventeen-volume magnum opus.

admiration for Massillon was pronounced and, after Martingale graduated as a bachelier in 1771, the two of them remained close and, if subsequent events had turned out differently, Martingale might even have followed his mentor into a career in medicine.

Anatomy of a young man

The few physical descriptions and the one reliable image we have of Eustachius Martingale portray a slender but not athletic figure, his pale complexion hinting at either childhood malnutrition or the night-owl habits of the inveterate academic. His eyes are blue-grey and wide, child-like and curious. Even at nineteen (the age at which he sat for the painter Adelaide Labille-Guiard) Martingale's hairline was receding rapidly and lent his appearance some much needed maturity.

These descriptions and the accounts of his early life might leave us with the impression of a pious, diligent and resourceful young man. Such appellations are accurate but they do not paint a true picture of Martingale. Like all men, Martingale was not without his vices and his secrets.

It appears that almost from the moment of his arrival at the Collège Mazarin, Martingale had taken to both alcohol and gambling. The wide eyed expression that Madame Labille-Guiard had captured so skilfully was one of drunken vacancy, not wonder, and Martingale's anaemic frailty was that of a man whose money was spent at cards, not on food. Martingale hid his habits well. He managed to wheedle increasing amounts of money out of his cousin in order to fund his intemperate lifestyle without Claude suspecting a thing. But this alone was not enough to cover his escalating debts and the small money that Massillon paid him for his services became vital in staving off his creditors.

Massillon paid Martingale on a rigid piece rate system. There would be a set payment for a copying up a page of notes, or for preparing surgical instruments. There would be different payment for the vivisection of a pig to the vivisection of a Barbary Macaque. Martingale was also paid handsomely for sourcing corpses from city morgues and assisting in their dissection. When the dead were in plentiful supply, Martingale was at his busiest and indeed he recalled the fiercely hot summer of 1769, when there was an outbreak of typhus fever in Paris, as the "happiest days of my life." Conversely, when there were relatively few dead, Martingale faced lean and desperate times.

It is in this context that we must view the events of autumn 1772 when Martingale asked Massillon to lend him a considerable amount of money to pay off his gambling debts. Since graduation, Martingale had made a little money as a writer but had otherwise lived off his inheritance. Massillon was initially scornful of Martingale's lifestyle and his impertinent request but Martingale pleaded with him. It was said that Massillon loved Martingale as a son and so it was perhaps with the stern love of a father that Massillon told Martingale he would not lend him the money but pay him for the procurement of corpses as he done when Martingale was his student.

There were others in Paris who dealt in corpses, buying them from morgues or directly from those bereaved families whose grief was overshadowed by their financial hardship and selling them to universities, medical schools and anatomists. Competition between corpse traders was fierce. Martingale struggled to give Massillon the constant supply of cadavers that he required and therefore strove only to procure the bodies of those who had died from unusual ailments and which he could therefore sell to Massillon for an elevated fee. One such corpse was that of a youth who had died of a ruptured oesophagus brought on by excessive vomiting. The dissection of the body led to the publication of Massillon's paper, *Anatomy of a Young Man* (1773). It also brought Massillon to the attention of the Parisian judiciary. It transpired that Massillon had dissected, not the young man named on the chit Martingale had given him, but one Xavier Petit, a local hoodlum whom the prévôts des maréchaux (provosts) had been seeking for some time.

From fragmentary and elliptic comments we have from him, we can assume Massillon realised that Martingale and Petit were known associates and indeed it was probable that Petit was one of Martingale's many creditors. There is no record of this information ever coming to the attention of the prévôts and it is likely that Massillon strove to shield his protégé from accusations of being a resurrectionist or even a murderer. In May 1773, the London Gazette denounced Massillon as a "ghoul" and revelled in reports that Massillon had been threatened in the streets by men of "low character." In July of the same year, it reported that shortly before he was due to attend an investigative judicial hearing, Massillon died. He was found on the floor of his study at the Collège Mazarin, having ingested a quantity of poison. Exactly one week after Massillon's death, Martingale boarded a ship bound for the Americas.

Saint-Cyr

By some circuitous route, Eustachius Martingale came to the Caribbean island of Saint-Cyr. With the remains of what little money he had brought with him from France and with a substantial loan from a local gen de couleur called Alexandre Villeneuve, Martingale bought a share of a large sugar plantation.

Martingale was no businessman and paid scant attention to the day-to-day workings of the plantation. In all likelihood he stayed in Saint-Cyr simply to avoid his legal and financial woes in France. Martingale's account of his years in Saint-Cyr would have us believe that his time there was predominantly devoted to the study of the local avian fauna. It is true that he spent some time exploring the countryside of Saint-Cyr, even spending a brief time as a captive of escaped slaves, the Maroons, in the forest highlands, and his ornithological studies there were the foundation of his first published book, *Histoire naturelle des plus beaux oiseaux chanteurs de Saint-Cyr* (1881). But Martingale, that character of many facets, did much more and much less than that. Though Basseterre, the administrative capital of Saint-Cyr, was no metropolis, Martingale was able to partake of all the vices he had enjoyed in the saloons and backstreet card rooms of Paris. He remained a profligate gambler and took as easily to Saint-Cyr rum as he had to the wines of France.

Furthermore, Martingale developed a habit for making freely with the women slaves who worked on the plantation that he part-owned. The treatment of slaves on Saint-Cyr was brutal and led to a particular social structure on the island. At the top were the French colonialists who held the reins of power. However, much of the wealth of Saint-Cyr lay in the hands of gens de couleur (freed slaves) and the mulatto population, who were nearly all the descendants of French men and female slaves. Male slaves rarely lived long enough to have children of their own and therefore Saint-Cyr had no native slave population and had to import thousands of souls from the Dahomey coast each year. Consequently, Saint-Cyr slaves had a distinctive African culture and, despite all prohibitions and punishing beatings, retained their tribal languages and practices. One such slave on Martingale's plantation was a woman called Akosiwa. She was "plain and unshapely[4]" and Martingale showed no interest in her until he heard a rumour that Akosiwa claimed to be a princess of an African royal household. Martingale had her brought to his house and questioned her. She was a skilful and witty storyteller, despite her clumsiness with the French language, and told Martingale of a kingdom, west of Mount Sokbaro (perhaps somewhere in what is now British Togo), and her father, the king, who was defeated in war by King Tegbessou of Dahomey. After the destruction of her homeland, Akosiwa's father was beheaded and the entire population of the kingdom either sacrificed to the Dahomey gods or sold into slavery in Ajudá.

What happened in the months after that meeting is not certain and the few historians who have shown interest in the matter have either admitted bafflement on the matter or posited specific viewpoints without justification. Some suggest that Martingale, captivated by the woman's mental adroitness, savage sophistication and the perverse contradiction of the noble slave, fell in love with Akosiwa and made her his wife in all but name. In his book, *Jean-Baptiste Martingale: Hero of the Caribbean* (1892), the American 'dime novel' writer Chapman Oliphant luridly describes how Martingale violently debased and degraded the "African princess" on successive occasions, keeping her as prisoner in his house until the final months before her death. One account relates that Martingale asked Akosiwa to marry him, to even accompany him back to France, and that she refused his offer. Another speaks of the slave woman being brutalised, beaten and left for dead in a field. The truth, perhaps, lies somewhere in the midst of all of these versions. We might find enlightenment of a sort in the reports of

---

4 Remy-Claire, *Martingale et Saint-Cyr* (1902).

Martingale's other affairs on Saint-Cyr. In the royal museum in Basseterre, beneath glass, visitors today can see a letter dated October 1779 from Alexandre Villeneuve to Martingale, demanding the repayment of the loan made five years earlier. The letter speaks plainly of Martingale's "wanton habits and frequent inebriation" and less clearly of "the brawl outside Monsieur Loubet's" and "the dead girl, drowned." What we do know is that in January 1780, Akosiwa gave birth to a boy. Akosiwa died in the hours that followed. Such a thing was not unusual. Before she died, Akosiwa apparently asked that the boy be called Kwámè. However, the child was christened with the name Jean-Baptiste and, because there was no doubt in the locals' minds as to whom the father was, given the surname Martingale.

Martingale left Saint-Cyr in February 1780.

The resurrectionist

Eustachius Martingale had lived two lives, one in Paris and another on Saint-Cyr and he had done an effective job of destroying both. One might argue that if there were ever such a thing as natural justice then Martingale's should have been to meet an ignoble and unrecognised death, perhaps succumbing to fever on the long journey back to France or meeting a drunkard's knife blade on the docks of Marseille. However, the infinitesimal and ineffable cogs of destiny had no such plans for Martingale.

Martingale, to his credit, did not attempt to resume the life he had left behind in 1773. The returned Martingale reinvented himself as something entirely other, obtaining a modest but secure position as a writer on the *Bulletin des Lois*. He collated his ornithological notes and, after the publication of his first book, swiftly followed it with *Histoire naturelle et générale des colibris et oiseaux-mouches de la zone torride* (1782). Simultaneously, Martingale began work on a new project. Drawing on his knowledge of ornithology, anatomy and clockwork, he poured his efforts into the construction of an automaton device. It took the form of a short wooden box upon which stood a carved model tree (about two feet in height), abounding with scores of etched brass leaves. Nestling in the trees were four brass birds, exact replicas of species that Martingale had observed in the Americas. From a main spring within the box and along gyrating arms concealed within the tree, counterfeit life was impressed into the birds, causing them to stand, flap their wings, waggle their tails and raise their heads in what Martingale assured his audiences was an authentic reproduction of their song. In 1784, he displayed this automaton, along with a number of earlier, experimental efforts, to members of the Académie des Sciences. He told them that his design was a variant of a design by Heron of Alexandria although historians of automata have disagreed as to which 'design' he might have been referring. Automata were enormously popular in France at the time and regarded as scientifically important. Martingale's offerings to the Académie were politely received and his contributions to natural history and to the fledgling system of ornithological classification were both recognised and applauded.

Despite this praise, Martingale was not entirely able to escape his dubious past. Much had been forgotten or forgiven but not all. During his absence from France, Claude Martingale had died of a bladder infection and, with no other living relatives, left his not inconsiderable estate to his cousin. Unsurprisingly, Claude had placed a number of draconian stipulations on the inheritance. One was that Eustachius must attend confession at least once a week. Another was that he should not drink to excess and not drink at all "away from the dining table." Thirdly, it was decreed that Eustachius must never again lay his hands on dice or cards. These were not idle requests; a portion of Claude's estate had been set aside to employ a lawyer's clerk "for not less than three years" to follow Eustachius day and night and report back on any infringements.

And it is not a coincidence that, at roughly the same time, Massillon's niece made herself known, accused Martingale of having a hand in his old tutor's death and demanded reparation. Martingale neither caved into her demands nor denied the accusation but chose a third course of action. He made a wager of sorts with Mme Massillon; he drew up a will, making her his sole beneficiary. If he died before her (and being both ten years older than her and aged even further by his years of drinking this seemed a reasonable assertion) then she would have everything. And, of course, if he did not then she would receive nothing at all. She readily agreed and made no further accusations against him.

Martingale paid Auguste Belloc, the lawyer's clerk hired to spy on him, a second wage to be his research assistant and amanuensis and this seems to be a genuine arrangement. Indeed, rather than try to bribe or dupe Belloc, Martingale made every effort to fulfil the provisions of his inheritance. Having managed to keep his wealth out of the hands of the opportunist Mme Massillon, at least for the time being, Martingale now consolidated his hold on it. Through an act of supreme will that had not been seen in him before, he foreswore all alcohol and stayed clear of Paris' numerous gambling dens, instead throwing himself into his work. With Belloc as his apprentice, Martingale worked on his second great automaton: the card-player. He completed its construction in July 1785 and displayed it to an invited audience of friends and scholars at a party that September. Martingale arranged his presentation as a piece of theatre which began with the demonstration of the automaton birds and another mechanical item described as "the wooden duke."[5] He then spoke to his audience at length on the themes of determinism and of chance. In florid language, he discoursed on predestination, free will and the self-contradictory omniscience of God and then reflected upon man's trifling obsession with games of chance and capricious fate. He then flung back the makeshift curtain arranged before his stage to reveal the card-player, his fusion of determinism and chance, "the gambler forged from inhuman clockwork."

The card-player took the form of a life-sized wooden mannequin seated behind an enclosed playing table. The figure was dressed in a shirt and waistcoat, held a pack of playing cards in his inarticulate left hand, with his right hand resting protectively on top of them. The card-player's face was carved into the likeness of a negro with a sly and watchful expression. Martingale invited two gentlemen of the audience to come up and play against the machine at a game of La Bete, a trick-taking game not dissimilar to Whist. A college master and Belloc's elderly father came forward

---

[5] The account we have of the demonstration from Friedrich von Grimm does not explain this particular automaton in greater detail.

and perched themselves on the stools that Martingale had laid out. Martingale produced a large key, inserted it into a slot in the side of the box table and wound it round three times. The card-player raised its head smoothly, nodded genially at the two men before it and dealt out cards to all three of them, taking them with the thumb and fingers of the right hand and placing them down in three neat rows of overlapping cards. The card-player then tapped the table and Martingale, much to the audience's amusement, explained that it was asking for each of them to place an ante in the painted circle at the centre of the table. Once the men had put down some small coin, the automaton then gestured for the man to his left, Monsieur Belloc, to begin play. When it came to the card-player's turn, the automaton selected a card from those laid before it, dragged it to the edge of the table, turned it over and laid it down. The card-player won that trick and, indeed, won each and every hand in that game. Once its victory was complete, it brought its hand down with a thud and swept its opponents' money off the table and into its lap. Martingale then removed the used cards and placed them at the bottom of the pile, the only action that the card-player could not perform by itself. The audience laughed and cheered to see the two men bested by a machine and they took it in good humour.

There have been attempts since to explain how this automaton was able to play so skilfully, given the obvious fact that it could not see its own cards, let alone the cards of its opponents. Suggestions that Martingale manipulated the apparatus through magnets or invisible wires simply do not tally with accounts of its demonstrations, for Martingale often took a seat in the audience whilst a game was in progress. In 1804, Joseph Jacquard proposed that the cards used in the game might have had punched holes in them by which the automaton could read them whilst dealing. This is a charming and ingenious notion but patently untrue and quite unnecessary. In 1846, Jean Robert-Houdin, "the father of modern magic," demonstrated how the blind card-player's trick was effected. With a carefully prepared deck (the automaton's deck was never shuffled before play), Robert-Houdin played blind-folded against two other men and won every hand, much as Martingale's card-player had done.

Word of the card-player's uncannily human-like abilities spread quickly and it is probable that Martingale would have achieved a degree of fame through it alone, but what happened in the month following that first demonstration ensured that Martingale would become, for a time at least, the most famous (or perhaps infamous) man in all Paris.

Death's apprentice

On the morning of the twenty-ninth of September 1785, Mme Massillon was passing by the church of St-Germain l'Auxerrois when a pigeon alighted on one of the gargoyles at the top of the bell tower. It appears that the pigeon's slight weight was sufficient to dislodge an ill-fitting stone from its housing and the gargoyle fell, striking Mme Massillon on the shoulder and back, snapping her spine and killing her instantly.

It was impossible to suggest that Eustachius Martingale was responsible for the woman's death. The roof of the bell tower was virtually inaccessible.Several people claimed to witness the pigeon landing on the fateful stone and Martingale himself was, at that time, in a coffee house three miles away with the Baron d'Holbach, a man of dubious philosophy but impeccable reputation. These factors did not deter speculation as to how Martingale had managed to kill her, for his morbid wager with her was well-known.

The Parisian newspaper, *Gazette*, published a lengthy article about the peculiar incident and, weaving in details of Martingale's earlier life as a corpse-trader and student anatomist, and spuriously describing his mother as a Romany fortune-teller, it labelled Martingale "Death's apprentice," a title that would follow him for the rest of his life. His notoriety sealed, Martingale was summoned to Versailles shortly afterwards to present himself and his automata to the royal court. Bizarrely, Martingale refused the summons, sending a letter in reply that said, if given six months, he would be able to "present their royal majesties with a new automaton of superlative wonder." Such an impertinent response would normally have been met with considerable indignation but it appears that the court acceded to his request, and waited.

Martingale's angel

In May 1786, Eustachius Martingale came to the court of Louis XVI. He had prepared well for his performance in front of the young king and his courtiers and brought with him a number of automata and mechanical novelties. As with the demonstration of the card-player, Martingale had his showpieces set up on a stage with a retractable curtain. Again, as before, Martingale's routine began with the showing of his lesser pieces, the mechanical birds amongst them. He then launched into his revised speech on the nature of life, clockwork and the laws of chance, now considerably longer and, at times, utterly impenetrable. However, when he saw the young king yawn, Martingale became nervous, cut his speech short and unveiled the card-player. The audience was deeply impressed by the automaton's skill and life-like movements and nobles of the court clamoured to be the next to be beaten at its table. The courtiers might have had the card-playing going all night but the reservoir of cards it held ran out and Martingale, with a show of reluctance, wheeled it behind the curtain explaining that restocking the deck of cards took "time and delicacy," (thus perhaps giving credence to Robert-Houdin's explanation of the automaton's secret).

The king had not forgotten Martingale's boast of presenting an "automaton of superlative wonder" and requested to see the new creation. While his assistant, Belloc, set up the automaton, Martingale addressed the audience. Returning to his beloved theme of predestination, he spoke of the order of the universe, the theology of Augustine of Hippo, of God's omniscience in all matters and of how the destinies of all humanity are written in the "great book." Alluding to the improbable death of Mme Massillon (this causing a titter of excitement amongst an otherwise indifferent audience), Martingale explained how he had become fascinated by death, specifically the hour and manner of death as preordained by God. His fascination, he told the assemblage, led him to discover an incomplete automata design by Agostino Ramelli, the sixteenth century Italian engineer, itself based upon an unnamed work of Heron of Alexandria, which was intended to measure the life given to a person. The design was incomplete, Ramelli's idiosyncratic notation was difficult to decipher, but Martingale had persevered, adapted and invented anew.

At Martingale's signal, Belloc swept aside the curtain to reveal the finished work. Two metres in height, Martingale's Angel (as it was universally known) took the appearance of an angelic figure of indeterminate gender and was carved entirely from a single block of wood. The sculptor[6] had shaped the flowing robes to suggest that the angel was standing in a stiff breeze or perhaps walking at speed. A single, sandaled foot poked out from beneath the robe's edge. The angel held an open book against its chest with its left hand, the curving polished pages facing outwards. There was a small aperture in the pages of the book, revealing a blank wooden panel beneath. The angel's right hand was half-outstretched as though in greeting or to receive something. Neither limb was articulated, merely another part of the carving. The angel's face was beautiful, bland and benign. The hair was shoulder-length and, though immobile, flowed with disconcerting realism. The wings, partially opened, were imposing, detailed and delicate. Sadly, the amateur application of paint to the angel's exterior had done much to undo the beauty of the sculpture. The robes and wings were painted a uniform white, the hands, foot and face a bright, fleshy pink and the hair an unnatural sunny yellow.

Keen to show the court that his device was no mere statue, Martingale turned the angel round so that they might see its exposed and hollow back and the workings within. Amongst the cogs, gears, lever arms and music-box drums, sat a complex arrangement of bellows and tubes. This, Martingale pointed out, provided the angel with the capability of speech. Martingale then produced three keys, wound up the clockwork mechanisms in three separate locations and turned the angel to face the audience once more.

---

[6] Our knowledge of the angel's appearance comes from numerous sources, including the diaries of Maria Leopoldina, wife of Emperor Pedro I of Brazil. There is no record as to who the sculptor might have been. Martingale had numerous talents but this level of artistry was almost certainly beyond him.

Martingale then asked for a member of the court to come forward and have their destiny read by the angel. There were numerous volunteers and Martingale warned them that this was no trick and that only those willing to know the number of days left to them should come forward. The first volunteer was a young chevalier. Under Martingale's instructions, he stepped forward and took the angel's outstretched hand in his own. The holding of the hand depressed dozens of closely packed studs embedded in the angel's palm. At once, the inner workings of the angel began to whirr and click and then, much to the amazement of all, a voice issued from the angel's half-open mouth. The mechanical being's pronunciation was uneven and irregular but it spoke clearly enough for all to hear the words, "Eight thousand, five hundred and four days." At the same time, the circular panel within the angel's carved book turned slowly until a small painted picture of crossed swords presented itself to the aperture. The young chevalier stepped back in astonishment. He allegedly turned to an acquaintance and asked what it meant. Directly the reply came that he had a little over twenty-three years remaining to him. Martingale pointed out that the image of crossed swords was an indicator of the manner in which the man would die. The chevalier was unsure as how to take this news and returned silently to his seat.

We cannot say what reaction Martingale had hoped to draw from his audience but at that moment the audience was at once intrigued, cynical, fearful, repulsed and thrilled. A second man came forward, urged on by his friends, and took the angel's hand. The mechanism whirred once more. "Five thousand, two hundred and seventy-one days," the angel said as the image of a horse appeared in the angel's book. Slowly, as a sense of macabre fascination gripped the room, a third, a fourth and a fifth man took the angel's hand and each was given his allotment of days. A courtier put it to Martingale that his "death predictor" simply spat out random numbers to frighten the credulous but Martingale was ready for such a challenge. He called for one of the five men who had already been tested to take the angel's hand again. The young chevalier who was fated to die in 1809 gripped the angel's hand a second time. "Eight thousand, five hundred and four days," said the angel, exactly as before. There were gasps, of horror and excitement in equal measure.

Some reports say that his majesty, Louis XVI, offered to buy the automaton from Martingale there and then and that Martingale refused. Other, less credible reports suggest that Louis himself strode forward and took the angel's hand and quailed at what he heard.

As with the card-player, there has been speculation as to how the angel's trick worked. Given that the angel's fortune-telling ability is demonstrably beyond the capacity of man, let alone machine, inquisitive minds have pondered the question of how the automaton was able to recognise an individual who had held its hand before. The fanciful notion that the studs in the angel's hand comprised some sort of fingerprint reader is untenable and should be disregarded. Since both Martingale and Belloc often stood near the angel when it was in use, a more credible solution is that the angel accessed some form of mechanical memory, perhaps punch-card based, when certain concealed buttons were pressed on the angel's painted exterior. As for the angel's facility with language, such a thing was not that remarkable. The Hungarian, Farkas von Kempelen, had created an automaton capable of primitive speech several decades before and Martingale is known to have studied his work[7].

The grand tour

For the following decade, Martingale displayed his automaton marvels throughout the great nations of Europe. Whether he had planned to spend so long on the road is uncertain but it is likely that the grand European tour was prolonged by the advent of the French Revolution in 1789. Evidence suggests that this extended time on the road bored Martingale enormously. His private notebooks overflowed with unrelated jottings: principles of ornithological classification, incomprehensible mathematical

---

[7] This is being more than charitable to Martingale whose final, unpublished work on automata contains entire sections copied from von Kempelen's *Mechanismus der menschlichen Sprache nebst Beschreibung einer sprechenden Maschine* (1791).

theories, sketches for unworkable devices, letters to (amongst others) Pierre Joseph Bonnaterre, the naturalist, and to Jaquet-Droz, the automaton maker[8], written but never sent. Between 1786 and 1796, Martingale gave hundreds of demonstrations both public and private. For a fortnight in the spring of 1788, fly sheets advertising "Death's Apprentice and the Angel of Days" drew hundreds of people to nightly demonstrations in Vauxhall Gardens, London. The rough woodcut image on the handbill (clearly executed by an artist who had neither seen the angel nor met its maker) showed a spindle-shanked and heavily bewigged Martingale standing beside a colossal carved figure which was more grim reaper than angel. Belloc received no mention on the fly sheet but he certainly acted as Martingale's agent in all matters for the duration of the tour.

From the Low Countries, the mechanical circus travelled eastward into Greater Germany, spending more than eighteen months in Brandenburg alone, before turning south towards the Holy Roman Empire. In Vienna, the clockwork birds, card-player and angel were demonstrated before the imperial court. Emperor Francis II, recently crowned and too busy with affairs of state, was not present but his wife, Maria Theresa of the Two Sicilies, was seen to be quite taken with the marvellous machines. She put many questions to Martingale after the demonstration, about his formative years and the craft of automaton manufacture. Finally, she asked him whether he had ever taken the angel's hand.

Martingale replied plainly that he had, and wished he had not.

12th April 1799

Martingale lived out the final two years of his life in Rouen and devoted his energies to so many projects that none of them reached notable fruition except one: the restoration and fortification of a tall house on the outskirts of the city. Bars were fitted to all of the windows apart from the small window to Martingale's study on the third floor. Locks and deadbolts were

---

[8] The letter to Jaquet-Droz was actually dated two weeks after the Swiss watchmaker's death.

46

fitted to all of the doors, both internal and external and Martingale had the front door and the rear door to the house reinforced with iron plates.

During 1799, the last year of his life, Martingale employed two boys of the city to act as his doorkeepers and watchmen with specific instructions to be on the guard for "strangers and men of sinister character." They also acted as Martingale's personal messengers as, by that time, their master refused to step outside the confines of his home. Furthermore, he did not allow his servants to enter the house beyond the kitchen and ate his meals at the kitchen table alongside his housekeeper. Thus the universe was neatly divided in two. On one side of a locked door was Martingale's private and rigorously controlled domain and on the other, the world.

Auguste Belloc had left Martingale's employ upon their return to France, to take up a legal post in Paris. However, they remained good friends and Belloc frequently came north to Rouen to visit the increasingly eccentric Monsieur Martingale. In March 1799, Belloc received a letter from Martingale in which he had written the words:

"Come to me on the morning of the 12th of next month. If all is as it should be, I will have had a visitor on the previous day and my business with him shall be concluded. I trust only you to set my affairs in order."

Belloc actually arrived in Rouen a day early, coming to Martingale's house on the evening of the eleventh. Martingale's juvenile doormen knew Belloc well and let him in, informing him that their master was alone in his study and that Belloc was to go straight up. Belloc entered the dark fortification and made his way up the stairs. He came running down the stairs minutes later, clutching his travel case, his face ashen, his breathing rapid. Belloc was barely able to speak but dragged both lads upstairs to the study.

The window overlooking a sharp slope and a neighbouring courtyard was open. Papers on the desk were rustling softly in the breeze. On the floor lay the body of a man and, a short distance away, his severed head. Blood pooled in the cracks between the floorboards. A white feather, too large to be a goose-quill, sat precariously on the window sill. From the corner of the room, the eyes of Martingale's Angel looked on.

The local magistrate and several men of the city were roused from their beds and a thorough search of the house was conducted. Martingale could not be found, either alive or dead. The boys on the door were adamant that no one had entered the house in the past day nor had Martingale left it. The doors and windows were checked but found to be secure. The body of the man was laid out for identification but he was a stranger, recognised by no one. He had a ragged beard, several teeth missing and wore clothes that were old and ill-fitting. The wounds around his neck indicated that his killer had taken several blows to finally sever the head. As neither a murder weapon nor Martingale's body was ever located and the dead man had no known kin, a legal investigation was never made into the incident. For a life governed by the laws of *what must be* and games of *what might be*, it must be judged either wholly inappropriate or utterly fitting that Martingale's impossible departure from this world belongs to the realm of things that *cannot be.*

In his will, uncovered several days later, Martingale had bequeathed the angel to Maria Theresa of the Two Sicilies. The majority of his automata and his journals and notes were left to the National Institute of Science and Arts (which had superseded the Académie des Sciences during the Revolution). On inspection, most of notebooks were deemed indecipherable or simply nonsensical and placed in storage, where they mouldered for decades until they were thrown away. The automata were sold at auction in 1810. To Belloc, Martingale had left the card-player and enough money to cover his funeral expenses.

The unexplained feather disappeared shortly after Martingale's death. There are claims that it appeared as an exhibit in Jean Robert-Houdin's museum of magic in Blois but these cannot be confirmed.

• A Feast of Bats

March 12th

Was discomfited to find O'Farrell, Sir William Harrington's man, at the rectory door with a large net in each hand. He demanded entry to the church & when asked for what purpose, said it was on account of the bats in the belfry. As this made virtually no sense to me (the Irish are renowned for being intemperate fools, taken with fancy & nonsense), I had him sent on his way, although he was loath to go & insisted that he had come upon strict instructions from his master.

March 13th

Reviewed Sunday's sermon. Decided to read from John, chapter 5 in the hope that the phrase 'take up thy bed & walk' might resonate with Mr Bath, the ostler, who is a known malingerer.

Sir Wm Harrington called on me in the afternoon & accused me of interfering with his business, namely the matter of O'Farrell, nets, bat, etc. Over coffee, Sir Wm declared that he was on the "cusp of a scientific breakthrough" & I invited him to elaborate.

"Do you not notice, reverend," said he, "that at the end of a tiring day one's limbs feel heavy & leaden, like great weights?"

I proposed that this was the result of exhaustion stemming from the day's exertions.

"So thought I!" exclaimed Sir Wm. "But a more satisfying reason occurred to me as I lay on my couch not six nights ago. Is it not so that our world is held in a ceaseless & perfect orbit of the sun by the sun's gravitational pull, that all heavenly objects of mass exert a force on that around them?"

I demurred that I had read as much but was not a natural philosopher of any stature.

"Surely, the mighty sun must also exert its same powers over us, raising us up by day and, as it passes across the antipodes, pulling us down into our beds at night."

I conceded it was an interesting notion & invited him to stay for supper which was to be fish in parsley sauce though what fish it was I could not say.

"Furthermore," said he, "do we not feel energetic & uplifted when the sun shines upon us but downcast & laggardly when the skies are overcast & the sun's gravitational power is... diffused & diminished by cloud cover? Indeed, do not the birds stay in their roosts when it is dark & stormy? Bees cannot fly at all when the sun does not shine."

"Are you suggesting that the birds' powers of flight come from the sun's lifting rays?" asked I.

Sir Wm smiled broadly at me & I felt honoured to be treated so amicably.

"It seems obvious now it has been shewn to you," said he.

But I put it to him there were many creatures which eschewed the day in favour of the night, foxes, owls, bats & the like.

"Ah-hah!" exclaimed Sir Wm loudly. "You find the very nub of my theory & thus my need for the bats from St Ciricus' fine belfry. I trust you agree."

I nodded in fervent agreement although I did not understand him fully & he left me then.

Spoke to Cook regarding the unidentifiable & frankly dubious fish she had served for supper. She expressed puzzlement herself as to its type & origin.

March 14th – Before Dawn

Troubled by unexpected & cacophonous bowel movements in the night. Had Maid prepare a cup of Fuller's All-Purpose Tonic. Retired to bed with a copy of Pliny's *Naturalis Historia*.

March 14th

Woke late. Had stern words with Cook regarding last night's fish & the state of my innards. Insisted she take up the matter with Mr Moulding, the fishmonger.

Sir Wm & his man, O'Farrell, called on me in the late a.m. O'Farrell once again armed with nets. Took them across to the church & let them in. Sir Wm, having his own chapel up at Raithby (though I doubt he ever sets foot in it), is not one of my flock & I drew his attention to the church's fine architectural features. He ignored these without any pretence of polite interest & made for the stairs.

As we climbed, discreetly enquired about Sir Wm's recent health though made no reference to my own night time troubles or the questionable fish. Sir Wm declared himself to be in the rudest of health and, as though to prove it, harried his man to greater speed up the steps to the top. Arrived in St Ciricus' belfry somewhat out of breath & wishing there was a chamber pot to hand.

Sir Wm pointed upward at the many pipistrelle bats hanging from the rafters of the belfry. O'Farrell sought out a way to climb up to them.

"That there are creatures who are not drawn down by the sun's pull & who make the night time their own is an indisputable fact," said Sir Wm to me. "It is clear that some other force has a greater influence over them."

"What is this force?" asked I.

"The moon," announced Sir Wm, loud enough to cause some of the bats above to flit from one perch to another. He continued in a quieter tone. "I recalled my Newton, watching the tides at Selcombe. The course of the moon about our Earth drags the tides of the sea with it. & yet, I realised, the waters of Raithby pond nor the coffee in my cup seem inclined to move with the moon. Why is this?"

I blustered in search of an answer, although my mind was undoubtedly on other more *fundamental* matters.

"Clearly," said Sr Wm, "there is some aspect, some element that causes both the seas & the creatures of the night to respond to the moon's silvery pull. Perhaps the answer lies within the sea's salt, some form of *Substantia Luna* which is similarly found in the badger, fox and other nocturnal creatures. Moreover, have you not witnessed how the eyes of cats & foxes glimmer in the night?"

"I have," I averred.

"That is the *Substantia Luna* in action, I warrant," said Sir Wm.

By this time, O'Farrell, whose Irish ancestry had granted him not only the aspect & intellect of an ape but the agility also, had managed to net more than a dozen bats without disturbing the entire group. NB: Must look up the collective noun for bats.

"But what of bats?" I said to Sir Wm. "I believe they have no eyes to speak of at all."

"But the effects of the sun & moon are evidently strongest upon them out of all creatures," said Sr Wm.

"How so?" I enquired.

"I put it to you, reverend," he said with great pride in his words, "that these bats before us are not *hanging* from the rafters but *standing upon them*! Should one of them fall now, it would fall not downwards but upwards towards the heavenly bodies above them, like angels tumbling towards their maker!"

I was prepared to say that Sir Wm's words were madness but respect for my social betters held my tongue in check.

"But bats must flap their wings in order to stay aloft," I argued instead.

"Yes," said Sir Wm. "But in which direction do they flap? Which force are they resisting? Can you answer that?"

I admitted I could not. Vexed in both mind & stomach, I took the opportunity to thank Sir Wm for his time & excused myself. Am ashamed to say that though I raced down the steps, I did not make it back to the rectory before a foul urge overtook my bowels.

Did not see Sir Wm before he left. Sent Maid over to the church to lock up & retired to my rooms early with more Fuller's Tonic & my copy of Samuel Johnson.

A group of bats is known as a cloud or a colony.

March 15th

Rose with great difficulty & prepared to do the Lord's work. Had it not been the Sabbath I think I might have remained in bed all day.

Sermon went pleasingly well despite my decrepitude. John, Chapter 5 did not have the desired effect on Mr Bath the ostler as he was apparently at home in his bed, having been taken with the flux.

Hastening from church to rectory, found O'Farrell on my doorstep once more, hat in hand & wringing it in a most consternated manner. Ignored his initial greetings & entreaties, but went indoors to attend to my bathroom before speaking with him.

The man is a half-wit by birth & doubly so when flustered & I had to reprimand him sharply before he could be made to make sense. Eventually, was given to understand that the cause of the man's anxiety was the apparent & inexplicable disappearance of his master, Sir Wm Harrington.

Reluctantly agreed to go with him. Had Cook's Boy saddle up my horse & rode out to Raithby, with O'Farrell capering on ahead like a court jester. We were at Raithby Hall shortly before luncheon. Sr Wm is a widower with no sons & his daughters are away with family in Tiverton. Lacking its master, the household was much like a headless chicken, flapping about in hysteria with no reason or purpose.

O'Farrell directed me to Sir Wm's rooms. His library was sparsely populated & the Raithby Hall tapestries of which I had heard mention required, in my humble opinion, either cleaning or burning, for moths & the dust of ages had dulled them considerably. The door to Sir Wm's bedroom had been broken in. O'Farrell explained that his master was in the habit of bolting the door at night & he, O'Farrell, had broken in when he had been unable to rouse his master that morning.

Sir Wm's bed was ruffled but had not been slept in. The window was cast wide open & rain had fallen on the floor within. Looked out & observed the gardens below but no sign of Sir Wm or of any disturbance that might indicate a fall from the window.

Declared that this was all very interesting but did not confide with O'Farrell that I had no notion of what had happened to Sir Wm.

Whilst sat in Sir Wm's kitchens, consuming a plain luncheon of bread & pork haslet, I did observe with some surprise a bat's wing atop the swill bucket Cook kept for her master's pigs. I questioned Cook & she went on to describe with no hint of shame how she had prepared a meal of one dzn bat for Sir Wm's supper the previous evening. She was at pains to explain how she had gently roasted them so as not to damage the "moon stuff" within.

There was little else that I could do that afternoon, so gave instructions to the household staff, ordering all to be about their business as though their master were at home & went on my way, with the intention of speaking to the town magistrate about the matter in the morning.

Ate a dinner of tripe & onions. Constitution much improved.

As I was undressing for bed tonight, happened to look out of the window & thought I saw a large dark shape passing high above in the moonlight. Went to my bedside to fetch my spectacles but upon my return the apparition had vanished.

• Osloff and the Turk

Dear Mr Houdin,

It gives me pleasure to comply with the requests contained within your letters (August 3rd and 8th). Do not take my tardiness in responding to be any form of disinclination. On the contrary, my association with the great mechanician Wolfgang von Kempelen and his chess playing Turk,* being one that historians and men of science have chosen to ignore (I have not spoken or heard talk of it these last twenty year), I am only too glad to relate what little I know to a man such as yourself, one whose mind is free from prejudice and stifling dogmatism.

My recollections of the chess player are intimately linked to the story of my association with the great Dr Osloff, and to recount one without the other would be meaningless folly. And therefore it would be prudent to begin this lengthy account with a description of Dr Osloff, if you would permit me this indulgence.

As a relatively young man, Semyon Osloff, recently widowed (as you may know) was accorded the position of chief physician of the city hospital at Vitebsk. A few years later, he was appointed to the medical department of the ministry of the interior and came to the attention of the Empress Catherine and the Grand Duke Paul Petrovich, Catherine the Great's son and heir. Grand Duke Paul was so enamoured of the mighty doctor that in 1796 he entrusted to him the management of the Cholera Asylum of St Petersburg.

This infatuation with the doctor was transparent and justifiable. Grand Duke Paul recognised that Osloff possessed a rare mind, incisive, analytical and not given to false modesty or idle flattery. The brutal honesties of death (by which I mean his parents, his wife and infant son) had inculcated in Osloff a brutally honest demeanour and an outward manner that lacked any sentimentality or notion of selfishness. Osloff spoke freely and plainly even in the presence of royalty, was rarely turned to laughter or tears and

---

* Which I am given to understand is presently in the possession of Dr John Mitchell of Philadelphia.

walked through life with barely any acknowledgement that he himself existed. In truth, I have never met a man who used the personal pronoun 'I' so infrequently.

Osloff had few personal pleasures, if any. He played chess well (as I shall later relate) but professed to dislike the game. He would drink at social occasions but did not indulge to excess, as was the habit of his fellow countrymen. He was an acquisitive reader but read only to further his understanding of the nature of the world. The only book I ever knew him to treasure was a copy of the New Testament scriptures in Greek in a modest binding. I believe it had originally belonged to his father. At most, Osloff found a discreet contentment in the resolution of philosophical conundrums and in the contemplation of God.

In his lifetime, the good doctor was given many opportunities to solve riddles (both real and imagined) and it was his faculty with these that made him the darling of the grand duke's inner circle. In 1790, a man was arrested for two most gruesome murders committed in the walled gardens of the hospital at Vitebsk and it was only through Osloff's powers of observation and inference that the true culprit was discovered and the falsely accused man (a member of the local Jewry) was exonerated. The story of this investigation was one that Osloff was required to recount *ad nauseam* at the grand duke's social gatherings. At the very same gatherings, the grand duke would publicly present Osloff with riddles and puzzles of obscure origins and delight in seeing him make his methodical way to the truth, never once managing to confound Osloff. Perhaps Osloff objected to being treated as little more than a performing animal. Perhaps he saw that Grand Duke Paul had genuine affection for his astounding mental powers and only wished to bask in his brilliance. Osloff never spoke of this to me, but since he did attempt (at great personal risk) to warn the grand duke about his impending assassination, we can assume Osloff bore the monarch little ill will.

In August 1796, Grand Duke Paul Petrovich held an extravagant ball at his summer residence. To some, such frolics seemed monstrously insensitive as, not more than five miles away, the grand duke's mother was struggling through the last months of her final illness. Indeed her declining health had caused her to become so fat that her 'greatness' was more aptly attributable to her corpulent size than to any of her earlier deeds. It is true that the empress and the grand duke held no love for one another, she seeing him as a fey and impotent wastrel and he despising her for holding to that opinion, but even someone as naïve as the grand duke (who had few friends and admirers as it was) ought to have comprehended that his decadent entertainments would engender feelings of disgust and derision amongst the kingmakers of the Russian aristocracy.

Nonetheless, the grand duke did hold his ball and, despite the repugnance they would later voice, the guests came. It was a sumptuous and profligate affair and it was said that the food laid out for his five hundred guests would have fed half of St Petersburg with ease. The evening's entertainment featured the performance of a conjurer from Milan. The grand duke enjoyed conjuring acts but, more than that, he took pleasure in asking Osloff (who was in attendance, naturally) to explain how the conjurer's tricks were performed. As ever, Osloff's explanations, given within moments of the end of the magic act, did not disappoint and the Milanese conjurer was dismissed from the palace with the audience's laughter ringing in his ears.

The grand duke asked Osloff if there had ever been a conjurer's illusion that he had not been able to uncover. Osloff admitted without arrogance that there had not. The grand duke was mightily pleased by this. He then asked Osloff if he had heard of Wolfgang von Kempelen and his chess playing Turk. Osloff admitted he had heard of the device but had not had the honour of inspecting it himself, it being located in far off Vienna. The grand duke, Osloff knew, had had this particular honour, having visited Vienna with his second wife during his European travels some twelve or more years before. Grand Duke Paul Petrovich had met Kempelen in the court of the Holy Roman Emperor Joseph II and been impressed by the clockwork automaton that could best the most skilful of chess players. The grand duke had been mystified by the machine. He had heard it said that the Turk was operated by some sort of 'trick' but, like many, he harboured the opinion that the Turk was a genuine mechanical marvel and *constructed* with the ability to play a superior game of chess.

The grand duke owned a number of automata, including a mechanical bird's nest and one of Vaucanson's flautists, and told Osloff that he wished to add Kempelen's Turk to his collection. Kempelen was presently touring the Turk around the cities and towns of Europe, giving demonstrations to nobility and to paying customers. Petrovich had determined to send one of his most trusted clerks to a demonstration in the town of Wittenburg and approach Kempelen with an offer to buy the Turk. However he was loath to pay a considerable amount of money for the Turk if it turned out to be nothing more than an ingenious conjurer's trick. With that in mind, the grand duke wished Osloff to travel with the clerk and inspect the automaton before any money was handed over. Osloff demurred at the suggestion, having no great desire to travel on what he regarded as a grocer's errand, but the grand duke was adamant and so, within a week, Dr Semyon Osloff and the court clerk, a young man by the name of Dmitri Koroshilov, were on a coach bound for Wittenburg, bearing between them a considerable amount of Russian gold.

Osloff and Koroshilov arrived in Wittenburg on 23rd October, a full week or more before Wolfgang von Kempelen and I. Once the two Russian gentlemen had made their introductions, Kastner*, the Bürgermeister of Wittenburg, offered them rooms in his own house rather than at one of the local inns. So it was that when our coach drew into the town square (we had been on the road for more than fifteen hours having spent the previous night in a small village south of Hof) we were received at the town hall or Gerichtslaude by the Bürgermeister, his wife and the two Russians.

Kastner made the introductions with an air of over-familiarity and not a great deal of accuracy. Osloff was introduced as 'Dr Semyon Osloff, a member of the Russian court and personal physician to Catherine the Great.' His companion, Koroshilov, was suddenly elevated to the status of 'imperial treasurer.' Kastner's description of Kempelen was flowery but reasonably true but I, I

---

* A curious man whose full range of emotions, from toadying servility (directed to his honoured guests) to poorly affected contempt (directed at his underlings), was conveyed entirely through the raising and lowering of his eyebrows.

must relate, was introduced as 'Captain Jan Worousky, Kempelen's secretary, a war hero and a learned man of science.' Captain I once was and, as you know, Kempelen's personal assistant and thus privy to all his secrets, but I have never claimed to be a student of the sciences, let alone a 'learned man.'

At this meeting I had my first chance to appraise Osloff's physical appearance. He was a man of precise movement and posture. When standing, he stood erect which gave the impression that he was an extremely tall man, though perhaps in truth no taller than myself (I am three inches short of six foot). He was balding, though he was not yet forty years old, and this lent exaggeration to his high, curving brow and sharp and unfavourable nose. As I have already mentioned, he was not a man given to smiles or frowns but his face was alive nonetheless. His gaze, shadowed by thick dark eyebrows, was wide, roving and all encompassing. When his gaze met mine, I had the distinct impression that he was memorising every detail of my person (although perhaps my memory is now clouded by my subsequent reflections upon his personality and reputation).

That meeting was short but cordial. Night had fallen and we were keen to take to our beds. The Bürgermeister had also provided us with rooms in his house but Kempelen would not allow himself to rest until the mechanical Turk (which, carefully stowed in three crates, had followed our coach upon a heavy wagon) was safely stored indoors. The Bürgermeister's servants ferried the crates from the back of the wagon to the house, while Kempelen fretted over the manhandling of his precious crates like a mother hen clucking over her eggs, a habit of his which I had seen acted out in countless towns and cities. I took myself slowly up the stairs to my room whilst the other people of the house were engaged elsewhere.

We had arrived one day before Wittenburg's Hallowe'en celebrations, a carnival of fools and monsters. Each October, the townsfolk celebrated the eve of All Hallow's Day with a parade of masked and costumed Hofnarren, earthly recreations of the evil that the risen lord has overcome. The carnival was not limited to the parade and attracted entertainers, travelling markets, sideshows and professional freaks from far and wide. It was intended that the mechanical Turk's demonstration games (the first of which was to be held after the carnival on Festnacht) would prove to be the chief cause of celebration that year.

On 31st October, Kempelen and I set to rebuilding and checking the mechanisms of the Turk. Kempelen asked the Bürgermeister for a secure room in which to assemble the machine, far from prying eyes, and the Bürgermeister duly provided us with a large room in his own house with but one door and a sturdy lock to which only the Bürgermeister himself and the housekeeper had keys. The room had shuttered windows. It was bare of all fixtures and fittings save for a single chandelier, and thus perfectly suited to our needs. Kempelen closed and bolted the shutters, had the candles upon the chandelier lit and in that empty seclusion we prepared the mechanical chess player for its evening performance.

We had finished our work by late afternoon and, in due course, we joined the Bürgermeister's party on the balcony of the Gerichtslaude to watch the beginning of the revelries in the square below. I observed Osloff watching me as I climbed slowly and stiffly to the balcony. Being espied, I made an effort to carry myself up those last few steps in a more natural fashion but Osloff was not deceived.

"Are you in pain, captain?" he asked.

"Not at all, doctor," I replied. "Simply tired. It was a long journey yesterday and the reconstruction of the chess player today required all manner of strenuous contortions."

"Perhaps an old war wound haunts you."

I hid my surprise well and simply nodded.

The party on the balcony consisted of the Bürgermeister and his wife, the other esteemed bürgers of the town and, of course, the two Russians. Within moments of arriving on the balcony, Koroshilov had drawn Kempelen aside and began to speak to him in low, confidential tones. I knew well not to involve myself in Kempelen's financial affairs and, taking a glass of wine from one of the Bürgermeister's servants, found a place from which I could best see the parade of fools.

I know that you have travelled through Europe, Mr Houdin, and have perhaps witnessed such things but let me say that there is nothing in the Americas to compare to the Hallowe'en carnival. Perhaps it is because the United States of America is a young

60

nation, a juvenile, and only in great age can a nation dredge up such spectacles of darkness and grotesquery. A vile and disquieting parade of Hofnarren, many with God-given deformity, others merely aping it, had begun to wend its way through the crowded square below, accompanied by enthusiastic but disharmonious music played on the horn and fiddle. Many of the Hofnarren wore "zottelgwaender" suits of ragged patchwork. All wore masks of wood or moulded paper and, in the flickering light of many torches, those gargoyle faces seemed to take on a life of their very own.

The capering fools were dressed to represent specific evils and vices and many of them I was able to recognise. A misshapen brute wearing a jacket stuffed with pillows and a mask with enormous jowls and even larger mouth was the epitome of gluttony. Two dwarfs with hooked nose and curved horns jabbed little pitchforks into the thighs of a gaunt creature whose many chains and long cloth tongue (which hung right down to his waist) marked him as an unrepentant liar. With each stab of the pitchforks and each yelp of pain, the crowd let forth with laughter and cheers. However, one of the figures in the parade seemed curiously out of place, a young and shapely woman (she wore no mask at all) dressed in yellow finery with bells and mirrors hanging as ornaments about her.

I turned to the man next to me, a rotund Bürger with an impressively proud set of moustaches who had been sharing a private joke with the Bürgermeister's wife, and asked him what the woman in yellow signified. He asked which woman I was referring to but when I tried to find her again in the crowd she was gone from sight. The moustachioed Bürger returned to his conversation with Kastner's wife.

At that moment, Osloff joined me at the rail. "She is the Weissnaar," he said. "A beautiful woman but guilty of the sins of vanity and self-obsession."

Kempelen and Koroshilov were with him. I remember seeing a curious expression upon Kempelen's face that seemed comprised in equal parts of exhilaration and trepidation. Not knowing what he and Koroshilov had been discussing, I was mystified by his expression and much of the following conversation

"I believe I have just committed either the most wonderful or most calamitous act of my life," said Kempelen, smiling at

61

Koroshilov and Osloff as though he had uttered the wittiest bon mot but his eyes were fixed solemnly on mine.

I asked Kempelen what exactly he had done to warrant such a dramatic exclamation but, before he could answer, Koroshilov interrupted.

"Nothing is certain yet, Kempelen," he said, somewhat pompously. "We have not inspected the machine."

"You will see it tonight," said Kempelen confidently.

"At close quarters," insisted Koroshilov. "We are not witless theatre-goers to be fooled at a distance by cheap trickery."

Kempelen protested loudly at the insinuation and vowed that Osloff and Koroshilov would be placed in the foremost seats at that night's demonstration.

"As it happens," he went on, "we have yet to elect an opponent for tonight's game. I have heard it said that the Russians are masters of the chessboard, although I must add I have only ever heard it from the lips of Russians!"

Koroshilov immediately deferred to Osloff, confessing that the doctor was by far the better chess player.

"So be it," said Kempelen. "Dr Osloff will play against the Turk!"

Such was his ire and passion at this point[*] that Kempelen said this loud enough for all on the Gerichtslaude balcony to hear. The Bürgermeister declared this excellent news, prompting cheers and small applause from the assembled guests.

With the hour of the chess game approaching, Kempelen and I decided to go back to the Bürgermeister's house in order to make our final adjustments to the Turk. I took a moment to shake Osloff's hand and wish him good luck.

"Will you not be watching the game?" he asked.

"I am sure it will be an excellent example of gamesmanship," I told him, "but I have witnessed the machine play a thousand times and, as I said before, I am quite tired. I would rather retire to bed and rest these weary legs of mine."

Kempelen and I returned to the Bürgermeister's house to prepare both the machine and the room. Once the machine was

---

[*] Which may have owed something to the wine, I cannot say

readied, my weary legs were carted off to bed and Kastner's servants were allowed in. As one closed and locked the shutters, another climbed a stepladder to light the chandelier and a third set out chairs for the spectators according to instructions given earlier by Frau Kastner. Kempelen also requested that a candelabra be brought in and placed beside the chess playing automaton. (I must stress once again that, apart from these items, the room was entirely empty.)

As the clock in the hallway struck one, the door was opened to admit our audience. There was some excitement and a less than dignified rush for seats, but Kempelen had ensured that chairs were reserved at the front of the room for Koroshilov, Kastner and Kastner's wife. One bürger, the rotund fellow with proud moustaches, arrived late and was forced to sit in the back, complaining that guests such as himself would not have been treated so shabbily in the days when his father was Bürgermeister. His truculence notwithstanding, the assembly was animate with good-natured curiosity and high expectations.

It would be well to describe now the chess-playing automaton, although I am sure you have read many descriptions of it including the not entirely accurate article by Mr Poe. The machine took the form of a perfectly proportioned wooden mannequin seated behind a large wooden cabinet measuring four feet in width, two feet in depth and three feet in height. The mannequin was arrayed in fur-trimmed robes and wore a turban atop its head. It is from this attire that the "Turk" gained its common sobriquet. The Turk's face was carved and painted with an expression of deep concentration and dark intent and by the light of the candelabra took on a fearful, even demonic aspect. The candlelight also illuminated a chessboard set into the top of the cabinet upon which the game would be played. On the front of the cabinet were two doors, one significantly larger than the other, and a wide drawer beneath them.

Once the guests were settled, Kempelen stood before them and, with a manner more akin to a circus master than a scientist, gave them a much rehearsed and elaborated introduction to the mechanical chess machine they were about to see. As he spoke, he opened the larger of the two doors on the front of the cabinet, revealing a space within that, apart from three brass quadrants, was entirely empty. Kempelen next opened a corresponding door at the back of the machine and turned the automaton around on its wheeled feet until all of the guests had seen straight through the cabinet, from front to back and from back to front. Following his set routine, Kempelen then closed the large doors and directed the audience's attention to a small door on the side of the cabinet. He also opened the smaller door at the front and invited the audience to note the mechanisms within, which consisted of numerous cogs, springs and ratchets and a set of studded rotating cylinders. It was these cylinders to which many observers have attributed the Turk's chess playing skills, claiming that Kempelen had somehow codified the various chess moves and strategies into the careful arrangement of those tiny studs. Kempelen opened a second door at the back of the machine and held up a candle so that the audience might make out its faint glow through the layers of densely packed machinery. Having demonstrated to the satisfaction of all that there was nothing untoward concealed within the cabinet, Kempelen closed the doors and opened the drawer beneath, from which he then removed the chessmen, a large key and a small wooden box (the purpose of which he did not explain). Kempelen quickly set out the chessmen and then finally invited Osloff to sit down before the Turk.

Kempelen informed Osloff and the audience that the automaton would play white and therefore move first. Furthermore, Kempelen warned, the automaton would not countenance any cheating and would confiscate any piece that was moved illegally. This last caused some amusement in the audience but Osloff merely nodded curtly to show he understood. Kempelen went to the side of the cabinet, inserted the key into a hole and wound the mechanism six or seven times. At once there was a loud clanking sound from within and the Turk juddered into life. Its left hand, which until that moment had lain perfectly still by the chessboard, lifted up into the air, swung over to the king's pawn, picked it up with a jerky click of its wooden fingers and advanced it two squares. Though there were several loud gasps of amazement from the audience, Osloff calmly surveyed the board and then made his own opening move.

And so the game progressed. Kempelen would return to the cabinet to wind up the mechanism every few moves and, at other times, he would take a peek inside the small wooden box he held but, apart from that, the only actors in that gripping drama were Osloff and the Turk itself. The Turk was, by far, the more animated of the two players. As well as moving its hand, it made a wobbly nod of its head whenever it placed its opponent in check and would, on odd occasion, rap its fingers on the table top when it felt that Osloff was taking too long over his move. By contrast, Osloff was quite inert, always sitting alert and erect but only ever stirring to move his piece.

A record of that game was made by a young man in the audience but it has since been lost and I do not recall the very details of the moves made. What I do remember is that the players were evenly matched and took up strong positions on the board from early on. The game held the attention of all and there was fierce debate as to who would win. I should imagine that a number of wagers were also made on the outcome. Koroshilov was very much taken with the Turk and clearly heard to say, "If your machine is the victor in this game, Kempelen, the Grand Duke will definitely be making a purchase." However, he was not forced to make good on his hasty offer because shortly afterwards the Turk made a poorly judged move and Osloff took white's queen. The game concluded five moves later when the Turk tipped over his own king, signalling resignation.

There was applause and hearty congratulations for Osloff, who then complimented Kempelen on having such a gifted chess player in his service. The Bürgermeister also praised Kempelen for laying on such absorbing entertainment and then announced that the drinking and merriment would continue next door in the parlour. Kempelen told Kastner that he needed to perform some small repairs on the chess player and would join the party later. The Bürgermeister would hear nothing of the sort and, guiding Kempelen firmly by the arm, led him from the room before locking the one door with his key.

I was not privy to the conversations that went on in the Bürgermeister's parlour and only heard details of them later on, but I can surmise much of what was said. There is no doubt that many people were in deep discussion about the Turk and the means by which it was able to play such an accomplished game. The Bürgermeister's wife had been notably impressed by the demonstration and was almost insensible with the desire to know how the contraption worked. I have heard many theories put forward over the years in answer to this question. Perhaps (some argued) there was something within that little wooden box that Kempelen kept looking into from time to time. Perhaps Kempelen kept a magnet or several magnets in his jacket pocket and the machine was operated through the manipulation of these. Or perhaps Kempelen directed the automaton's game with wires of catgut, so thin as to be invisible to the naked eye. Of course, there were a few who were either naïve enough or farsighted enough to recognise the possibility that the machine did truly play chess under its own cognisance but these individuals were truly few in number. Koroshilov was amongst these few and, convinced of the chess player's authenticity, was keen to hear Osloff's judgement but the doctor would not be drawn into making a conclusion at that time. (In fact, his thoughts lay elsewhere.) Kempelen was also strangely subdued and kept looking at the clock on the wall.

At some hour when the rest of the Christian world was surely asleep but the Bürgermeister's party was still alive with talk and wine, Kastner spoke briefly to his wife and then, apologising to his guests, said that he would be back in a moment and left the room. Nothing was thought odd of this until, less than a minute later, there came an unmistakeable thumping sound and a small cry from the room next door. Some of the guests were either inebriated or too engrossed in conversation to recognise in the cry some unknown misfortune. But most of those assembled made haste towards the source of the sounds: the room in which they had witnessed the defeat of the Turk. The door was found to be locked and attempts to knock it down were entirely without success.

A great cry went up of "Find the keys!" and people moved off in all directions, calling for Kastner or the housekeeper to come and open the door. I am convinced that some of the more immoderate drinkers thought this to be some peculiar parlour game as they called out with enormous relish and no real sense of alarm. Eventually, the housekeeper was found on the servant's stairway and was hurried along to the locked door. She slowly produced her key and, with trembling hands, unlocked the door.

The guests rushed in, much as they had done earlier that evening, only to find a very different scene awaiting them. The automaton still stood at one end of the room, the candles by its side almost burnt to nothing. And in their light (for the other candles in the room had gone out) it was possible to see the body of the Bürgermeister, Kastner, laid out on the floor in the very centre of the room. Dr Osloff and the housekeeper were quickly at Kastner's side. The Bürgermeister was laid out on his front, blood coursing freely from a wound on the side of his head and so Osloff turned the Bürgermeister onto his back to better tend to the man. The doctor then proceeded to inspect the wound and seek out a pulse or other sign of life. There was however none to be found and Osloff quietly declared the man to be dead.

At this announcement, Kastner's wife began to wail in a most awful manner and Osloff was amongst others in demanding that the woman be taken from the room. Death, I have noted, brings out a great variety of emotions. Some members of the audience, for indeed this was a corpse with an audience, were filled with curiosity and excitement at this dramatic conclusion to the evening. Other less ghoulish persons were filled with an unnecessary shame at having been involved in revelry and celebration in one room whilst Kastner lay dying next door. Amongst them all, only a few had the presence of mind to address the practicalities of the situation.

Osloff instructed the housekeeper to find a room in which the body could be laid out. The town doctor, a red-faced little man by the name of Freidmann, called upon three servants of the house to carry the body up to the room. Kempelen advocated that a priest be found and brought to the house to administer whatever last rites were appropriate. With all these instructions given, one man asked what they should do now. Osloff suggested that the man (and all the gentlemen guests) should take their wives home for there was nothing more to be done that night and the scene of a bloody death was not a fitting place for women to remain.

"But what about the murderer?" cried Freidmann.

"Murderer?" said Osloff, seeming quite surprised. "Yes. I suppose the servants could search the house but any killer who has made it to the street will already be lost in the crowd. There will be many strangers in town to-night."

In the hour that followed, the priest came and nearly all of the guests were persuaded to leave. Soon, the only people remaining in that room were Kempelen, Osloff, Koroshilov, Dr Freidmann and two senior bürgers (a very sober gentleman by the name of Bremner and the rotund, moustachioed man, whose name was Seiler). The main preoccupation of the group's discussion was what was to be done now, namely in finding an explanation for Kastner's death.

Seiler seemed to be of the peculiar opinion that no explanation would be found. The shutters on the windows were firmly closed and bolted and the door had been locked when the guests had tried to come to Kastner's aid.

"Where is Kastner's key?" asked Bremner.

"Here," said Osloff and produced the key from his pocket. "I found it on the body when we first came in. I assume that he locked himself in here when he came in."

"But why did he come in here?" asked Kempelen.

"A good question but one that can wait," said Osloff.

There were no other entrances to the room save a small fireplace, the flue of which was too small for even a child to gain access through. Furthermore, there were no places in the room in which a concealed killer could hide.

"What about inside the chess machine?" said Seiler.

"I showed you that it was empty earlier," said Kempelen.

"Then show us again," demanded Seiler.

"Very well," said Kempelen loudly and crossing to the automaton, repeated his demonstration of earlier that evening, opening doors at front then back and then the second set of doors to the side.

"As you can see," he said, "the machine is quite empty. There is no killer here, unless you think that the Turk itself murdered Kempelen."

Koroshilov chuckled morbidly and without humour.

"If not the Turk, then who? The devil himself?"

"There is also the housekeeper," said Bremner. "She had a key."

Osloff did not think this relevant, saying, "Do you think it possible that she had time to murder the Bürgermeister, leave the room, lock it and flee from sight before any of us came out into the corridor? It seems unlikely."

"What other explanation can there be?" asked Seiler. "I personally found the woman on the servant's stairs. If she was quick she might have done all that and walked there unseen before being discovered."

"Very well," said Osloff. "We will interview her in the morning. However, I think it time we all went to our separate beds. I for one will need fresh eyes and a clear head with which to address this problem. May I suggest that I lock this room when we leave and retain the key so that any evidence that might be found in the morning will remain undisturbed until then."

There was agreement from Koroshilov, Freidmann, Bremner and Seiler but Kempelen objected, not forcefully but with calm reasonableness, and asked that the key be entrusted to him for he had to perform those small acts of maintenance upon the automaton that he had wished to carry out earlier. There were certain springs to be unwound and levers to be reset which might become damaged if left any longer in their presently tensed states. Osloff assented to this request but asked that Kempelen make as little disturbance to the room as possible. With this agreed by all*, each man took to his own room or his own home and by the time the first grey lights of dawn touched the rooftops of Wittenburg, even Kempelen himself was abed and the room in which Kastner had died was locked once more.

Mr Houdin, in desiring to give you a full account of these events I have come to the end of my very last sheet of paper. Have no fear, I shall spend my last few cents in getting this important letter posted to you. As you are no doubt aware, I am an old man now and poor, and such small items are a heavy toll upon my meagre income. It hurts my pride and dignity to ask you for charity but if you could spare me a small amount of money (which I will

---

* Osloff's reputation as a man of wisdom and insight had preceded him and such was his decisive and authoritative manner that the bürgers of Wittenburg were loath to dispute his judgements.

pay back to you in due course) I will be able to write to you again all the sooner.

Your sincere and humble servant

J. Worousky

Boston, December 12th 1844

Dear Mr Houdin,

I am extremely grateful for the generous and entirely unexpected gift of $20 that you have sent to me. This day I have been able to purchase some fine ink and paper with which to continue our correspondence and to pay off some debts that I have regrettably incurred with certain businessmen.

In answer to your first question, nearly all the discourse that took place in Wittenburg over the duration of our stay were conducted in German. Wolfgang von Kempelen was Hungarian by birth but chose to speak German wherever possible to demonstrate his personal devotion to the empire and the Holy Roman Emperor. As a Pole, German is not my first language nor even my second but I speak it well enough to be accepted in polite society (though my written German is quite atrocious). One of the criteria upon which Dmitri Koroshilov was selected for this mission of acquisition was his faculty with German and Dr Osloff knew several languages, although mostly in a dry and academic manner. Osloff occasionally slipped into Russian when in conversation with me, knowing full well that as a former Polish officer I spoke it fluently. I am also sure that Osloff and Koroshilov conducted their private discussions in their mother tongue. With regard to your second question, my memory for dialogue is good but not perfect. Given that I am translating as well as transcribing what I remember, you will have to forgive me if I paraphrase from time to time and do not quote each person verbatim.

If I recall correctly, my narrative had reached the point at which Kempelen himself went to bed. Before going to sleep, he spoke to me about all that had occurred that evening and, by the time morning was truly upon us, I was fully briefed on the events that I had happened to miss the night before.

Few, I imagine, had slept well that night (save perhaps Kastner's wife who had been given a sleeping draught by Dr Freidmann to combat her hysterical nature) and when I descended the stairs that morning I expected there to be no one about. However, I found Dr Osloff by the parlour room window, looking rested and alert, a cup of steaming tea poised most artfully in his hand and his gaze upon the quiet scene outside. Without turning his eyes from the view, he addressed me by name.

"Good morning, doctor," I replied. "I have heard the terrible news."

"I beg your pardon?" said Osloff, giving me a most studious look as though I were something being inspected through a microscope.

"About the Bürgermeister," I explained. "It is terrible news."

"Of course. I am surprised that you managed to remain asleep through all the clamour and commotion of the evening."

I explained that I was a deep sleeper.

"There were screams and shouts in the house last night," argued Osloff, "not least from Frau Kastner, who would have been carried right past your room on the way to hers. You must be a very deep sleeper."

I nodded calmly and said, "It is a soldier's gift. Warfare, you see doctor, consists of long periods of excruciating boredom interspersed with brief moments of action. A good soldier learns to sleep through the boredom and remain awake during the moments of action. A poor soldier stays awake with fear and dies because he is too tired to carry out his duties. I have slept through entire nights of cannon fire before."

Osloff appeared to accept this explanation. "Well, as a soldier you have no doubt witnessed violent deaths in many forms."

"Indeed I have," I said but added, "though I wish it were otherwise."

"Then perhaps you will be able to assist me shortly. Dr Freidmann will be arriving to examine the Bürgermeister's body with me. I would value your opinion also."

And so when Dr Freidmann came to the house shortly afterwards, the three of us went to the room in which Kastner's corpse had been placed. It was laid out on a small cot and covered with a white sheet. The Bürgermeister's wound had not been cleaned up or bandaged in any way and the side of his head and a small area of the bed were darkened with a crusted layer of dried blood. Osloff possessed a narrow metal rule and used this to measure the width of the gash in Kastner's skull.

"Any thoughts, Dr Freidmann?" enquired Osloff.

Dr Freidmann puffed out his cheeks and, after a momentary pause for thought, said, "Death must have been instantaneous."

To elucidate his point, Freidmann reached into the wound and with a delicate touch pulled out a bloodied but shiny fragment of skull, a shard the shape and size of an ancient arrow head.

"But what kind of weapon did this?" asked Osloff of both of us.

"A heavy instrument to be sure," said Freidmann.

"A sword perhaps," I offered but Freidmann was shaking his head.

"A sword blow is a clean blow," he said. "This skull has been pulverised."

"A blunt instrument then. A fireside poker."

Osloff inserted his forefinger into the wound and such was the depth of Kastner's injury that Osloff could penetrate it fully without his finger becoming bloodied.

"Do you know of any man who could drive a poker quite so deeply into a man's head?"

I admitted that I did not.

Osloff surmised, not without irony, that the murderer must have been a man of enormous strength, who was able to enter a room through a locked door and disappear again without being seen.

"And our only suspect so far is the housekeeper, a woman of advancing years who seems neither fleet of foot nor exceptionally strong," said Osloff. "Nonetheless, we must speak to her."

In the late morning, bürgers Seiler and Bremner came to the house and, along with Osloff and me,* interviewed the housekeeper.

The poor old maid seemed quite terrified as she stood before us in the parlour but I was astute enough to not equate that fear with guilt. So used to being unnoticed by her betters, she was now subjected to scrutiny by four men who, she no doubt presumed, thought her responsible for Kastner's death. Osloff made no effort to put her mind at ease but questioned her directly.

"Who has keys to the room next door?" he asked.

"I do, sir," the housekeeper replied meekly. "And the master. He had a key too."

"Are there any other keys for the lock on that door?"

"Not that I know of, sir."

"Not that you know of?" he said accusatorially. "How long have you been the housekeeper here?"

"Eight years, sir. I was maid of the upper stairs for ten years before that. Longest serving member of the household, if you do not mind me saying, sir. I was housekeeper before Herr Kastner was made Bürgermeister and saw that key passed from his predecessor to him."

"Then you will know if there are any other ways into that room excepting the doorway."

"None, sir," said the housekeeper.

"Where were you at the time of the murder?" asked Bremner.

"I would have been upstairs, sir. That is where I was when I heard the shouting and such."

"What were you doing upstairs?"

"I was making sure my girls had finished their evening duties. And I could hear a window creaking so I was looking into the rooms to see if one had been left open somewhere. I did look in on the captain," she said and gave me a blushing bow of the head. "I do beg your pardon, sir, but I thought your window might have been open so I went in not realising you were already asleep."

"Did you speak to Captain Worousky?" asked Osloff.

"No, sir. I opened the door and saw him lying in bed. I could see his feet poking out of the end of the bed, you see. So I

---

* Freidmann had gone to tend to the continually distraught Frau Kastner and both Kempelen and Koroshilov were still in their beds.

apologised to him and left. It was maybe then that I heard the first cries from downstairs."

"Did anyone else see you upstairs at that time?" asked Osloff.

"No, sir, not until Herr Seiler met me on the stairway and he told me to come down to the hall. I came as quick as I could, sir."

"Of course you did," said Osloff, his tone gentle now. "You have clearly been a loyal and hardworking servant and you have demonstrated that again to us this morning with your precise and honest answers. Thank you."

The housekeeper curtseyed and went to the door, only to be called back by Osloff.

"There is one last question for you," he said and pointed a long stiff finger at her. "What is that on your collar?"

I had not noticed the mark until Osloff had mentioned it but now I could make out a tiny, dark and round stain on the woman's uniform. The housekeeper also seemed to have been unaware of it.

"I do not know, sir," she said.

"It is a blood stain, made by a small drop of blood," Osloff informed her. "How might that have got there? Were you wearing those clothes last night?"

"I was, sir."

"Then it must be Kastner's blood," interjected Bremner. "I distinctly remember that she was crouched beside you when the body was first discovered. Surely, she must have touched the body or the blood on the floor and then accidentally transferred the material to her collar, smearing it with a thoughtless caress of her fingers."

"An excellent explanation, Herr Bremner," said Osloff, "but with one flaw. This stain is not a smear of blood. It is a drop of blood. Come see that the stain is almost perfectly circular. This drop of blood has *landed* on the housekeeper's collar either from Kastner's wound, naturally assuming that it is the Bürgermeister's blood, or-"

At this juncture, Osloff broke off and raised his eyes heavenward in sudden and deep contemplation. None wished to break the man's silence, for it was as if we could hear the great doctor's thoughts in motion, almost see the great wheels of his mind revolving, but the housekeeper could not contain herself.

"I did not kill him, sir!" she ejaculated with as much fervour as her station could allow. "I was never anything but loyal to him! Though times is lean and I've had to take a cut in pay, I've had nothing to complain about. Always loyal, that's me."

"But of course you did not kill him," said Osloff most abruptly and, without seeking the concurrence of the rest of us, dismissed the woman from the room.

Once she was gone, Seiler snorted and slapped his belly and said, "Dr Osloff, your reputation for intellectualism means naught to me! You must be entirely insensible to think that woman is innocent. She was the only person with access to the room and she has even been marked with her victim's blood."

I decided that I must speak at that point.

"Herr Seiler, you forget that she was in my room at the very moment the Bürgermeister was killed," I said.

"You were asleep. She could have invented the episode to divert our attentions."

"I may have been asleep but she entered my room with more noise and fuss than a she elephant. It was to rouse me momentarily. I do recall seeing her shadow in the doorway."

Seiler was displeased but mollified in some measure and there was no more talk of the housekeeper having committed the foul murder. That meeting ended with no better understanding of the Bürgermeister's demise than with which it had begun. Bremner reported that a search had been made of the town and inquiries made of all foreigners and transients in the town's hostelries but there had been no discoveries of note. Furthermore, he explained, there had been a serving man by the front door all last night and various kitchen servants by the rear entrance to the Bürgermeister's house and none had espied a stranger trying to exit the building around the time of Kastner's death.

"The people of the town have heard the details of this incident," added Seiler. "They fear that witchcraft has played a part in Kastner's death. The day's festivities may not proceed if the townspeople are afraid to leave their homes."

"Very well," said Osloff at last. "We must tell them that the Bürgermeister's death was an accident. Inform them that Kastner fell whilst drunk and dashed his head against a chair."

Neither of the two bürgers approved of disseminating such lies but they saw the prudence in allaying the public's fears and left to make such announcements as were necessary.

"God does not look kindly upon liars, even those with noble intentions," said Osloff, so quietly that at first I thought he was musing to himself, but then he turned and fixed me with such a steely glare that I was put in no doubt that he knew I had spoken falsely about seeing the housekeeper in my room the previous night.

"But the housekeeper is innocent," I insisted. "Your investigation of Kastner's murder must now be at an end."

"Not at all, captain! There is still more to be discovered," said Osloff, "Let us inspect the room again. If I am not mistaken, I perceive the weight and shape of the key in your coat pocket."

Surprised though I was at Osloff's perceptiveness (for Kempelen had in certainty entrusted the key to me before taking to his bed), the doctor was not at all mistaken and so we proceeded to the nearby room whereupon I unlocked the door and we two entered. As the room had remained unopened since last night, with the shutters still closed and the chandelier and the candelabra unlit, it was now in complete darkness. I made my way cautiously over to the windows and unbolted and opened the shutters one by one. Daylight now illuminated the scene, the neatly set out rows of chairs, the inert form of Kempelen's chess playing automaton and the dark and irregular patch of blood in the centre of the floor.

"What do you hope to discover in here, doctor?" I asked.

"Inspiration," Osloff replied. "We must establish what riddle faces us and thus find its ultimate resolution. We must think what questions we wish to find answers to."

"Who killed the Bürgermeister?" I suggested.

"The most obvious question. What else, captain?"

I thought for a moment and said, "How was the Bürgermeister killed?"

"Go on," said Osloff.

"Why would someone want to kill the Bürgermeister?"

"Good. Can you think of any more?"

I could tell that I was being tested and, though Osloff displayed no outward signs of enjoyment, he was taking unmistakable pleasure in testing me so. I considered the matter more intently and, being struck by an original thought, added, "What was the Bürgermeister doing in here at all?"

"Indeed!" said Osloff, his eyes afire. "What was he doing in here?"

"I assumed he had come in here to take a closer look at the automaton whilst no one else was about, wishing to uncover the secrets of Kempelen's machine."

Osloff agreed with my hypothesis.

"Shortly before he left the parlour to come in here, Kastner and his wife were engaged in serious debate regarding the machine's workings. What strikes me as unaccountably odd is how the murderer knew Kastner would be in that room. It seems unlikely to the point of foolishness that the murderer would wait in here for him on the chance that the Bürgermeister's curiosity would get the better of him."

I put it to Osloff that the murderer had perhaps followed the Bürgermeister into the room.

"And yet the room was empty and locked, almost certainly from the inside, when we entered," he said.

"Can you be sure?" I said. "Perhaps the assassin hid behind the door when you entered and then simply joined the back of the crowd when all attention was on the body."

Osloff admitted that this was an intriguing notion. The theory was put to the test. I stood behind the door whilst Osloff opened it but such was the arrangement of the door and wall that even I, a man with no spare flesh on my body, could not fit comfortably behind it.

"Besides, hiding behind the door simply does not seem in accordance with the *ambience* of this murder," said Osloff.

I asked Osloff what he meant by this cryptic comment and he proceeded to explain.

"Look at this room, dear captain. What do we see? Chairs arranged in an orderly fashion, the automaton immobile and much as it was left, shutters and door that were firmly closed and, in the very middle of the room, a significant pool of blood. A murder was committed in here. So what is missing from the room?"

I was not immediately aware that this last question was directed at myself but Osloff prompted me to answer. I confessed that I could not see what essential items were missing.

"If a murderous attack took place in here, where are the signs of a struggle?" said Osloff. "Where are the overturned chairs? Where is the bloody handprint? Where are the footprints? Where is the hastily discarded murder weapon? I speak in figurative terms, captain, but I hope you understand my point. We stand at the scene of a brutal murder and yet the scene offers not one hint that the murderer was ever in here."

Osloff had come to stand by one of the windows and his gaze had fallen upon a small knothole, no wider than a thumbnail, in one of the shutters. He slipped his finger partway into the hole and regarded it with an absent minded aimlessness (although I have since come to realise, Mr Houdin, that Dr Osloff never acted in a manner that was either absent minded or aimless).

"Then perhaps the murderer was not in this room at all," he said.

I was about to ask what could be meant by such apparent nonsense but I was forestalled by the arrival of Kempelen. My master, who had only recently arisen, was in a foul temper and of capricious mood and had few good words for me that morning.

"I have been looking everywhere for you," he said.

I explained that I had been helping Dr Osloff with his investigation.

"And have you idly stood by whilst he inspects our automaton?" Kempelen demanded. "The protection of my scientific discoveries is part of your most vital duties."

"Herr Kempelen, your 'scientific discoveries' are not my primary concern this day," said Osloff, his tone both appeasing and reproaching the mechanician. "We have been attempting to ascertain the details of the unfortunate Bürgermeister's death. I would only be interested in your automaton if that Turkish gentleman's eyes could truly see and were witness to the criminal act."

The Turk's dark gaze held us all in that moment and I felt a singular chill of fear when meeting them.

"But see they cannot," said Osloff. He turned to face me. "I thank you for your assistance this morning, Captain Worousky. It seems you are required elsewhere. We shall speak later."

He bid us farewell and left me in the disagreeable company of my normally congenial friend and employer. I was glad that Osloff was not in the room in the hour that followed for Kempelen and I, who always shared a frank and honest relationship, had much to say to each other that was not pleasant to hear. Let me say for now that Koroshilov's planned purchase of the automaton filled Kempelen with glee but held nothing except uncertainty and consternation for myself. We kept our voices low (for we were in a house of mourning) but unkind words were said and in time I felt a need to leave the house lest I say something truly unforgivable.

I left the Bürgermeister's house to find that the streets of Wittenburg were once again host to the stalls and sideshows of the Festnacht carnival. Seiler and Bremner had evidently succeeded in allaying certain fears amongst the townsfolk and enticed them back to their revels. The revels were more subdued this day and rightly so! There was music but it was modest in tone and lacking excessive gaiety and there were smiles but none of the uproarious laughter or cheering of the previous day.

I ate a light meal and drank a small beer at one of the local inns before taking a stroll through the market place. There was a great deal of entertainment to be seen in the town but nothing retained my interest for long. Eventually, in my meandering tour, I came upon Dr Osloff once more. He was watching the performance of a marionette theatre that had been erected in the yard beside the church and was so thoroughly engrossed by the actions of the miniature figures on stage that he did not at first realise I was standing beside him. I was somewhat perplexed by the intensity of his concentration and after regarding the puppets' play at length, asked him if it was appropriate for a man of his standing to be so enamoured of an entertainment whose principal devotees were children and halfwits.

In hindsight I can perceive that my question was ill couched and it was entirely probable that my voice still carried some of the anger that my argument with Kempelen had earlier engendered.

Whatever the case, Osloff did not take kindly to the question or the interruption and told me so.

"You speak as though I should be ashamed to stand here," he said. "Is there something unseemly about this presentation, sir?"

I replied that I had no moral objection but that the marionette theatre was a simple and childish diversion and lacked any of the high artistry that marked out more worthy entertainments.

Osloff thought this argument lacked merit.

"You eschew something for its simplicity," he said, "somehow equating complexity and sophistication with a higher artistic ideal. I myself find that most strange. As a child, I spent many hours in the fields and the grassy plains near my home, studying the animals and plant life and collecting specimens in jars. Many specimens I was able to identify myself but others I would have to take home and ask my father's opinion on. I would happily watch the movements of a beetle – a *simple* creature – for hours. The years moved on and, yes, life does become more complex and more sophisticated but I have never forgotten what can be learnt in the contemplation of the simple things. For it is true that adults learn to ignore simple things, mistaking simplicity for unimportance. Regard the marionettes, captain. Do you see them dance?"

"I see them dance," I said. The four little figures, two male, two female, jiggled about in accompaniment to a rough and rustic tune that the puppeteer's accomplice played on pipes that were not unlike the penny whistles that our American children are given as Christmas presents.

Osloff asked me then, did I think myself able to dance as well of those puppets. I laughed and said that my legs were not up to such exertion. Osloff went on further to say that even the most proficient of dancers could not hope to match those marionettes. I scoffed at this and made it clear that I could not agree with such an assertion.

"Look closer," he said. "Ignore the pipe player - he cannot even keep in time with himself – but simply observe the marionettes. See how the knees and hands rise in co-ordination. See how the elbows bend, the feet tilt, each describing a perfect arc through the air."

I did as he bid me do and, slowly to be certain, a transformation took place in what I saw. Osloff was quite right. Though I find it difficult to explain, Mr Houdin, the movements of the figures' limbs were flawlessly unified with one another. They were separate from each other in time and movement and yet together in harmony, perhaps in the same way that the component parts of a beautiful face, though obviously distinct from one another, in congruence conspire to create a well-proportioned and harmonious whole.

"They possess a graceful quality," I conceded.

"Graceful," said Osloff, much taken with my choice of words. "And where does this grace derive from? Does the puppeteer possess a grace and a skill which somehow eludes the world's finest dancers? Hardly. Besides, you will note that the puppeteer does not control all the puppets' movements. There are but two strings to each puppet and yet – the flex of that wrist there, the tilt of the head – it is as if the marionettes have a life, an anima of their own."

"It is gravity and the laws of physics at play here," I said, truly understanding at last. "The limbs are pendulums."

"Exactly," said Osloff. "The marionettes act as though controlled individually and with minute precision but in fact all of their movements are focused around a single centre of gravity. The puppeteer is a complex and, in all likelihood, a graceless creature but he creates a graceful piece of theatre through the simple action of pulling a couple of strings. The marionette is mindless but achieves a beauty that we, for all our intellect, cannot attain. Perfection, dear captain, is found in grace and simplicity and innocence."

This last was spoken with a particular fervency and I perceived that Osloff had revealed something of his own philosophy with this remark and indeed he continued to speak in a manner that was most personal.

"*Pluralitas non est ponenda sine neccesitate**, captain. It is in the contemplation of the simple that we find truth. In contemplation of the simple cross we find God's truth. And it is also

---

* Mr Houdin, I trust you are familiar with these most famous words of William of Ockham.

said that the monks of the Far East find their own truth through meditating upon the most simple thing of all: nothingness."

His good humour (such as there was of it) had returned and it was with some small cheer that he said, "I have at least found my own portion of truth for the day."

"And what is that?" I asked.

"I now know who killed the Bürgermeister," he said.

Mr Houdin, a full two days and two nights have passed in the writing of this letter and now the lamp on what passes for my table is burning low. I have no more lamp oil in the house but shall use what remains of my money in purchasing some on the morrow. The winter is particularly harsh in New England, it is not yet even Christmas and I constantly worry that I have not put aside enough money, food or firewood to see me through to the spring. If you could send some small token of your friendship to me, my spirits would no doubt be elevated and that golden springtime would not seem so distant.

Your loyal and thankful friend,

J. Worousky

Boston, January 20th 1845

Dear Mr Houdin,

I thank you for your most kind letter and gift. Such a sum of money will not last long, particularly so since my landlord has with the turn of the new year decided to raise the rent, but the spirit in which the gesture is made is appreciated nonetheless.

In the evening of the day that followed Kastner's murder, Dr Osloff called together a number of people in the Bürgermeister's house. Osloff chose to hold that extraordinary meeting in the very room in which Kastner had died and Osloff made it clear to all upon invitation that the purpose of the gathering was to expose Kastner's killer. Before the arrival of the others, Osloff had had the shutters on the windows closed and bolted and the chandelier and the candelabra by the automaton chess player lit in the same manner as the night before. Amongst those invited were bürgers Seiler and Bremner as well as Dr Freidmann, Koroshilov, Kempelen, Frau Kastner,* the family priest, Kastner's housekeeper and myself and, although I was possibly not alone in thinking the chosen location and brazenly stated purpose of the meeting altogether too macabre, none of those invited refused to attend.

I remember vividly how, whilst we sat down on the arranged seats, Osloff took a position at the head of the room next to the Turk and adopted the position of an academic master about to give a lecture, one hand tucked inside his jacket and his face raised in order to project his voice more clearly. He briefly thanked those present for attending at such short notice and then, without preamble, launched into a speech which bore echoes of the discussion he and I had had earlier that day in front the marionette theatre.

"The murder of Herr Kastner was a most curious thing," he began. "There were numerous baffling details surrounding his death, not least of all the unusual business of the keys and the locked door, but most curious of all to my mind was the sheer simplicity of the murderous act."

Osloff paused and cast his eyes across the assembled persons but, as no one in the room (myself included) yet understood what he was talking about, he continued.

"Let us consider the events of last night. Herr Kastner was enjoying an evening of drink, merriment and pleasant conversation. At some point in the early hours of the morning a propos of nothing discernible, Herr Kastner excused himself from the party, made his way into this room, unlocking the door and then locking it again behind himself, walked across the room and was suddenly struck down by a single blow of enormous strength."

Frau Kastner gave out a sob at this and pressed an herbal pomander firmly against her nose and mouth to stifle her sorrow. Osloff ignored the interruption.

---

* who spent much of the time sniffing an herbal pomander that Freidmann had given her to calm her nerves.

"The door was not unlocked again for some minutes but, once the door was opened, the room was found to be much as we see it now. There had been no sounds of a confrontation between Herr Kastner and his assailant, and no signs of a struggle were found within the room. There are no material clues as to who had attacked the late Bürgermeister. This, I can assure you ladies and gentlemen, is not normal. I have been the sombre witness to scenes of death in the past and I have never seen an act so perfectly executed.

"Think if you will about the character of Herr Kastner's killer. This act of murder was premeditated and Herr Kastner's killer had therefore carried deadly intent in his or her heart for some time – weeks, months, or even longer. Herr Kastner's killer is a twisted and sinful creature and sinful creatures cannot act with such precision as was shown here. The guilty and sinful mind is a thing in flux, turbulent and complex, and incapable of such perfection."

"Are you daring to describe the Bürgermeister's death as 'perfect'?" demanded Bremner hotly.

"Not morally perfect," Osloff assured him. "The perfection lies in its complete flawlessness. But, as I am trying to indicate, perfection and the sinful heart are quite incompatible. Perfection is the bedfellow of grace, simplicity and innocence. So, I was forced to ask myself, how could our complex and sinful murderer give life to this one simple and perfect act of murder?"

"I hope you have an answer," said Seiler, yawning, "because so far I have heard nothing from you but empty and meaningless waffle."

"I do have an answer indeed, Herr Seiler," said Osloff. "The answer came to me this afternoon whilst regarding the dancing of a marionette. The marionette, you see, is a simple and elegant thing but the man pulling the strings – he is as graceless and sinful as the rest of us. It occurred to me that this puzzle of Herr Kastner's murder also featured a marionette of sorts."

Dr Freidmann professed that he did not understand Osloff's meaning.

"We must look for something that acted on the murderer's behalf," explained Osloff. "The murderer himself was not able to be in this room. Herr Kastner had locked himself inside and, whatever fancies we might choose to concoct, there is no other way in or out of this room. The chimney flue is tiny and the shutters were firmly closed. The murderer was definitely outside the room."

"I have it!" I declared loudly. "The murderer was outside the house, armed with a long bored firearm of some sort. He fired through the window, killing the Bürgermeister with a single shot to the head."

"An interesting conceit," said Osloff not unkindly, "but entirely ridiculous. First of all, captain, the murderer would have to fire through the shutters."

"And there is a hole in one of the shutters right there," I said. "I saw you put your finger through it this morning."

"It was a knothole, not made by either man or firearm," said Osloff. "But you have failed to grasp my point. If the killer fired through the wood of the shutter, how could he have possibly known at what to aim? Furthermore, Herr Kastner's wound was in the top of his head, not the side, and there was no lead shot in that wound when Dr Freidmann and I inspected it. The Bürgermeister was not shot and though the murderer was outside the room, the murder weapon was not. In fact, the murder weapon is in the room at this very moment."

Osloff's assertion that the killer's weapon remained in the room caused an amount of dismay. The priest gave a shout of disbelief, Frau Kastner sobbed once more into her pomander and I was amongst several men who began to scour the room for sight of a likely weapon. And then Bremner let out a cry of inspiration.

"The Turk!"

Kempelen was at once on his feet, placed himself before the Turk with arms spread as though protecting a loved one.

"Herr Bremner, Herr Kempelen, calm yourselves!" commanded Osloff. "This inanimate lump of wood could no more kill Herr Kastner than it could best me at chess. It had nothing to do with Herr Kastner's death except for the fact that the Bürgermeister had come in here to get a closer look at the machine."

Kempelen returned slowly and reluctantly to his seat and order was restored to the room.

Osloff gave a mighty sigh and said, "There are too many individuals in this world ready to act on a hastily reached conclusion. We should not be among them. If we were only to think clearly for a minute, the answer would become obvious. Let me present you with five noteworthy facts relating to this incident. Firstly, there is the extraordinary strength of the blow that killed Herr Kastner, far more violent and penetrating than most men could possibly deliver. Secondly, there is the fact that the killer could not possibly have been in the room with Herr Kastner. Thirdly, there is the small but perfectly round blood stain on the housekeeper's collar."

"Yes," said Seiler triumphantly. "You now admit that the housekeeper had some part in this."

"Only in that she was a witness to the murder," said Osloff, "insomuch that the fourth fact, which many of you might have forgotten, is the creaking sound that the housekeeper heard upstairs shortly before Herr Kastner's death. And the fifth fact is the most telling of all. If you remember, when we entered the room and discovered Herr Kastner's body, the only illumination in the room came from the candelabra that had been placed next to the chess machine. I thought that most odd at the time. The candelabra and the chandelier would have been lit at the same time and bearing identical candles and yet the candles on the chandelier had gone out. How could this be? When, of course, the answer did come to me I knew at once what the creaking sound had been, how the blood had appeared on the housekeeper's collar and how the Bürgermeister was murdered." Osloff lifted his gaze to the chandelier that hung from the ceiling in the very centre of the room, directly above the spot upon which Herr Kastner had died.

"The candles were extinguished when the chandelier fell from the ceiling and onto Herr Kastner's head," explained Osloff. "It was the rounded end of the centre spike which pierced the Bürgermeister's skull with such force, killing him in but an instant. The speck of blood on the housekeeper's collar must have fallen from the chandelier above as she and I tended to the dead Bürgermeister below."

"Amazing," said Dr Freidmann, who was truly impressed by the ingenuity of Dr Osloff's logic (as was I). "But tell me, doctor.

How did the chandelier come to fall and why was it not on the floor when we entered the room?"

"You might not be familiar with chandeliers such as these," said Osloff. "As you can see, the rope which upholds the chandelier runs through a hole in the ceiling and into a room on the floor above, most likely a cupboard or storeroom. The rope is tied off in such a way that it cannot fall of its own accord. However, should the rope be untied, a person in the room above can drop and then pull up the chandelier with relative ease. The hole that the rope passes through is just wide enough for the person in the room above to see part of this room and thus determine when the victim was passing underneath. The creaking sound that the housekeeper heard upstairs was undoubtedly the Bürgermeister's assassin moving about in that room and preparing to drop the chandelier on Herr Kastner's head."

"But who dropped the chandelier on Herr Kastner?" asked Koroshilov.

"It would have to have been someone familiar with the house, someone who lives in the house or who had lived in the house at some point in the past. Furthermore, it would have been someone who stood to benefit from the Bürgermeister's death. Tell me, Herr Bremner," said Osloff, fixing his attention on the sober gentleman, "who will be the next Bürgermeister?"

Bremner was slow in answering and evasive.

"We have not even yet begun to consider that matter, doctor. To do so before the incumbent Bürgermeister has even been laid to rest would show the utmost disrespect."

"But once the due respect has been shown to the late Bürgermeister, who would be likely to take his position?" asked Osloff patiently.

Bremner said that there were numerous candidates and reeled off a list of about five or six names, including his own and Seiler's.

"Oh, yes," said Osloff, as though a thought had suddenly struck him (although, of course, this was the point he had been leading to all along). "Herr Seiler, your father was the previous Bürgermeister, wasn't he? You lived here in this house as a younger man. I remember you saying so last night. It must have been galling that the exalted position of Bürgermeister did not pass from father to son, as you unquestionably felt it should. Is that why you killed Herr Kastner?"

Seiler was dumbfounded but Osloff paid no heed to the man and addressed his next question to the housekeeper.

"On the night of the Bürgermeister's death, is it true that Herr Seiler found you on the servant's stairs?"

The housekeeper replied that she had.

"You see?" said Seiler. "How could I have been messing about with ropes on the floor above, if I was seen coming upstairs from the ground floor?"

Osloff asked the housekeeper if she had in fact seen Herr Seiler coming *up* the stairs. She hesitated at first and he asked her to think clearly and answer honestly. She finally answered in the negative, saying that she had met Herr Seiler at the top of the stairs.

"He had his back to me at first, facing the stairs," she said.

"As I suspected," said Osloff. "May I suggest that it was not Herr Seiler who found the housekeeper as he climbed the stairs but in truth it was the housekeeper who found Herr Seiler about to go downstairs."

"Such lies!" roared Seiler, getting to his feet. "The woman is obviously lying to save her own skin!"

"Is she?" asked Osloff. "I wonder if anyone here can remember being in your company in those few vital minutes before Herr Kastner's death. Anyone?"

No one was able to speak in Seiler's defence.

Seiler thrust a quivering finger towards Osloff. "The impudence of your accusations, sir! I endeavoured to offer you every courtesy in our humble town, even though you have trampled on our hospitality and lorded about the place as though you were the emperor himself! I won't listen to this a moment longer!"

Seiler drove a path to the door, pushing chairs and also the poor priest aside in his haste to make an exit. None moved to stop him. Indeed, Bremner felt that Osloff was very much the man in the wrong.

"You have no evidence to support these allegations, doctor. Your manner is most inappropriate. See what distress you have caused to the widow Kastner," he said, gesturing towards the weeping woman who clung to Dr Freidmann for support and whose breaths were ragged and undignified sobs.

Osloff told him to save his concerns for those who deserve them

"Frau Kastner's tears are only for herself," he said. "Her grief is but an act."

This remark was a shade too severe for even me to stomach and I wondered whether Osloff had lost all sense of decency. At a time and distance removed, I now perceive that Osloff had at that moment revealed one of his few notable faults: a certain lack of empathy with his fellow man. Osloff's unwavering honesty and emotional aloofness had removed from him certain elements of tact and sensitivity that the likes of myself take for granted. Osloff was a phenomenal master of logic and a man whose objectivity in observation was unsurpassed but that objectivity came at a cost.

However, I had not come to these conclusions until some years later and at that moment, in the Bürgermeister's house, I was roused to displeasure by his words. Others shared my sentiments and Osloff came under a sudden barrage of harsh criticism but one that he weathered with great stoicism.

"Frau Kastner cannot weep honestly for her husband for she assisted Herr Seiler in the murder," said Osloff.

Bremner instantly demanded that Osloff substantiate his allegation or withdraw it at once. In response, Osloff explained that Seiler must have had an accomplice for there were certain events that he could not have engineered alone. He directed everyone's attention to the chandelier once more.

"As a murder weapon, the chandelier has one particular defect. The victim must pass directly beneath it. How convenient it was for Herr Seiler that the chairs in this room had been arranged in such a manner that the Bürgermeister was obliged to walk beneath the chandelier in order to reach the chess playing machine, here. Furthermore, Seiler could hardly have gone up to the room above and merely *hoped* that Herr Kastner's inquisitiveness would impel him to come into this room. No, while many in the parlour discussed the mystery of the Turk, one person's desire for an explanation was so strong, so insistent, that Herr Kastner was all but forced to come in here to unmask the machine."

Osloff glared at the widow Kastner with a dreadful expression of contempt.

"There is nothing in God's creation that drives men to action so much as the nagging ways of women, is there? It was also you who instructed the household servants to set out the chairs in this formation."

"That is all conjecture and supposition," said Bremner. "It is not proof."

Osloff conceded that this was true.

"Even I was not convinced that my hypothesis was correct," said Osloff, "until Frau Kastner gave herself away, not ten minutes ago."

"How did she do that?" I asked. "I have seen nothing improper in her behaviour."

"Perhaps you did not notice," said Osloff, "but when I told you that the murder weapon still was in this room, Frau Kastner's eyes darted instinctively to the chandelier. It was an unintentional act and a moment later she attempted to hide what she had done with another of her theatrical and unladylike wails but she had laid bare her guilty heart for all to see. She knew how her husband had died because she had orchestrated his death."

"But why?" demanded Freidmann. "For what reason would she want to kill her husband?"

"For the promise of a better life," said Osloff, "by which I mean marriage to a wealthier man, the new Bürgermeister of Wittenburg no less. Some amongst us heard the housekeeper admit this morning that Herr Kastner, though a holder of a prestigious position, had fallen on lean times. That was unacceptable to Frau Kastner, whose very character is comprised of vanity and self-obsession: a Weissnaar if you will."

The widow Kastner (whose feigned weeping had ceased) stood up now and, in a quiet but scarcely restrained tone, told Osloff that he was no longer a guest in her house and was to leave immediately. Osloff remained where he was and said nothing in response. At this, Frau Kastner discarded all sense of self-control and screamed such invective and insults at the doctor that I could not bring myself to repeat them in this letter.

Irrespective of what conclusions each of us had drawn that evening (and there were various opinions as to whom guilt should be attributed and for what particular sins), it was hastily decided that, for the sake of good taste and civility, the gathering should be brought to an end. Kempelen and I retired swiftly to our rooms whilst Osloff and Koroshilov decamped to one of the local inns. Before taking to our beds, Kempelen stated that we would leave town the next day, as early as was decently possible. I heartily agreed with him. Neither of us spoke of the evening's proceedings but each went to bed with nothing else in our thoughts.

The following morning, the Bürgermeister's house was silent. It was not a restful silence, nor the sombre silence of the tomb, but the silence of a ruffian hiding in an alleyway: deliberate and menacing. Kempelen and I rose early, dressed swiftly and went downstairs to dismantle the Turk with all haste. Once done, Kempelen instructed the servants to bring our carriage about and have the Turk, in its crates, loaded onto the wagon whilst we went over to the inn to meet with Osloff and Koroshilov.

We found the two Russians taking their breakfast. Koroshilov was delighted that Kempelen had thought to meet them. Interspersing his every sentence with apologies, Koroshilov expressed his worries that the embarrassing *shutovstvo*** of the night before had prejudiced Kempelen against selling the Turk. Kempelen sought to allay Koroshilov's fears and said that the automaton was still for sale at the price they had previously agreed. I held my tongue though there were things I wished to say at that time. Osloff however, came to my aid although perhaps not in a manner I would have liked.

"The Grand Duke Paul Petrovich will not be purchasing your machine," he stated bluntly. "Your invention is a fake."

It was evident that Osloff had not yet shared this opinion with Koroshilov for the clerk protested quite vociferously. Kempelen however was amused by Osloff's denunciation of the

---

** This was the Russian word that Koroshilov used but, for once, my English fails me and I am unable to think of a suitable translation. It means something akin to 'misbehaviour' or 'joke' but without the purposefulness of either.

automaton and asked Osloff to give account of his reasons for calling it a fake. It was my impression that Kempelen thought Osloff, with his accusations against Seiler and Frau Kastner, had humiliated himself once and was to do it a second time with a clumsy attack on the Turk.

"The mistake many people make is in thinking that chess is a logical game, a pursuit of pure intellect, when it is nothing of the sort," said Osloff. "It is a graceless game, burdened by an over preponderance of rules, exceptions and peculiarities. That it is so complex blinds the average man to the fact that it is an easier game to master than sjaski.*** Chess is not a game of the intellect. It is a game of observation and memory."

"You speak of intellect and memory as though they were distinct and separate things," said Kempelen.

"I have known university doctors who can name every article within the human body but cannot find the way to their own operating theatres. I have met a court genealogist who can recite the lineage of every noble in all the Russias but cannot add three numbers together without recourse to ink and paper. And yet I have also met an idiot savant who, given any date in the past thousand years, can recount what day of the week it was. Knowledge and intellect are quite distinct and separate, sir. Throughout history, we humans have accumulated an ever-growing library of knowledge and yet seem to slide inexorably towards senseless brutality and irrationality. With each footstep we take away from the Garden of Eden, so our knowledge grows and our common sense decreases."

"What is your argument, doctor?" asked Kempelen.

"My argument is that man is graceless and entirely suited to the graceless game of chess. Machines are simple, graceful and much more suited to the graceful arts. Herr Kempelen, if you had presented us with a counting machine or a harpsichord player like the ones Vaucanson is purported to have made then I would have accepted its authenticity much more readily. But a chess machine? No, sir. Furthermore, for a precisely engineered machine, your

---

*** A Russian board game not dissimilar to the game Americans call checkers.

chess player is quite ungainly. Whereas all the true automata I have seen move with a fluidity and grace that humans cannot match, your chess player's head and hand move in faltering irregular jerks. It is the arrogance of man to assume his superiority to machines and it would be quite in-keeping with that arrogance for a man who wished to emulate the actions of a machine to make such actions appear less graceful than his own, even though such an emulation would be quite inaccurate."

"Are you suggesting that the Turk is a man?" asked Kempelen.

"I am suggesting that the Turk is operated by a man, concealed within the mechanism," said Osloff.

"And you base this speculation on the nebulous notions that the Turk's capabilities are too advanced and yet that it is not graceful enough to be a true machine," said Kempelen. "To my mind, you contradict yourself, sir."

"Not at all," Osloff replied. "However, there was one other detail that convinced me that the machine was counterfeit. Your machine, if machine it is, does not want to be sold."

Kempelen expressed confusion at this remark, as did Koroshilov.

"Two nights ago, I sat in contest with your Turk," said Osloff, "and I will acknowledge freely that I was the significantly weaker player."

"How can you say that? You won the game," said Koroshilov.

"Only because I was allowed to win," said Osloff. "I fared badly for much of the game and was on the verge of inescapable defeat when you, dear Koroshilov, made the rash proclamation that we would buy the machine if it proved to be the victor in our little game. On the move immediately following your statement, the Turk sacrificed its queen for no marked reason and subsequently lost the game. To my eyes, it was clear that the Turk had deliberately thrown the game in order to avoid being sold to our master, the grand duke. For a machine to do such a thing is impossible but, for a human operator who fears for his continuing livelihood, it seems quite a rational action."

"Most interesting but nonetheless how can you possibly contend that my automaton conceals a human operator?" said

Kempelen. "Twice now I have shown you the inside of the machine. Where could a man possibly hide?"

"That did trouble me at first," said Osloff, in a reflective mode, "but then an answer of sorts did come to me. I noted that on both occasions you opened the automaton's doors you made certain to open only one set of doors at a time. Furthermore, it occurred to me that the drawer at the base of the cabinet probably was not as deep as the cabinet itself. Making some rough calculations, I would surmise that with certain sets of sliding panels and concealed doors a small person, perhaps not taller than four feet, could lie in the recess behind the drawer when the larger door was opened and then squeeze into the larger portion of the cabinet when the smaller doors were opened. Once the doors were closed again, that person could sit in the larger compartment and direct the Turk with ease. My guess would be that the operator is somehow able to slip a hand into the forearm of the Turk's playing hand, in which there is no doubt some sort of wire-worked mechanism for moving the Turk's fingers. The operator also perhaps observes the game through the furred cloth of the mannequin's torso. The clanking noise of the clockwork mechanism probably serves to hide any noises that the operator might inadvertently make. As a parlour trick, it is one of the more ingenious ones I have seen. On that at least you must be congratulated, Herr Kempelen."

I could see a conflict of emotions on Koroshilov's face. Part of the man was astounded by Osloff's astute rationalisation of the Turk's workings and yet another part of him still wanted, desperately wanted, to believe that the automaton was genuine. It was this part of him that caused him to question Osloff's conclusions.

"But where is this four foot high chess player?" he asked incredulously. "Is it possible that Kempelen has brought a six-year-old chess master to Wittenburg and kept this child prodigy hidden from sight?"

"Of course not," said Osloff. "You have met Kempelen's chess master and spoken to him on several occasions. He is no child."

"I do not remember meeting any such person. Who is he?"

"The young Polish captain here," said Osloff, meaning myself of course.

Koroshilov frowned and gave a snort of disbelief.

"You are talking nonsense now," said Kempelen. "The captain here must be six feet tall if he is an inch."

Osloff shook his head, reached towards me with his hand and rapped his knuckles on the top of my thigh. I did nothing to stop him. Osloff's argument was in full and majestic force and to stop him at that point seemed a churlish thing to do. As Osloff's knuckles struck my leg there was the clear and hollow sound of wood.

Koroshilov was struck speechless by this turn of events.

"That we could not spot your false legs for what they were is a credit to the artisan who fashioned them," said Osloff. "I hear that there are English craftsmen who are skilled in such things and can make an artificial leg that bends and flexes in much the same manner as a marionette's limbs."

I conceded that my legs were indeed English in make, purchased by Kempelen and given to me as part payment for my services as the Turk's operator. I went on to explain that I had lost both legs to enemy cannon fire two years earlier. Osloff mused on this.

"The Kościuszko uprising," he said.

There was no need for him to say more on the matter for he had landed upon the truth of my situation. I was in exile, unable to return to my homeland or enter any part of Russia's great empire for fear of immediate arrest. I had not wanted the Turk to be sold to the grand duke for it was my source of employment and Russia was the one place where I dare not follow the Turk.

"Well, you have given us your hypothesis, doctor," said Kempelen stiffly, refusing still to admit that his secrets had been revealed. "Are you adamant that you will not purchase the machine?"

"Quite certain," said Osloff and Koroshilov was compelled to agree. "But do not be in such low spirits," Osloff went on. "This whole episode has ended more happily than it might have done."

"How so?" asked Kempelen.

"What would the assembled guests in the Bürgermeister's house have said yesterday evening if I had revealed the true nature of the Turk then?" said Osloff. "I suspect that the captain here, who we must remember was within the machine before, during and after Herr Kastner's murder, would now be facing the hangman's noose. For who would believe stories about chandeliers and jealous bürgers when an obvious culprit was found to have been in the room all along?"

"There is inconsistency here though," said Koroshilov, who was somewhat confused. "Did not the housekeeper see Captain Worousky in bed moments before the Bürgermeister was killed?"

"No," I said. "She saw my legs and the shape of several cushions beneath the sheets, piled in such a way as the present the facsimile of a sleeping person and enough to fool the casual observer who might wander into my room."

"I remember you were keen to corroborate the housekeeper's account of her presence in your room that night," said Osloff. "At first I thought it a gallant but misplaced attempt to come to the innocent woman's aid but now I see that you had an ulterior motive, that of providing yourself with an alibi."

"Please do not think harshly of me because of it," I said.

"Worse though is that, inside that cabinet, you were witness to the act of murder. How much simpler it would have been if you had told me earlier what you already knew."

Kempelen shook his head.

"You are wrong," he said, happy to wrangle some small victory from the day. "Captain Worousky, though indeed inside the machine, could not see out of it. The position of pieces on the board is communicated to him by other means I will not describe. He only heard the thump of the falling chandelier and nothing more."

"A shame," said Osloff. "If he had been able to see, he would have been able to confirm my account of the Bürgermeister's murder."

Kempelen laughed heartily at this.

"No one can confirm your flights of fancy, doctor," he said. "Your version of events is quite ridiculous. I only hope that one day Herr Seiler will forgive you for falsely accusing him of Herr Kastner's murder."

"Did you not hear the news?" said Osloff. "I spoke to the potboy earlier this morning. Herr Seiler was seen to leave town in a hurry last night, taking only money and that which a fast horse could carry. By his actions, he has condemned himself."

This was indeed news that Kempelen and I were unaware of but the four of us did not remain together to discuss it. Osloff and Koroshilov's coach had been made ready and all of us had long journeys ahead of us. Farewells between Kempelen and the two Russians were cordial but nothing more. I, though, had developed a warmth for the curious character of Doctor Semyon Osloff with his unflinching honesty, his detached manner and his ever-watchful eyes. I shook his hand and asked that God's blessing went with him.

Though our relationship had become fraught, Kempelen and I continued our tour of the empire, the secret of the Turk still unknown to the common man. Some months later I heard that Frau Kastner had eventually confessed her part in her husband's death, first to the priest and then to the council of bürgers, chaired by the new Bürgermeister, Herr Bremner. In her confession she admitted that the murder was committed in much the same manner as Dr Osloff described. She was hanged for her crime and buried in the forest in an unmarked grave. To my knowledge, Herr Seiler was never caught.

The travelling tour of the mechanical Turk went on for several months and it was only in November of 1797 that we returned to Vienna where I played my last ever game from within the cabinet's cramped, smoky interior.* The day after that performance, Kempelen informed me that he was dismantling the automaton for good. True to his word, Kempelen had the Turk put into storage and retired to his home town of Pressburg where he devoted his remaining years to more serious scientific study, including the development of a mechanical head complete with

---

* In order to see what I myself was doing inside the cabinet I was required to light a small candle. A metal tube was supposed to divert the candle smoke up through the body of the mannequin and out of a small chimney in the top of the Turk's turban. The candelabra that Kempelen always placed by the Turk's side disguised any smell that the Turk's opponent might detect. Despite all these ingenious arrangements, by the end of any game the air within the cabinet was quite poisonous to the lungs and brain.

teeth, tongue and larynx which, when suitably instructed, could utter several words in German, French and Italian. Mr Houdin, I must express how pleased I am to say that Kempelen and I parted in Vienna as good friends, for the next time I saw the dear man was at his funeral.

I end this letter with the promise that future missives shall detail another narrative concerning the brilliant Dr Osloff and his solution to the Martingale Mystery. I shall await your next letter (which I assume will include a suitably generous imbursement) before writing to you again.

I trust these words find you well.

Your ever-reliable correspondent,

J. Worousky

And children love kittens

Hedley was on him in an instant, first tripping the lad onto the ice and then hauling him up by the collar of his jacket.

"I'm quite fine," I protested as the chestnut seller's boy helped me to my feet.

"The boy assaulted you, sir," said Hedley, shaking the lad with one hand while threatening him with the shillelagh stick he carried in the other. "He would have robbed you too given the chance."

"As would half the people here which is why I have you by my side," I replied. "It was an accidental collision, I'm sure."

"The ice can be treacherous," agreed the chestnut seller.

The urchin lad wriggled in Hedley's iron grip like a church pond tiddler.

"Oh, do let him go, Hedley," I said.

Hedley scowled and then dropped the lad onto the frozen Thames. The lad shot me a scowl of his own although he did not have Hedley's years of experience and there was something pitiful in his gaze that a scowl could not conceal.

"What's your name, boy?" I said.

The straw-haired lad did not speak, possibly imagining that I would be passing that name to the Southwark magistrate.

"The gentleman asked you a question," barked Hedley and slapped the lad across the ear.

"William," he said.

"And where are your parents?"

He pointed across the frozen river to where a trio of similarly pitiful types clustered around a brazier beneath a jetty.

"I'm with my friends."

I hesitated for a moment, fearful of Hedley's possible reaction, and then spoke, if only to see Hedley's actual reaction.

"Would you and your friends like some hot chestnuts, William?"

"Would I!" he said enthusiastically.

"Sir..." growled Hedley warningly.

I looked fondly at my man Hedley. I found him quite endearing when he became over-protective, like an ugly bull terrier that had no redeeming trait but its loyalty.

"Hush, man," I said. "Let us spread a little cheer."

I had the chestnut seller make up half a dozen bags and with Hedley glowering at the lot of them and ready to knock their skulls with his lead-loaded shillelagh, I had the troupe of tatterdemalions lead me on a tour of the Frost Fair. I had visited this Frost Fair not two days before and, unlike these children, had also known two Frost Fairs earlier in my life, but they squired me about the fair as though I was visiting London from far off Timbuktoo.

While young William was expounding on the wonderful nature of Mr Trimble's mystery bags (which the butcher was cooking in a pit on the ice and selling for three times their worth), I realised that one of the urchins, a poppet of a girl with hollow cheeks and forget-me-not blue eyes, had taken my hand in hers. A glance was sufficient to stop Hedley from ripping the impertinent lass away.

"Well, don't you have pretty eyes?" I said.

The girl didn't smile. Her kind rarely had chance to learn how.

"As I boy, I had a dolly with eyes like yours," I said. "We probably still have it somewhere."

The boy William was looking at me, as were his friends.

"Sausages all round then?" I suggested.

"Thank you, mister," said the tallest lad and even doffed his cap.

I had Hedley pay the man but did not partake of Mr Trimble's wares myself. Instead, I looked up along the Thames, frozen beyond the westward curve. Frost coated every window and rooftop.

"Twenty years it has been since the last big freeze," I said. "Since the last fair."

"Was you a little boy then?" asked William.

His sausage was too hot to eat, so he broke it in two and steam rose from both halves.

"Oh, you're very kind," I said, amused. "It's at times like this that I can imagine why your ancestors worshipped the Viking gods of snow and thunder."

"What's that then?" said William.

"On a day like this, one could imagine trolls and giants, white monsters striding across the frozen land."

"'Ere, mister," said the oldest girl, "did you see the elephant?"

"What elephant would that be, dear?"

"The one they led across the river on the first day of the fair to show the ice was safe."

"I can't say I did. How novel. I wonder what menagerie they inveigled it from."

A strange and imprudent notion came to me.

"I do have an elephant in my house," I said.

"A real one?" said William.

I nodded.

"Part of one. He looks after my walking sticks. I wonder if you'd like to come to luncheon tomorrow, after church, and I might just show him to you."

"Sir, I must protest," said Hedley.

"I thought you might," I said.

"This is not wise."

"Possibly not. Nonetheless, I would like William and..."

"Mary."

"James, mister."

"And that's Elizabeth," said William, pointing at the girl on my arm.

"... to join us tomorrow. You can have Mr Jelks search them for weapons if you must and have the ostler's boy stand guard over the dining table if it makes you happy," I said.

Hedley grumbled and gave each of the children a fierce glare, packed with more gristle and threat than one of Mr Trimble's sausages.

There was a pause of several minutes between the first knock at the door and the arrival of the four children in the dining room. From the slightly surly look on the tall boy's face – James, wasn't it? – I deduced that Hedley and Mr Jelks had indeed given them a stern word and frisking in the hallway. Additionally, judging from the dampness around William's collar and the fresh ruddiness of pretty little Elizabeth's face and hands, they might have also been taken to the back kitchen and introduced to the cook and a damp facecloth.

I stood to greet them by name and gestured for them to sit. Awkwardly, they sat at the places arranged for them. James' eyes went from the polished table silver to Hedley and back to the silver again. The older girl, Mary, stared at the empty plates intensely as though willing food to appear on them.

"Where's the rest of it then?" said William.

"The rest of what, William?" I asked.

"The elephant."

"Ah," I said. "You saw the elephant's foot cane stand in the hallway. I should imagine his other feet are doing sterling work in other households. His ivory tusks might be gracing an organ or piano somewhere. The rest of him... I can't say. The person to have asked would have been my brother."

"Is he an elephant hunter?" said Mary.

I laughed at that.

"Lord, no. He was a taxidermist, a mounter of animal remains. You might have spotted him in his chair as you passed the study. I dabble but my brother was the true artist."

I gestured to the examples of mounted birds and mammals beneath bell jars on the corner tables of the room.

"My efforts are juvenilia by comparison," I said. "Look."

I stood briefly and retrieved the white kitten from the japanned sideboard behind me. I do not know if any of the children had spotted it as they entered and whether they had taken it for a real cat, curled up in sleep.

I placed it in front of little Elizabeth, gently as though I might accidentally wake it. The girl looked at me with those forget-me-not eyes.

"Go on. Touch it," I said.

A pink hand, lines of grey grime in the knuckles, reached out cautiously. Elizabeth prodded the kitten's side and then suddenly, possessively, stroked its fur.

"It's dead," she said, barely a whisper, the first words I had heard her speak.

"It has been dead a long time, Elizabeth," I said. "If it had lived, it would have grown up into a fat tom cat and died many years ago. Do you like it?"

She nodded silently, not taking her eyes off it.

I laughed to myself, a thought coming to me entirely unbidden.

"My mother used to say that men love women, women love children, and children love kittens. That was the natural order of things."

I looked at the children at my table and could see the point was lost on them.

"She was, perhaps, a somewhat bitter and ungrateful woman. But is it any wonder that, in the knowledge of such unreciprocated affections, my brother and I remained unmarried?" I said.

The maid came in with luncheon and the children were presented with hams, cheeses, bread and preserve. The four of them had clearly been given brief but strict instructions regarding table manners and appeared to strain at invisible bonds while the maid served, hands automatically rising to take food but pressed down again by virtue of will. Amusing though I found it, I am not a cruel man and said the shortest of graces before inviting them to tuck in. Again, they made their best efforts to show restraint in the taking and eating of what was probably the finest meal they had seen in their lives. I could even see James counting under his breath, consciously and deliberately holding himself back between mouthfuls, between snatching one item and the next.

I did not partake from any plate until the children had slowed from their initial restrained gluttony to relaxed and unhurried nibbling. I saw that Elizabeth – sweet, unblemished child! – ate with only one hand, keeping the other firmly on the stuffed kitten. I told her that she was quite the most enchanting creature and would soon blossom into something quite beautiful. Elizabeth simply nodded in response, accepting not questioning.

"Are you saying that she's not beautiful as she is, mister?" said William.

There was a twinkle in the young rogue's eye. Oh, he was a sly one I would wager and perhaps, one day, his youthful cheekiness would give way to a criminal cunning. But not yet.

"All things have potential for greatness and some achieve it," I replied. "Plato tells us that there is a realm of perfection, a world of forms, in which every perfect ideal is to be found. The most beautiful woman, the most cheesy piece of cheese, the most kittenish kitten. We mundane creatures might move towards or away from those ideals. The French as a nation reached their prime more than a century ago and are now descending into the most awful mess. We, by comparison, are fully entering our prime only now and reaping the rewards of being everything that we can be. That, my friends, is why we will soon have that scoundrel Napoleon taken in hand."

James and William gave a cheery little patriotic cry at this.

"But Elizabeth here," I said, "perhaps like the fledgling nation of America, is approaching the ideal of innocent beauty at tremendous speed but is not there yet."

I felt a sudden heaviness in my chest as I looked at the girl.

"And we achieve that perfection or near perfection for but a moment and then it is gone," I said, sadly.

At once, I slapped the table to rouse myself from my momentary melancholy.

"Cakes!" I declared and, within minutes, seed cakes, fruit tarts and sugar-coated Chelsea buns were upon the table.

While we all feasted anew, I questioned the children a little about their lives. In all honesty, I had no interest in the dreary comings and goings of guttersnipes, but I was interested in the London that they knew. We spoke of the local markets, of public houses and the street sellers with which we were all familiar. Talk turned to tavern singers and, with some coaxing, Mary sang a tuneful air that was doing the rounds that winter. We clapped and cheered and set to playing parlour games, many of which were new to my young friends.

The children were utterly without schooling and knew almost nothing of the world beyond the local streets but the three older children were undoubtedly quick-witted and possessed of a fine humour. Elizabeth did not join in with the games, but sat and watched and brought her own radiant charms to the room. It was quite dark outside and Hedley had rebuilt the fire in the grate more than once before we took pause to draw breath.

"Well, the evening is upon us," I said, "and soon enough we will all have to retire to our beds."

A glance, both amused and dark, passed between Mary and William and I wondered only for a moment what foul lodgings they would be in that night. But then I reminded myself that I had brought an afternoon of gaiety into their otherwise squalid lives, that we – they and I – had known moments of true happiness together and that I had done more than my Christian duty.

"This has been a marvellous day," I said. "We must do it again."

"We must," agreed William, grinning.

Hedley growled in the shadows but said nothing.

"Next year then?" I suggested.

William blinked.

"Next *year*?"

I nodded and considered a moment.

"The first Sunday in February. After church."

"But mister," said James. "That's a terrible long time."

"The gentleman has spoken," said Hedley. "It's time to go."

"Well, quite," I said.

As Hedley briskly ushered the children from their chairs, William grabbed at a pair of buns still on the table and thrust them inside his jacket. Such spirited opportunism, I thought.

"Make sure all four of you come," I said. "I think we've made the perfect quintet, haven't we?"

Elizabeth stood at the table-side, no taller stood than she was seated.

"And how will you have blossomed before we meet again?" I said.

She looked at me but her hand remained fixed on the white kitten on the table. Its fur had darkened slightly now under the touch of her grubby hands and I could even see crumbs and smears of butter in its fur.

Many people come to my door throughout the course of the year and the discretion and judgement of my household determines which might be brought to my attention. It is entirely possible that my four young friends had appeared on my doorstep more than once in that year, seeking my company or a hand-out but Hedley did not inform me if they did and I did not ask. However, once the year had turned and the winter deepened (although without the severity to freeze the Thames and warrant another Frost Fair), I looked forward to our meeting with an uncontainable glee. I had cook buy the best meats, pies and works of confection and bought a splendidly colourful waistcoat for the occasion.

On that Sunday, I stood in the dining room and listened to the sound of boots in the hallway and low and indecipherable voices and could have capered about in my excitement if my legs were up to it. When the four of them entered, I had to restrain myself from rushing forward to embrace them.

"James! Mary! William! Elizabeth!" I cried, beaming like a drunkard.

"It is good to see you, sir," said James, and Mary even offered a curtsey of greeting which was both clumsy and touching.

How the year had worked its changes on them! All were taller, although James not much more than he had been last winter, and like rolled pastry they had thinned as they had grown. There was no prosperous weight to any one of them and the clothes on their backs were threadbare rags but I hoped that the bountiful feast we were about to consume might do a little to rectify one of those.

"Ah, Elizabeth," I said, unashamedly appraising her directly. "My rare beauty, one step closer to perfection. Did I ever tell you that I had a dolly with eyes just like yours?"

She shook her head.

"Well, I did. I do. Please, sit."

The children took to their chairs and maid brought in luncheon and it was as if the months had fallen away from us and not a moment had passed since we were last at table together. We shared our news of the year and of the changes we had seen in our city but, perhaps because there was not one this year (or likely to be one again for some years) our talk turned time and again to the Frost Fair of the previous year. It appeared that the children had spent nearly every day out on the ice, working for pittance, scavenging when there was no work and enjoying the festivities.

"Did you hear about the Wandsworth girl, mister?" said William.

I nodded, knowing full well.

"They pulled the poor thing out once the river began to thaw," I said.

"They say she spent more than a month under the ice," said James, drawing a distasteful look from Mary.

"And yet she was as fresh of face as the moment she went under," I said solemnly. "Oh, to be frozen and unchanged forever."

Reminded by a flurry of interconnected thoughts that I would not be able to explain, I turned to Elizabeth.

"My dear, do you still have that kitten I gave you last year?"

There was a sudden sadness – and did I note a flicker of fear? – in Elizabeth's eyes.

"It was... it was stolen from her," said William.

"Oh," I said, initially disappointed, then unaccountably irritated and then, a moment later, moved to sympathy. "Oh, I am sorry to hear that. You seemed particularly fond of it."

"I was, sir," she said.

I cannot explain but each time this girl – this girl who was silent and demure – each time this girl spoke, I felt a shiver of bliss run through me. Her words were rare things, diamonds, snatches of birdsong.

"I did not show you any of my brother's work last year," I said. "May I suggest that before we have our puddings, I take you on a little tour."

"Is that advisable?" said Hedley.

"Isn't it?" I replied.

My man pulled a face.

"I wouldn't let these children see any more finery than they already have. It might give them... ideas."

I laughed.

"You know, Hedley here counted the knives and forks at the table the moment you left last year."

"Is that so?" said William with pretend disbelief.

"And had the staff do a full inventory the day after. Come."

I led them upstairs to rooms that were rarely opened, except for a weekly dusting by the maid. In truth, the children were perhaps as astounded by the richly coloured carpets and printed curtains as by any of the items of taxidermy on display behind glass but what did it matter when I sought only to entertain, not to boast?

"These are some of my brother's more classical pieces," I said. "His attempt to create his own world of forms if you will. Here, the most stoaty stoat. Here, a particularly gibbonish gibbon. Here, a divinely heronite heron. British fauna on the right. More exotic creatures down towards the windows. Notice how we ensure the light does not shine directly on them. It causes them to fade over time. Fade faster I should say. All things fade eventually, don't they?"

"'Ere, is that an eagle?" said Mary.

"Ah," I said, stepping forward to join her at a boxy case of glass and French-polished mahogany. "One of his finest pieces. It is not an eagle but a red-tailed kite. It can be found all over the New World but here my brother has captured it in the act of attacking a proprietor amazon – that's a kind of parrot. These two came from the island of Saint-Cyr in the far Caribbean, a gift from a French explorer by the name of Martingale. A strange and unseemly gentleman who met a most mysterious death."

"Mysterious?" said Mary.

"He retired to his room one night, locking both door and windows. He was a cautious gentleman – Hedley would have approved no doubt – and had men guarding the entrances to his home. A friend came visiting the next morning, his lawyer or somesuch, and entering the house alone, found Monsieur Martingale to be gone and the body of an unknown ruffian on the bedroom floor. The ruffian had had his head cut clean off."

"Lord above!" said James.

I nodded.

"A body appearing from nowhere. Another man vanished."

"Witchcraft," said William.

"Nothing so outlandish," I said. "The appearance of magic through intelligent human agency. Shall I tell you how it was done?"

Despite the emphatic affirmatives and several entreaties, I decided that it would be a story for another time and diverted them with the less baffling yet nonetheless enchanting witchcraft that was taxidermy.

"Taxidermy. From the Latin for the arrangement of skin," I said. "The true skill of the taxidermist is in the preservation of the hides. My brother was one of the first Englishmen to master the arsenical soap method. True, the mounting and positioning of the subjects takes an artist's eye but it is only because of the preparatory work that we can still look on these lustrous exhibits, years, decades later. This way."

I led them on, with Hedley obtrusively close on their heels, to the room that contained my brother's 'fancies'.

"The poisons in the preservatives took their toll on my brother's health," I said. "Night blindness made him a misery and a recluse. I don't know if they had a debilitating effect on his senses or whether age brought out a certain whimsy in him..."

In one case, a dozen field mice sat at school desks, taking instruction from a hedgehog with a schoolmaster's cane. In another, a long-haired terrier strode on its rear legs, arm in arm with a ginger cat.

"Frogs dancing round a maypole!" exclaimed William. "Who'd have thought it?"

"And look," said Mary, pointing at the most vulgar tableau that took up the full corner of the room.

"What is that thing?" she said.

"It's a bear," said James. "We saw one at the pits in Greenwich."

"The other thing," said Mary, tutting. "Is it a hairy pig?"

"A javelina," I said. "A wild pig of the Americas. Although quite what it is doing taking tea and cake with an Andes bear is anybody's guess."

"You should ask your brother," said William.

"As with many issues, he refuses to be drawn and is silent on the matter these days," I said.

Elizabeth touched the honey-smeared muffin in the bear's hand and then looked at me.

"Fakery," I said. "Plaster and glue. However there are real cakes aplenty downstairs. Shall we?"

We trotted downstairs, five household adventurers returning from our explorations to a much-deserved feast. We passed the door to the study. The top of my brother's head was just visible above the back of his high-backed chair. I did not pause to make any introductions; the children were my guests, not his.

In the autumn of that year, there were callers at the door to my house who engaged Hedley in fierce argument. I did not step from my rooms to investigate. I did not want to know. Once my man had chased them off, he appeared in my room, his shillelagh gripped with white-knuckle tightness. He glowered at me in a manner I perhaps ought to have taken exception to but he was a long-trusted and treasured servant and I was inclined to allow him some freedom of expression. He stood before me, stock still, glowering in silence and then departed. We did not speak of the matter again.

A third February came and another bitter winter, although the Thames remained ice free again. My elation at seeing the children was as high as ever. James was almost a man now. There were the beginnings of whiskers on his chin and a round-shouldered stoop to his back. Mary was herself almost a woman and I suspected from their closeness that the two of them were perhaps living as common-law husband and wife, although they gave me no palpable grounds for that suspicion. William, despite the fact that he wore no boots, his feet bound in rags, was now as tall as James. Some of the boyishness worked from him so that his cleverness and impudence now made him something more interesting and dangerous than a mere scoundrel or scamp.

"And who is this?" I said, inspecting Elizabeth at arm's length.

The girl looked to William for confirmation and he nodded.

"Elizabeth, sir," she said.

She had grown for certain, changing the aspects of her body and even face. She was wearing that same pinafore dress as the year before but now it barely stretched past her knees. The blonde hair, matted and dirty though it had always been, was now darkening to a mousy brown. And even her eyes...

"You used to have such blue eyes," I said.

"Yes, sir," she said.

I retrieved the two glass eyes that I had put in my pocket that morning. I showed them to her and then held one up beside her own eyes.

"I couldn't find the dolly but I found these. You had eyes this very blue. But the colour has gone from them, made them more of a grey."

Oh, to be able to work that improvement on Elizabeth, to restore her eyes to dazzling forget-me-nots. I smiled with the deepest affection and, yes, with love.

"Near perfect," I whispered.

Hedley made a throaty noise.

I abruptly remembered that my guests were waiting and bade them all sit down.

When the food arrived, they ate with less decorum than I had recalled. Hunger, it seems, had robbed them of some of the manners that Hedley's doorstep threats had instilled in them. I asked what they were doing to earn a living. William explained that James had an occasional position in a tannery and Mary managed to find some work as a seamstress.

"Skilled with a needle, are we?" I said. I picked up the needle and fine wire I had been using to repair the large cat on the third floor that morning. "Maybe a career in taxidermy beckons," I joked.

Sadly and to my embarrassment, Mary failed to understand my jest and said, "If you could find me a position, mister, I would be ever so grateful."

I could not help but pull a distasteful expression.

"No," I said, gently but firmly. "Although I know a number of gentlemen engaged in the lower end of the trade, I make a rule not to mix friendship and business."

Mary stared at me, stunned and equally embarrassed.

"Eat," I said and savagely cut a hunk of bread for myself.

Partway through William's explanation of his own livelihood, which seemed to involve a combination of mudlarking, barge loading and a variety of other activities that might find him transported to Van Diemen's Land one day, James was overtaken by a fit of coughing. Although I called for maid, and tea and a cup of wine were pressed upon him, it was several minutes before the fit passed and he could breathe properly once more. I had risen from my seat in panic and now looked at it him with both anxiety and relief.

"A hunk of cheese went down the wrong way," I suggested lightly.

Mary rubbed her young man's back to ease his breathing.

"He has these attacks. They all pass eventually."

James mumbled his thanks for my concern and said he was quite all right, although I could see a tremor in his hand as he reached for his plate. I did not sit again. The young man was quite ill, that much was evident.

I looked down from the window to London Bridge which stood almost directly before my home. Even on this grim and unwelcoming Sunday, carts and carriages jostled at the junction. The bridge was a mess of people, carriages and the buildings that crowded its sides.

"They used to have heads on spikes at this end of the bridge," I said.

"They what, sir?" said William.

I turned to look at him.

"Heads, William. On spikes. Those people who had been executed for treason against the crown would have their heads put on spikes as a warning, as a message to others. They say that Good Queen Bess had more than two dozen heads up there at any one time."

I rolled the glass eyes in my fingers.

"What those empty sockets must have seen over the years. Time would have meant nothing to them, would it?"

"I couldn't say," said William.

"No, of course you couldn't," I said and then, "I never told you, did I?"

"What?"

"What happened to Martingale, the man in the locked bedroom."

Elizabeth looked to the others, apparently having forgotten the story I shared the year before.

"I got to thinking about it," said James, finding his voice once more. "I reckon that Mr Martingale and the dead feller with no head were the same person. That he'd put on a wig or something."

"And then cut off his own head?" I said, smiling. "Clever but no. I shall tell you the solution proposed by the most intelligent man I've ever had the privilege to know." I sat once more and popped a crumb of cheese in my mouth. "Martingale was alone in his house and entirely undisturbed until his lawyer friend arrived the following morning. The lawyer carried a leather bag and his cane. The appearance of the ruffian in Martingale's room has been a baffling mystery for years but is far less mysterious when one is aware that his lawyer friend worked for the French judiciary and that his cane was, in fact, a sword cane with a finely honed blade inside." I looked at the children, waiting for realisation to dawn. Confusion reigned on their faces.

William spoke first, naturally.

"The law man did his friend in. He killed him."

I nodded.

"But the other man..." said Mary. "Where did he come from?"

"The bag," I said. "The lawyer, working for the judiciary, had easy access to the remains of those criminals who had lost their heads to the guillotine. The lawyer beheaded Martingale and then swapped the head in the bag he carried for Martingale's. Perhaps he swapped some of their garments also to prevent witnesses identifying the body as Martingale's. I'm not sure. Clever though, isn't it?"

"Not half," said William.

"I think it's a perfectly horrible story," said Mary. "I don't like thinking about it."

"It?" I said.

"Death," she said.

I nodded in appreciation of her point.

"Death is inevitable. Surely, it's what we do in the time we have that's important. Like these gay parties of ours."

"Once a year," said Mary. "You have us one afternoon a year, and a year is a long time."

"Life between times is intolerably hard," said William and unaccountably looked at grey-eyed Elizabeth.

In the corner of the room, Hedley shifted, rocking silently from foot to foot.

"Are you not satisfied with my hospitality? My charity?" I said.

"We are, sir," said James quickly. "That we are."

"Do I share my table with any others? Are you not... chosen?"

"We are, sir," said James.

"And do other gentlemen and ladies of the city open their doors to the likes of you?"

"They do not," said William but without the contrite servility James had exhibited.

I gave a frankly hog-like huff of dissatisfaction and made sure that each of them met my displeased gaze.

Six nights later, I was woken from my sleep by sounds within the house. I sat up in darkness and listened to the silence. A minute or more passed in which I began to suspect I had but dreamt the noises and then there was a further flurry of sounds: harsh whispers, the rattling of a door handle, a dull concussive sound. I reached out for the bell pulls and rang first for the maid and then for Hedley. I intuited long before it became obvious that neither would come.

I climbed out of bed. By the time I had my bedside candle alight, there were footsteps outside my door. The door opened and there stood William, maid's evening lamp in one hand, Hedley's heavy shillelagh in the other.

"You shouldn't be here," I said, which was more courageous and less meaningful a statement than I might have hoped to make.

In the lamplight, the thick knobbly end of Hedley's shillelagh glistened darkly and wet.

"Am I then to take it that you have proved my man Hedley right?" I said.

William stepped into the room uncertainly. He was afraid. Of course, he was afraid.

"Hedley is – or is that was? –" I said, "of the opinion that the poor, the wretched, like untrained dogs cannot help but bite the hand that feeds them. That you cannot accept charity that is freely given but must demand more and more. Like the foolish farmer and his wife who cut open the goose in search of its golden eggs, you –"

"Charity?" said William, interrupting softly.

"Yes – I – "

"Sit down," said William and pointed at the chair by the window.

He placed the lamp on my dressing table beside a red squirrel posed on a piece of bleached wood. The lamplight brought a flicker of movement and greater life to the squirrel's eyes. William took a further step towards me. He was the smaller of the two of us and hardly in the rudest of health but he had youth, desperation and the shillelagh on his side. I sat.

"Why did you do it?" he said.

"Do what?"

"Why did you invite us in? Each year."

"I thought I might enjoy your company. I thought the feeling was mutual."

William frowned at him.

"Didn't you enjoy my table?" I said.

"We were hungry."

"And I fed you. We ate together."

William shook his head.

"Put your hands on the arms of the chair," he said and, once I had, he took a reel of something from his pocket and began to bind my wrists to the wooden chair. If there had been a moment in which I could have fought him off and perhaps made an escape, then that was the moment. But I did not.

I realised that it was my own taxidermist's wire with which I was being tied to the chair. Once my arms were secured, he unspooled the wire further and wrapped it about the head of the chair and across my throat.

"Please," I coughed. "You're choking me."

The reel dropped to the floor behind the chair, bounced dully on the carpet. William walked away to the dressing table.

"You know what the problem was?" he said. "We ate only when you wanted us fed, not when we wanted to eat."

"But I fed you," I said. "I did feed you."

William snorted.

"You gave us just enough to show us what it was like to not starve. You gave us crumbs, you ol' bag of bones, which was worse than giving us nothing."

"But those moments," I argued. "We were happy, weren't we?"

"Moments. I don't know nothing about moments," he said, "but a year in the cold..." He picked up the mounted squirrel with considered contempt. "Is that what you do, you and your brother?"

"What?" I said.

"Take something living, freeze it in a moment, let it only live when you want it to? Did we just stop existing, wink out like candles, when we weren't with you?" He swallowed, pained, as though he was the one with metal wire digging into his windpipe. "What did you want from us? What did you want from Elizabeth? Was it her you wanted? It was, it was."

I blinked.

"I have an appreciation of beauty that you perhaps lack," I said. "Maybe it comes with age. A solitary glance at the truly divine should be enough to sustain one through this vale of misery."

"Really? So you got what you wanted," said William, "and expected us to be – what? – thankful for the pittance you gave in return? You bastard. I bet you didn't even notice, did you?"

"Notice what?"

Violently, he flung the squirrel away and it cracked against something in a dark corner.

"She's dead!" he snarled. "She's been bloody dead for months!"

I frowned at the boy.

"Who?"

"Oh, I knew you wouldn't have us in your parlour without her. And I thought, we won't be able to fool him with another but..." Tears had sprung to his eyes. "It was a test, mister. I wanted to see if you noticed, to know if you cared." He dashed the tears from his cheeks with his filthy sleeve. "And that cat... it weren't stolen. We'd sold it within a week and she cried when we did because she didn't understand."

"William..."

He turned to leave but paused at the doorway.

"I'm taking the silver. Your stickman reckoned we'd steal it anyway so I reckon it's sort of owed to us. I think he's dead, by the by. I didn't mean to kill him. The kitchen staff is all locked up in the cellar. But I guess your brother will wake soon and come untie you." He gave me a final look. "You won't see me again."

"Wait," I said. "My brother isn't -"

But he had shut the door behind him, leaving me, bound and immobile. The candle by my bedside wavered in the breeze created by his departure. Long before dawn, it would gutter and go out. I watched it with only my thoughts for company.

• Blaubart

Waiting on the platform's edge as Aunt Etheline harangued the porters, I turned and saw him for the first time. Blaubart. I did not know his name then but even before I heard the stories, the gruesome fireside legends, I saw something striking about him, imposing and mysterious. He was staring straight at me with an expression of knowing admiration on his face, a self-disciplined pleasure much like that God must have felt when he created all and saw that it was good.

I felt his gaze pass right through me, as though he were looking not at me but at the polished steam locomotive behind me. In truth I cannot say how I perceived this, for his eyes were hidden behind round, dark spectacles of a kind I had never seen before. He stood in the shadow of an archway, a tall hat pressed upon his brow, his arms concealed within a long cape. He was darkness but for the jutting slope of his nose, the slab of cheek and the eloquent twist of his lips. Somewhat unnerved by his attentions, I raised a gloved hand and waved coyly. His expression abruptly altered and he nodded politely in response.

"Look lively, Dora!" said Aunt Etheline. "Nearly home."

I smiled brightly at my dear aunt though I was quite tired – it had been a seven hour journey from Salisbury to Edenport on the Flintshire coast – and fell in step with the portly little woman. I looked back at the archway. Blaubart had gone.

The family lawyer had made all the arrangements for our relocation to Edenport. Both my father and his brother had grown up there and my father still had property in the town. I suppose it was mine now: the victualler's shop by the harbour, cottages there and there, the tall white residence just west of the town and the household staff who were as much a part of my inheritance as the silver and china.

Mrs Rhybudd, the housekeeper, was a peculiar lady, so used to an empty house that she could not think of Aunt Etheline and me as anything but guests, although warmly welcomed and fiercely revered guests at that. Aunt Etheline came to despise the woman almost as quickly as I came to like her.

On the second afternoon, after a day of recuperation and unpacking, as Mrs Rhybudd laid on tea in the dining room, I mentioned my curious encounter with the dark-spectacled man at the train station.

"That would be Mr Giles Blaubart," said Mrs Rhybudd. "He's a strange one. You shouldn't pay him no nevermind."

"Really?" I asked. "Why?"

"It's not my place to say," replied Mrs Rhybudd. "He keeps himself to himself and that's the way we all like it."

Naturally, Mrs Rhybudd's words only served to tantalise and, if it wasn't her place to speak of Mr Blaubart, others I asked were far less reserved.

The morning maid told me that he lived in the wide, squatting mansion house on the hill above the train station.

"Alone?" I asked.

"He doesn't have a wife at present," the maid replied, "but he has been married before. More than once."

He had been married five times, explained the gardener as he clipped the border hedging. Blaubart had an eye for pretty, young ladies. He was wealthy and not an unappealing prospect for a certain kind of woman. There had been five wives but none of the marriages had lasted for more than year.

"Why? What happened to them?" I asked.

"Couldn't say," replied the gardener darkly, snapping his shears together.

"There are deep cellars in that place," said the victualler's wife, leaning over the counter. "Forgotten rooms, if you get my meaning."

"I'm not sure I do," I said primly.

"Thick walls in that house. A lass could shout fit to burst and none would hear her."

"He likes his meat," said the butcher's boy, leaning his bicycle against a bollard down on the promenade. "Loves a nice, bloody steak. And more besides, I hear. You know why he wears those dark glasses, don't ya?"

"No," I said.

"He can't withstand the daylight."

"Ah," I said, laughing. "He's a vampire."

The boy's eyes latched onto something behind me and his mouth snapped shut. I turned to follow his gaze. I saw my own reflection in those black, impenetrable circles.

"Mr Blaubart," I said, fixedly unruffled. "You startled me."

Behind me the boy fumbled for his bicycle, threw himself astride it and wheeled away.

"My apologies, Miss Everton," said Blaubart. His voice was like the wind: thin, quiet but penetrating. He smelt of leather and strange oils.

"You know my name?" I asked.

"I make it my business to learn certain people's names," he said.

"Which people might they be?" I said.

Four months later, I became the sixth Mrs Blaubart. Does that surprise you? The courtship was swift, yes, but it was carried out with such methodical sincerity that I could not help but be moved to accept his proposal. From the moment we met on the promenade, gifts began to arrive on strict weekly basis: velvety arum lilies, sugar-dusted Turkish delight, a slim volume of Baudelaire and a fine writing set so that I might send him letters. Walking out together after church, he spoke little of himself. He mentioned his businesses only circumspectly. He did not say from where his family hailed. A Cambridge education had erased any vocal clues to his origins. He asked me many questions and listened intently. This was a new experience for me and perhaps it was that, more than anything, which made me fall in love with him.

Love. A strong word to use. I became enormously fond of him and came to love those sensations I associated with him. The oily scent of his hands. The scratches in his breathy voice. The flourish of his signature in his frequent notes. The feel of his leather glove as it encompassed my hand.

Giles was older than me but not so old. Aunt Etheline approved of the match. Mrs Rhybudd looked on it with unconcealed horror. The rumours about Giles' other wives did not bother me greatly. I did not believe them to be true and they only added to the man's allure.

Not once during the courtship did Giles remove his dark spectacles. Nor did he on our wedding day.

We went straight from the church to his house in a fine carriage pulled by two beautiful white horses that had been brought over from Mold for the occasion.

My instatement as Mrs Dora Blaubart began with a wedding breakfast for two. My husband and I sat at either end of his long dining table, toasted one another and drank to our undying love. We spoke of the years ahead of us and the comforts of certainty.

Once the meal was concluded, my husband came to my end of the table and took my hand in his. My heart fluttered like a trapped moth. My thoughts turned nervously to our wedding night. However, I was too mistaken to be either nervous or expectant. Giles told me that there were papers, business matters, that he had to look at.

"On our wedding day?" I asked.

He nodded.

And so, I spent the evening of my wedding day touring the house with Giles' housekeeper. She was no Mrs Rhybudd but a pinch-faced Englishwoman called Strubby. She showed me the parlours, the library, the wine cellars – sadly lacking the horrors that the victualler's wife spoke of – the music room and the guest rooms. There was a lock on each and every door. Mrs Strubby locked and unlocked each in turn with a methodicalness that bordered on obsession.

"The master is very mindful of security," was Strubby's only comment.

The tour concluded at the base of a set of stairs, narrow and unlit.

"What is up there?" I asked.

"The attic."

"And what's it used for?"

Strubby's face twitched.

"The master's personal... effects. His... work."

I placed my first foot on the stair. Strubby put a restraining hand on my elbow. I may only have been nineteen but I was the lady of the house and was not going to allow the staff to touch me so readily.

"Get your hand off me, Mrs Strubby."

Her grip did not loosen fast enough. I fixed her with a fearsome glare. It was an expression copied from Aunt Etheline, one she reserved purely for insolent menials. I had clearly learnt well from my aunt. Mrs Strubby recoiled as though burned and bowed her head.

"Sorry, ma'am. The door at the top is locked. The master has the only key."

"I see," I said coldly.

I told Strubby to send up a girl to run a bath for me and then dismissed the woman. I spent an hour soaking in the tub. The water was hard and the soap refused to foam. Dried and feeling unnecessarily like a trespasser, I went into the master bedroom. I climbed into my side of the marital bed and waited for my husband. By ten o'clock, he still had not come.

I awoke at his touch. The morning light peered through the gap in the heavy curtains.

"Where have you been?" I asked.

"With you," he replied and nodded to the rumpled pillows next to me.

"But you are dressed," I said.

He nodded.

"I have to go to Crewe. There is rolling stock to be inspected. I shall be back this evening."

"But Giles..."

He kissed me.

"Our honeymoon can wait one day. Trains cannot."

And he was gone.

That day seemed to stretch on for an eternity. I was bored beyond measure. As before, most of the rooms were locked. I called

Strubby to open the music room and, grudgingly, she came. The harpsichord was riddled with worm holes. There were only five gramophone records – four disks of military marches and one of 'Music Hall Favourites'. The gramophone itself was in need of repair.

I wanted to make use of other rooms but could not bear the thought of having to suffer Strubby's exasperation once more. I took an early lunch, an early bath and retired to our bed, bored and lonely, before night had even fallen. I slept and awoke to find Giles at my side once more.

"Does marriage tire you so much, darling?" he asked.

"When did you return?"

"Shortly after six. You were already asleep."

I looked at his clothes. He was dressed for travel.

"You're not off again, are you?"

He nodded.

"An opportunity in north London. I cannot ignore it. I will be back tomorrow. Sunday at the latest."

At that, I broke down and wept and told him of my utter boredom. He held me and rocked me until I had regained my composure.

"Mrs Strubby can be a cranky soul but here..." He held out to me a ring with more than a score of keys threaded onto it. "You are the lady of the house. These should be yours now and you should not need to *ask* Mrs Strubby for anything."

I brightened a little. He paused in handing over the ring of keys. He took them back a moment, slid a small padlock key from the ring and then gave them to me once more.

"You won't need this one," he said. "A man's entitled to some privacy, is he not?" He made to put the key in his pocket, hesitated and then dropped the key into a slim-necked vase on the dresser. It landed with a tiny china clink. "But marriage is about trust."

He kissed me, tenderly, too briefly, and he was gone once more.

Of course I went into the attic. The only uncertainty was how long my curiosity could be kept at bay. Could I live out the rest of my life not knowing what really resided in that room? Could I resist it for ten years? Five years? One? No, I could not. And so I reasoned to myself, if I was going to cross that forbidden threshold, there was no difference between doing it now and doing it thirty years hence.

Ensuring that Mrs Strubby and the other servants were busy elsewhere, I climbed the narrow stair to the attic. The warped and unpainted door at the top was indeed held secure with a steel latch and a small padlock. I dashed down to the bedroom, almost broke the vase in my haste to remove the key and then ran back up to the attic once more.

With fumbling fingers, I thrust the key in the lock. The padlock sprang open with a powerful click. I slipped the padlock from the latch and, at that moment, a call came from downstairs.

"Dora? Darling? Change of plans, darling," called Giles, his footsteps resounding along the landing. "No need to go to London. A false alarm." His footsteps paused. "Darling?"

There was a creak: his foot on the bottom step of the attic stairs.

"Are you up there, Dora?"

He started to climb. I threw off the latch. It was loud enough. "Dora! No!"

His feet thumped on the stairs.

The attic was in darkness. I reached out for a light switch that I hoped would be there. My eyes widened in anticipation. If I was to be caught, it would be in full possession of the facts.

"Dora!"

His arms wrapped around my chest as my fingers touched the switch. Electric light momentarily blinded me and then I saw. His arms went limp against my sides.

"I told you not to," he said softly.

I stepped forward into the room. I'm not sure what I expected to find. The stench of congealing blood? A rack, surrounded by implements of torture? The heads of his former wives mounted on the walls, expressions of terror fixed on their faces? No. There was no blood, only the faint and familiar aroma of oil. Instead of a rack, there was a long table upon which a complex model railway had been erected. Pinned to the walls, instead of severed heads, were yellow sheets of paper: charts, timetables, names and serial numbers, mostly scrawled in a childish and enthusiastic hand.

"Is this your work?" I asked.

Giles shook his head.

"My income comes from investments. A legacy. I don't have to work. I'm just a railway enthusiast."

I frowned.

"You like to look at trains?"

"I love trains."

"You're some kind of – what? – train... spotter?"

He nodded.

I went to him and removed his dark glasses. He did not resist. His eyes were small, darting things. I looked at my husband anew. He wasn't a man. He was a child in a man's body, in a silly old-fashioned cape, in a dusty, lifeless house. A child with oily, unwashed hands and a pale, unexceptional face.

The marriage was never consummated. We were granted an annulment in the autumn.

• Appropriate Thunder

Having reached a point at which he was no longer heading away from one village but heading towards another, Josua Baum steered the motorcycle and sidecar off the road and into the broad forest. The woodland floor was a smoothly undulating carpet of hard earth, leaf mulch and the humps of tree roots. He could have driven deep into the forest but there was rain in the air and thunder in the distance and he could not risk his wheels becoming bogged down in the mud on the return journey.

Once he was out of sight of the road, he stopped the motorcycle on the far side of a tall, broad ivy-covered oak. He dismounted, took the blanket covered basket out of the sidecar – there was no sound or movement from within it, but he did not let himself dwell on that – and then retrieved the short-handled shovel from the carriage floor.

Josua raised himself on tiptoes and checked the forest in all directions before beginning to dig. The earth was packed hard but crumbled easily enough under the blade. Fifteen minutes later, he had a hole four feet deep and round enough to take the basket. He also had a sharp pain in his back, a hollow stomach of acid and a dull headache that he knew would not recede until he was back in the bar of the Wild Deer Hotel. It was raining constantly, though not heavily, and the loud but lightless thunderclouds were much nearer.

He straightened his back and groaned to himself.

"Hard work, hah?"

Josua gave a start and turned. An old man with thick whiskers was standing not three yards behind him.

"God in heaven!" he exclaimed.

The old man's bushy eyebrows went up as he considered this expletive at length before shrugging.

"Doing some digging, hah?"

He looked at the covered basket. Josua followed his gaze. It looked like a pile of washing or maybe a large picnic, Josua told himself. The old man had no reason to suspect it was anything more or less.

"Who the hell are you?" he said.

"Donar," said the old man. "And who the hell are you?"

Josua said nothing.

The old man, Donar, toyed briefly at his moustaches with grubby fingers.

"You looked like a... Josua."

Josua took a step back in surprise and nearly fell into his own hole.

"Right, hah?" said Donar. "I know *what* you are as well."

Josua shifted the shovel in his grip. Donar pulled out a hipflask from beneath the tails of the badly cured leather coat he wore.

"You, friend, are the persistent and occasionally repentant drunk." He unscrewed the hipflask, took a swig and offered it to Josua.

Josua hesitated.

"Takes one to know one," said Donar.

Josua took the flask and sipped. He gagged instantly on the earthy syrup.

"What is that?"

"A restorative," said Donar. "Speedy recovery and strength against the call of the beer."

"It's vile," said Josua, handing it back.

"Yup. It's that. Made from acorns." The old man slipped the flask into his coat. Josua saw a short-handled axe – or it could have been a small hammer – hanging from the man's belt.

Donar directed his gaze up to the boughs of the oak. "Amazing things, acorns."

"How so?"

"They only grow on mature oaks. Do you know how long that takes, hah? From acorn to oak to fresh acorns? There's strength and wisdom and patience in acorns."

For no good reason he could see, Josua found himself saying, "My mother once told me a story about a man who made a pact with Satan, promising to give his soul once his first harvest was in. The man planted acorns."

He studied the old man. He looked like a trapper but he was too well-spoken and his accent was definitely not Hessian. Far from the lights and familiar touchstones of his everyday life, Josua found himself able to believe that the devil walked the earth in human form and he was afraid.

"Place two acorns in a bowl of water," said Donar. "If they float together before floating to the edge it means that you and your love will be together forever. The wisdom of the acorn."

"Is that so?"

"You got a woman?" said Donar.

He nodded tersely. Donar smiled.

"Married?"

"Four years. We were married at the St Martinskirche in Solms."

Josua couldn't hide the emotion in his voice. He might as well have told the old devil the entire sorry story.

"Marry in haste, repent at leisure, hah?"

"Repent?"

Josua tasted the word, rolling it around his mouth. It was as sickly and unpalatable as Donar's acorn syrup.

"And you have children?" said Donar, looking once again at the basket. A raindrop, dribbled through the leaves above, splashed on his forehead. "More trouble than they're worth too, hah?"

Josua couldn't answer that. He had locked certain thoughts and feelings away from his conscious mind. The task in hand depended on that. If he was to stop and think about what he was doing now, he would fail.

"Tell me," said Donar. "Do you drink because your life is full of hardships and grief, or is your life full of hardships and grief because you drink?"

"Surely that's between me and my barman," Josua replied.

The old man laughed.

"The troubles I've had because of the beer. The troubles I caused my family. It drove my father to distraction. Miserable one-eyed bastard that he was." He paused. "Is, I suppose."

Josua frowned. The old man hardly appeared infirm – in truth, he bore himself with a straight back and something close to nobility and Josua suspected that underneath the stinking clothes were some sinewy and powerful muscles – but those wrinkles and those long whiskers, with the last traces of the man's once red hair all but gone from them, spoke of great, great age.

"Your father is still alive?" Josua asked, incredulous.

Donar stared vacantly, into the past.

"Mad bastard hung himself. From a tree." He stepped back to admire the mighty oak. "An ash tree, mind you. Nine days he hung there."

"Before someone found him?"

"Even after that, especially after that, he was more miserable than ever. Despaired at my drinking. The drinking and the fighting."

He raised two gnarly fists. Little white hairs sprouted from the dirt-encrusted knuckles.

"Show us your hands, Josua."

Josua, without thinking, let the shovel fall to the ground and held out his hands for inspection. Donar grabbed Josua's hands in his and peered at them closely, pawing and pummelling the flesh of the palms with his coarse thumbs.

"These are not a fighter's hands," he concluded soon enough.

"No."

"What do you do for a living?"

"I'm a school master," said Josua.

"Hah!" he barked, dismissively. "A school master. You're a Christian?"

Josua would normally have answered immediately but there was the matter of the basket and the hole and he could not answer that question now.

A peal of thunder boomed directly overhead.

Josua picked up his shovel.

"You should be on your way," he suggested. "The weather's turning."

Donar smiled broadly. There were teeth in his head and every one of them sunshine yellow.

"It doesn't worry me. This is my weather." He winked at Josua. "Literally."

Nonetheless, the old man ruffled his coat, gathered it about him and walked away, past the basket and the motorcycle, on through the forest.

Josua felt the sickening uneasiness within him subside a little and then Donar stopped and turned.

"Do you want to know how I knew your name?" he asked.

Josua hesitated, knowing he should say no, and not give the man any excuse to loiter.

"How?" he asked.

"The Great Oak at Shechem."

Josua shook his head.

"I don't understand."

"If you were a good Christian man you would. The Bible. I don't have much love for it myself but after all these years, you can't help but pick some of it up. Josua, leader of the Israelites, comes to Shechem and there, underneath the Great Oak that grew there, he digs a hole."

Donar walked a little way back towards Josua.

"In it, he buries the false gods of his people. The idols, the carved images, the little household deities. Josua takes all the things his people had once worshipped and he buries them beneath an oak tree."

"I see," said Josua, not sure if the man, who was an obvious lunatic, was speaking the truth or making it up.

"So, I saw you and a hole and an oak tree and I instantly knew that you must be Josua."

Josua could find no response to that.

"There is no originality in this world," said Donar. "You see the same things again and again and again. Old stories, old ways, old gods. They never die. Round and round they go. You've just got to learn to recognise them when they pop up."

Abruptly, in a move that made Josua's heart clench with fear, Donar tapped the basket with his booted foot.

"So, what's this?"

"Nothing," said Josua, quickly. Too quickly.

"I was wondering if you had false gods of your own to bury. Maybe something you once worshipped and adored but can't bear to look at anymore."

'He knows!' screamed a voice in Josua's head. 'He knows! He knows!'

What if the old man went to the police? He knew Josua's name, his profession, even where he was married, for God's sake! The police would be able to identify him within days. Josua considered, not for the first time, the shovel he held in his hand. Donar might have had that axe or hammer at his belt but Josua had his shovel and he had age on his side. And yet, in some indefinable way, Josua knew he would not be able to kill this man. He could already picture the hairy trapper sidestepping his first blow and then raising his fists – his worn and scarred fighter's hands – and that being the end of things.

"Because, you know," said Donar, "even if you don't want it anymore, there's always someone who does."

The blanket covering the basket moved. It was a small movement. Maybe the rain-dampened material was settling. Maybe not.

"Give it to me," said Donar.

"What?"

"Give it to me."

"You don't know what it is," said Josua.

"Yes, I do. And you know it too. Give it to me. Make an offering of it to me."

"What will you give me in return?"

"My blessings."

Josua's mind strayed dangerously close to that box of locked thoughts and feelings.

"What will you do with it?" he asked.

"Nothing," said Donar.

"Nothing?"

"Nothing. It's not what happens to it that counts. It's the fact that you will have given it to me. The offering is the important thing."

Josua looked at Donar in incomprehension and then, abruptly, recognised him at last. The ancient drinker, the fighter with the hammer at his belt, with the last wisps of red in his beard, with the thunder – how appropriate – in the skies above.

"Come, take it," said Donar. "Give it to me and go."

Josua stepped forward and picked up the basket. There was no sound from within as he lifted it. His heart ached with sadness for what he had done and what he was now doing. He put the basket in Donar's arms and the man's face suddenly flushed with warmth and life.

"St Martinskirche in Solms," he said.

"What of it?" said Josua.

"Lovely oak doors."

Josua tried to remember, could not think. Donar pressed a finger against the blanket but did not lift it.

"Taken from a tree dedicated to me not far from there. St Boniface himself cut it down."

With that, he turned and walked back into the forest. He did not look back but Josua watched him go all the same.

• Three Birds of Saint-Cyr

The Proprietor Amazon

The Proprietor Amazon is a small blue-green parrot endemic to the island of Saint-Cyr. It can be easily distinguished from similar birds, such as the Cuban Parrot and Hispaniola Amazon, by the hood of bright azure feathers on its head and face. These birds live in densely forested regions and make their nests in the hollows of rotting trees. They are unusually gregarious for parrots, living in social groups of up to twenty individuals.

Though it is a cautious creature, the Proprietor Amazon is both inquisitive and extremely noisy. They chatter incessantly whilst eating. In the forest their diet consists mainly of seeds, nuts, berries and flowers but they have adapted to take advantage of the fruit and maize plantations that are dotted about their island home and it is this penchant for thievery that has given them their name and caused them to be reviled in local folk tradition.

In the eighteenth century, on each plantation, there would be at least one slave whose job it was to scare off these opportunist scavengers. If a bird was spotted, up would go a cry of 'Yoto-toto' which was both an imitation of the parrot's cry and of the language of the French slavers (which was an alien mumbo-jumbo to many of the African-born slaves). In popular imagination, the amazon and the slave-drivers were one, taking the fruits of the land from those who had worked to produce it. And so the bird became known as the *propriétaire foncier*, or landowner bird.

Habitat destruction and the introduction of Martlesham's Jay to Saint-Cyr have since caused the Proprietor Amazon to retreat from many areas and to rapidly dwindle in number. Yet, even more than a hundred and fifty years after the emancipation of the Saint-Cyr slaves, this is seen by many islanders as a good thing.

The Saint-Cyr Lizard Cuckoo

It is curious that the Saint-Cyr islanders chose the Lizard Cuckoo over the Red-tailed Hawk as their national bird. Instead of favouring the bold and brutal bird of prey that feeds upon unwary Proprietor Amazons, the islanders expressed a preference for the cuckoo, which targets the same bird but takes what it needs through deception.

The Saint-Cyr Lizard Cuckoo is a large bird of about eighteen inches in length. It is uniformly light brown in colour apart from its eye-ring (which is orange) and the underside of its considerably long tail (which has white and black striping). Apart from lizards, it also eats amphibians, small snakes and insects.

Unusually for new world cuckoos, this particular species is a brood parasite and lays its eggs in other birds' nests, specifically that of the Proprietor Amazon. Though the Saint-Cyr Lizard Cuckoo's eggs are considerably larger than those of its victims, the cuckoo's egg shell has a similar colour and mottling to that of the Proprietor Amazon's and the rogue egg is usually accepted as part of the clutch by the female amazon. If the female cuckoo's egg cycle is out of synch with that of the chosen Proprietor Amazon hen, the cuckoo will usually eat all the amazon's eggs so that the amazon is forced to start another brood.

Once hatched, the cuckoo chick will methodically evict all other young from the nest. It will roll eggs out by pushing them with its back and peck any hatchlings until they either leap from the nest or die. Evicted amazon chicks are unlikely to survive the fall from the nest but those that do are nonetheless ignored thereafter by their mother. This behaviour seems callous but is necessary if the cuckoo chick is to receive sufficient food from its adopted mother; before it has fledged, the cuckoo chick will be nearly as large as her.

For islanders, the Saint-Cyr Lizard Cuckoo is more than just a bird. The folk hero, Kwami, who is sometimes a cuckoo and sometimes a man and sometimes both at once is the subject of Saint-Cyr stories in much the same way as Anansi is in other parts of the Caribbean. Kwami is sly and underhand and always manages to hoodwink Hawk, Propriétaire, Snake and Rat, often without them ever realising they have been fooled.

The Martlesham's Jay

The Martlesham's Jay, also called the crested pine jay, has a range that stretches from Alaska in the north to Mexico in the south. West of the Rockies, it has completely replaced the more well-known Blue Jay. The differences between the two species are slight but, confusingly, the Martlesham's Jay's plumage is of a more striking blue than that of the Blue Jay. To add further to the confusion, neither bird is actually blue. Their colour comes not from pigmentation but through the structure of their feathers which diffracts light in such a way as to give the impression of blueness.

The Martlesham's Jay lives in coniferous or mixed woodland and prefers to build its nest in the hollows of trees, constructing them from plant material held together with a cement of mud and leaf mulch. They feed primarily on seeds, nuts and berries but will also eat insects, eggs and the unprotected fledglings of other birds. Like many jays, the Martlesham's Jay produces a wide variety of sounds and is an accomplished mimic. When approaching a potential feeding area, the Martlesham's Jay will often imitate the cry of the Red-tailed Hawk, thus scaring away many of the birds with which it would normally compete for food.

The Martlesham's Jay was introduced to Saint-Cyr in 1918 when Anthony Sharp, a visiting historian, presented a breeding pair to Queen Honore. Being well-versed in the country's folklore, he suggested that the birds' mimicry of the Red-tailed Hawk might be used to drive the despised Proprietor Amazon from farmlands. The pair were housed in the royal menagerie and their offspring later released into the wild.

The extent to which Sharp's plan succeeded was not apparent for some years. Not only did the Martlesham's Jays chase the Proprietor Amazons away from prime feeding sites but they made their nests in the very tree hollows that the amazons favoured and so forced the amazons to go deeper into the forests to lay their eggs. This rout was so complete that in 1948, the queen declared the battle against the hated Proprietor Amazon to be won and the government issued a set of commemorative stamps to mark the 'victory'. Both the queen and the people of Saint-Cyr must have, for the sake of convenience, chosen to ignore the impact that the Martlesham's Jay was also having on their beloved Lizard Cuckoo. The Saint-Cyr Lizard Cuckoo's decline, whilst no more tragic than that of the Proprietary Amazon, is a story tinged with a note of cruel irony.

Even as the Proprietor Amazon retreats before the expanding numbers of Martlesham's Jays, the Lizard Cuckoo continues to lay its eggs in the tree hollow nests it had always frequented. It seems to matter little that those nests are now jay's nests. Unfortunately for the Saint-Cyr Lizard Cuckoo, the Martlesham's Jay's eggs are sufficiently dissimilar to those of the cuckoo to allow the mother jay to tell the difference. Subsequently, nearly all Saint-Cyr Lizard Cuckoo eggs are eaten within hours of being laid. Those few that pass initial detection hatch, only to be killed by their adopted mother and fed to their brood siblings.

For the cuckoo, thousands of years of evolution and adaptation have been undone in mere decades. The Saint-Cyr Lizard Cuckoos, unable to break the bonds of genetic conditioning, continue to lay their eggs in the jays' nests whenever possible. Naturalists have recorded instances of an almost symbiotic relationship in which an individual cuckoo hen will lay her eggs in the same hostile nest again and again, seemingly willing to offer her own young up as a sacrifice for the well-being of the Martlesham's Jay.

In recent decades, the constantly expanding oral tradition of Kwami stories has given rise to the character of Jay. Jay is the demon who tricks the trickster and his appearance is said to herald the end of the world.

• Numbers

"You can do anything with numbers."

"What was that?" said Finogen Gauk.

Peotr Spiakov looked up from the Weekly Sheet of Variable Integers, blinked rapidly to moisten his dry eyes and peered at Finogen.

"What?"

"You said something."

"Did I?"

He looked about himself. Their office on the third floor of the Department of Records (Quantities and Quotas) was large with a window overlooking Krasnaya-Prenya Street. An honour though it might be for the two departmental overseers to be given such a spacious office between them, Peotr did not like it. It was cold in the winter and the emptiness around his desk gave Peotr the feeling that something was always hovering close by. His mind was filled with ghosts and spies of late.

"You need a cup of tea," said Finogen.

"No. My bladder is full and I only have one page left to check."

"You look peaky, friend."

Peotr put his pen down.

"We received a letter this morning."

"Oh?"

"From the Judicial Appeal Committee. They've received our application and it's now being looked at."

"Did they say anything about Lukian?" asked Finogen. "Is he okay? Where is he being held?"

Peotr sighed.

"No. They did not say anything. It mentions the trial but they did not say if he is in prison or..." He smiled bitterly. "Serafima cried when I read it to her."

"Your wife misses her son. You have to be strong."

"Yes. Strong."

"You need a cup of tea."

"I need more than tea."

"But tea is all we have."

Peotr laughed.

"You are a clown, Fino*gei*. How did they ever let you work here? Koroshilov never liked you."

Finogen shrugged.

"Who knows? But Comrade Koroshilov is dead and you have his desk. All is well. Now, tea."

He sprang to his feet, bustled the cups and saucers from both their desks and was out of the door.

Peotr Spiakov was fifty-two years old. He had lived in the Presnensky District all his life. He graduated from Moscow State University in 1925, married a fellow mathematician and applied for a job at the freshly renamed Department of Records.

Peotr and Finogen Gauk sat the entrance exam together, a four hour exercise in copying, checking, totalling and comparing numbers. There were only numbers; no words, no meanings, no keys. Afterwards, Peotr was interviewed by Koroshilov in the office which he would later inherit. Koroshilov studied Peotr's test paper.

"Not one single error, in over a thousand actions. You are an excellent computer."

"Thank you, comrade."

"The meaning of that word will change soon. In the west there are plans to build mechanical computers. Boxes of cogs and wires. They will use them to collect their taxes, to run their banks and count their dollars. We too will make computing machines but we will not waste steel and glass on their manufacture when we have a far greater resource at our disposal."

Koroshilov looked at Peotr over the top of his national standard reading glasses.

"You will be part of that machine, Comrade Spiakov," he said.

"Yes, comrade," said Peotr.

Because of his government job, Peotr managed to avoid conscription during the Great Patriotic War. He had to cash in many favours to achieve the same for his son. He arranged a position for Lukian at the Office of Macro-Cryptography, working under the supervision of Peotr's university tutor, Belenki. Many of

Lukian's contemporaries were not so lucky. The sinecure that Peotr had bought his son had saved his life and so, naturally, Lukian despised his father for it.

After the war, though he lived in the same apartment as his parents, Lukian no longer lived with them. He was always out, with people he had met through his war work, with young angry students and disaffected academics. Peotr tried to reason with his son through Professor Belenki but the white-haired mathematician had also become a stranger to his former friends.

One wet September night in 1948, Peotr accosted his son on the street corner by their apartment block. They argued and then Lukian stormed off. Two days later, eight officers from the Ministry for State Security came to the apartment with authorisation to gather evidence and ransacked their home. The men in uniform took whatever books, letters and photographs they fancied, clearing Lukian's room of everything.

Six years after that, having received a letter from the Judicial Appeal Committee (acknowledging receipt of his own letter sent nine months earlier) and distracted by his aching bladder and ghosts of his own making, Peotr Spiakov signed off the Weekly Sheet of Variable Integers without bothering to check the last four columns.

"Bread rations have gone down."

Mrs Durakov, the apartment building superintendent, swept her broom back and forth across the step in front of Peotr, blocking his path. It had been an overlong journey home from the office, Peotr's body ached and he did not particularly wish to be waylaid.

"Is that so?"

"You know it is, comrade. Question is, what are your lot going to do about it?"

"My lot?"

"Quotas. That's you, isn't it?"

He grunted.

"We don't control anything, Mrs Durakov," he said. "We just juggle numbers."

He pushed his way past, half-stepping on her broom head.

"That wife of yours was crying again," said Mrs Durakov.

Peotr ignored her and trudged up the stairs.

"They sent another letter today," said Mrs Durakov, loud enough for all the ground floor tenants to hear.

Peotr turned.

"Who?"

"The Judiciary."

"Is that any of your business?" he said harshly.

The superintendent met his gaze.

"I think it is unpatriotic of you, comrade. Do not waste the government's time with letters."

"I want to know where my boy is. That is all."

She sneered at that.

"Not all of us know where our sons are," he muttered.

Sergei Durakov, twelve years dead, was buried in a mass grave outside the city of Golbega. Some days, Peotr felt a stab of jealousy because the superintendent possessed that small piece of knowledge. Most days, he would have gladly swapped the possibility of his son being alive for certain knowledge that he was dead.

"...you can do anything with numbers."

Peotr looked up from his work.

"What was that?" he said.

"I said, they think you can do anything with numbers," said Finogen Gauk, perched on the corner of his desk, tea cup in hand.

Peotr continued to look at him blankly. Finogen grinned wearily.

"You've not listened to a word I've said."

"I'm sorry," said Peotr. "I... My mind is on other things."

"Yes?"

"Another letter."

"Only a month since the last one? The wheels of justice are building up speed."

"Lukian's case has been passed onto the People's Committee for Political Rehabilitation."

"And that's good?"

Peotr shrugged.

"I'm sorry, Finogen. You were trying to tell me something."

"I was. You know the bread shortage?"

"Of course."

"Well..." Finogen waggled his eyebrows dramatically. "The government are blaming it on bureaucratic errors. In this department, no less."

Peotr laughed despite himself.

"What?" said Finogen.

"My building superintendent told me the shortage was our fault too."

"Then I'd watch what you say to her. State Security are launching an investigation."

Peotr's half-smile crumbled.

"You're joking, aren't you?"

"I am? Perhaps this is a work of sabotage."

"But we have no control over the food supplies. We just do the numbers. We only record."

"But those records are read and actions are made accordingly. There is power in numbers and only a single line separates a plus from a minus."

Peotr's mind flipped back to a Weekly Sheet of Variable Integers, maybe four weeks ago, and an unchecked set of columns.

"You think they'll find out who's responsible?" he asked.

"Not a chance. They'd be searching for one anomalous piece of data amongst thousands, millions even. They won't be able to see the wood for the trees."

The following week, when the threatened State Security investigation failed to amount to anything more than a brief inspection of the department by a junior Kremlin official, Peotr carried out an experiment. He introduced three deliberate errors into his department's output. He altered an underling's work, changing a one into a seven in a Transposition Matrix sheet, he swapped over the reference numbers on a pair of Throughput Dockets and he took a random sheet from a File Store Folder and binned it.

Then he waited.

Two months later, a passing acquaintance told him that the offices of the Ministry for Rural Mechanisation had taken receipt of an unexpected delivery of two thousand toilet rolls and that more than a dozen people had to have their workspaces relocated in order to make room for them.

Peotr might have left it at that but as the year drew to a close, he and his wife got another letter, stamped with the seal of the Judicial Appeal Committee. It was the longest such letter they had received.

It stated that Lukian Spiakov, arrested on the 25th September 1948 on charges of treason and sentenced to life imprisonment, would be exonerated and formally rehabilitated on the grounds that there was insufficient proof of guilt. However, as Lukian had died in a government work farm in February 1949, the rehabilitation was a posthumous one. The letter ended with thanks for the Spiakov family and an exhortation to see their son's death as a noble sacrifice in the ongoing struggle of the Soviet people.

Serafima Spiakov howled in grief and broke the china tureen that had belonged to her paternal grandmother. Peotr wept silently and consoled his wife and the next day he went into work with fury in his heart and thoughts of destruction on his mind.

His revenge on the Union of Soviet Socialist Republics may have been petty and small but it was not mindless. He did nothing obvious, nothing that would be spotted and changed, nothing that could be linked directly to himself. He changed dates. He moved decimal points. He turned minuses into pluses. He did it every day for a week and his minor acts of subversion slaked his savage hatred.

Peotr was surprised to the point of queasiness when Mrs Durakov offered him her sympathies.

"I heard," she said. "I am so sorry."

The superintendent placed her hand on top of Peotr's on the stair handrail. Her skin was rough, calloused by hard labour and caustic soaps.

"Thank you," he said.

"At least you know now," she said. "Did they say where he is... buried?"

Peotr sniffled.

"No. Somewhere in the Urals. I'm not sure I would want to visit..."

The sadness welled within him. He shook his head at himself and pulled himself together.

"Did you ever go and visit your son's grave?" he asked.

Mrs Durakov grunted.

"Minsk is too far. I don't have the money or the papers. I would but..."

"Minsk? No." He looked at her. "Golbega."

"Pardon?"

"Golbega. Your son died in Golbega."

She took a step away from him and put her hand back on the mop.

"I've never heard of that place."

"It's a city on the Svislach. Famous for its castle. Must be a million people living there."

"My son was killed by the Nazis in Minsk, Comrade Spiakov."

Peotr frowned at her, said a curt farewell and walked up to his apartment. He recounted his conversation with Mrs Durakov to his wife. Serafima shook her head and admitted that she too had never heard of any city called Golbega. Peotr got out his father's old atlas and tried to find it.

On a wet September night in 1948, Peotr Spiakov saw his son for the last time. Lukian had on the black tank commander's jacket that he had taken to wearing of late. They argued but they did not argue about the same thing. Their conversation was disjointed and non-reciprocal, like two mismatched cogs grating together.

"Just come home," said Peotr. "Your mother is cooking. The table is laid."

"There is no home anymore," said Lukian.

"Of course there is," said his father.

Lukian put a cigarette in his mouth and lit it.

"Do you know what I did in the war?" he said.

"It doesn't matter."

"We converted everything into numbers. We quantified everything."

"You worked in code-breaking."

145

"No. We converted everything into numbers. Soldiers. Tanks. Supply trains. Hills. Rivers. Nations. Ultimately everything can be expressed numerically. 'Understanding without the bias of language.'"

This last was a quote from a standard text on Soviet mathematics.

"Is this relevant?" said Peotr.

"We did it because you can change numbers," said Lukian. "With equations. With formulae. If you can transform a one to a zero, you can change a live soldier into a dead one. Macro-cryptography. We were decoding Hitler's armies."

"That's mad."

Lukian laughed, expelling a cloud of smoke.

"Tell me something about the war that wasn't. Numbers control the word. You can do anything with numbers."

Lukian's words were bitter as though he were disgorging lumps of rancid meat. Peotr didn't understand.

"That's in the past now. Come home."

Lukian shook his head.

"What do you think you do at work, father? You are part of the machine. You run the numbers now. Do you think it's fear or military might that hold Stalin's Russia together?"

Peotr instinctively looked around to see if anyone was listening. Rain had driven everyone indoors and the street was empty.

"You perpetuate it," said Lukian. "It's you. And your numbers. And I can't be a part of it anymore. Goodbye, father."

He spat a slither of tobacco on the floor and then hurried away, across the road, his shoulders hunched against the rain.

You can do anything with numbers.

Peotr put his hatred aside and set himself a new mission. He tinkered with numbers. He incorrectly totalled columns, fed false data into the system and watched the results. He studied the system of his own government's bureaucracy until it became like a live animal to him, responsive to his touch.

Peotr located Professor Belenki's research (that which hadn't been suppressed) and sought out the surviving members of the

Office of Macro-Cryptography. He listened to their ravings and, between the cracks in the idiocy, saw a glimmering light.

Peotr Spiakov was a mathematician and he learned once again to see the world as numbers. His malign influence became a ghost that haunted the corridors of the Department of Records. There was talk of sabotage but nothing could be proved. Peotr was too subtle. He was a computer, a piece of code in the system. He became a virus against which there were no antibodies.

There is power in numbers and only a single line separates a plus from a minus.

He knew that, given enough time, you could do anything with numbers. And he knew that, one day, he would make that one vital change and he would come home to find a tank commander's jacket hanging on a peg in the hall and a dinner table laid for three.

• Sanders

The parcel was heavy and square, foreign stamps clustered in the corner. The address read:

Sanders
Flat 7 - 32 Ashdown Terrace
NW6
England

"There's no flat seven," said Alice.

The postman sniffled and pointed at the grid of doorbells. There was seven, below five and to the right of six.

She began protesting that she was flat three, not seven, but stopped herself. The man looked frozen and she was suddenly curious about a flat she had never heard of in her six month tenancy.

"I'll take it up," she said and closed the door.

There were two flats on each floor and only three floors in the house. She was considering the possibility that the address was incorrect when, opening a narrow door on the second floor that was obviously a broom cupboard, she found a stair leading up and at the top a door with a plastic seven screwed onto it.

When there was no response to knocking, she decided to lean the parcel against the door for its recipient but the latch popped open and the parcel fell onto the floor with a slap.

"Hello?" she called. "Your door is open."

There was no reply. She picked up the parcel and stepped inside.

The living room sat within the sloping roof of the house. The round window at one end was open, letting in a chill breeze and barely any light. In the gloom, Alice made out pieces of dark furniture. There were three armchairs and in the largest was a pile of crumpled clothes with a wide-brimmed hat resting on top. A low bookcase on one wall drew Alice's attention. The volumes on its shelves were all tatty hardbacks and she had an abrupt inkling of what the parcel might contain. A musty aroma permeated the flat. She wondered if it was the ancient books although the smell had notes that were heavier, organic, animal even.

On top of the shelving unit stood a turntable and a stack of twelve-inch records. The top one was *Time Out* by the Dave Brubeck Quartet. Next to it was a pottery pagoda, pale pink and green. Alice touched it with her fingertips. Her nails made a satisfying 'tink' against its glaze.

"What?" rumbled a deep voice behind and then, much louder, "You!"

Alice whirled round to see the pile of the clothes in the armchair – no longer a pile of clothes – rise to its feet. He was a towering round-shouldered individual. The hat on his head brushed the ceiling and, in that thick duffel coat, he seemed nearly as wide as he was tall.

"How did you find me?" he growled in a thick accent.

She stepped back in fear, stumbling over a battered suitcase that she had not noticed before.

"Do you persist in breaking into people's houses?" he demanded.

Alice struggled to find words. She thrust the parcel towards him.

"Parcel," she said. "I just brought up your parcel. I'm sorry."

The giant figure was still. Dark eyes glistened and blinked beneath the brim of his hat.

"Oh," he said. "Your hair. I thought..."

She put a hand to her blonde locks.

"I'm sorry," she said. "I didn't see you, sleeping."

"My mistake. Sorry," he said.

Alice looked at the parcel.

"Are you Sanders?"

He nodded. She passed him the parcel and he took it with extreme care as though his enormous hands might crush hers in the exchange.

"Is Sanders your first name or last name?" she asked.

He made a thoughtful rumble in his throat.

"It is the name I live under."

In his foreign yet precise voice, he made it sound as though his name was something on a sign above his door and that he had lived under many such names.

Alice couldn't place his accent. It wasn't quite Eastern European, wasn't quite Indian, definitely not Hispanic. Perhaps, she decided, it wasn't an accent at all. He sounded like he had an obstruction in his throat, that his tongue was just too big for his mouth.

Sanders looked at the crammed bookshelves, at the cluttered surfaces, for a place to put the books down.

"Kitchen," he said and gently pushed past Alice and she realised that the fusty aroma in the room was him.

The kitchen curtains were drawn and the small room was as dark as the lounge. There was a round kitchen table and three mismatched dining chairs. The smallest appeared to have been comprehensively smashed and then rebuilt with string and tape.

Sanders placed the parcel on the table and tugged at its folds.

A sack of oats sat on the kitchen counter. The shelves above the oven were stacked high with tins and jars, several jars of honey but a whole shelf of orange marmalade.

"Wow," said Alice. "You like your marmalade."

Sanders grunted.

"Everyone likes marmalade."

"Yeah, but..." She gestured. "Are you expecting a world shortage?"

Sanders shrugged his huge hunched shoulders.

"It's winter," he said.

The weather worsened, more snow fell and Alice had to ask the landlady, Mrs Colebourn, to get someone in to look at the radiators in her flat. While the plumber fiddled with the pipes, Alice made tea for them all.

Through the kitchenette window, she saw a large bundled-up figure step heading away along Ashdown Terrace, leaving large round footprints in the snow.

"What do you know about the guy in flat seven?" said Alice.

"Flat seven?" said Mrs Colebourn.

"Sanders."

151

"He pays his rent regularly. Keeps himself to himself."

"Yeah, but what's he like?"

"Bit old for you, isn't he?"

"Mrs Colebourn."

Alice poured hot water into the pot.

"What does he do? For a living?"

Mrs Colebourn stood in the kitchenette doorway, her cigarette held halfway to her lips.

"Well, I've heard someone say he's a jazz musician," she said. "Keeps his saxophone in that shabby suitcase of his."

"Really?"

"I've heard. I've also heard he's an 'exotic dancer'."

Alice laughed and had to stop pouring milk into the cups to avoid spilling it.

"Puh-lease, Mrs Colebourn."

"Just repeating what I've heard. I've also heard he hands out leaflets at the covered market. You know, wearing a silly costume."

Alice put the milk back in the fridge.

"He seems like a very... interesting character."

"I should think he is."

"Is he foreign?"

Mrs Colebourn made a contemplative face.

"I assumed he was one of those... you know, the ones with the funny hats."

"Does that make him foreign?"

"A tragic history," said Mrs Colebourn. "You can see it in the eyes."

On Friday evening, on the way back from the bookshop, Alice saw Sanders walking a little way ahead of her. She hurried through the snow to catch up with him.

"Hello," she said, falling in beside him.

He looked down at her.

"Alice from flat number three. Hello."

He touched the brim of his hat with his free hand. Under his other arm, he held three long packets, wrapped in crisp white paper. A large salmon tail poked out from one under his elbow, level with her shoulder.

"Been shopping?" asked Alice.

"At the fish market. The best bargains are to be found at the end of the day."

"Uh-huh."

"I like driving a hard bargain," he said with relish.

"I wouldn't know how to haggle. It's not the British way."

He made a noise in his throat that might have been a laugh.

"I just give them a hard stare until the price is right," he said.

"You will have to show me that sometime."

"I thought I had." His feet crunched through the frozen snow. "I am sorry I startled you the other day."

"You've apologised already."

"Alice?"

"Yes?"

"Would you like to come to my flat for tea on Sunday?"

From his mouth, it sounded like a question from a Learn English language tape. She could not tell if he said it because he meant it or if he felt he ought to.

"I would like that very much," she said.

Alice appeared at Sanders' door in her best jeans and cardigan. When she knocked the door swung open but she knocked again and waited for Sanders to come to the door.

She had wrongly imagined that Sanders might have tidied his flat for his guest or at least opened the curtains. He had however dragged his kitchen table into the front room and laid out sandwiches and a pot of tea. Sanders, perpetually wrapped up against the cold, pulled out a seat for her and poured her a cup of tea.

"Too weak or too strong?" he asked.

"Just right," she said.

He sat down and they ate. The sandwiches were a choice of fish paste or marmalade.

She told him about her job at the bookshop, hoping to make some link with his obvious interest in books. He nodded politely and fed sandwich after sandwich into his mouth. His teeth were wide-spaced and pointed things.

"Where are you from?" she asked eventually. "Originally."

153

"We lived in the forest."

"Which forest?"

"Long ago. Far away. A small wood really. No more than a hundred acres."

"Sounds nice."

"It was a wood. A place to gather nuts, sleep and shit."

"A long way from Ashdown Terrace though," she said.

He grunted in agreement.

"I have lived in London a long time," he said. "And you?"

She recounted her life story, short though it was, and he nodded in interest and finished off the sandwiches.

As soon as the last sandwich was gone, Sanders went to the kitchen and fetched a long Battenberg cake. At Sanders' suggestion, they sat in the armchairs to eat it and Sanders put a record on the turntable. The sound that emerged from the speaker was a complex brew of brass, woodwind and piano, the volume turned down to an almost impenetrable whisper.

"Charles Mingus," said Sanders and sat heavily in his huge armchair with a cube of Battenburg.

Sanders chomped on the cake, spreading crumbs over his coat and faded checked trousers, and then proceeded to tell Alice about the history of the album they were listening to, the musicians featured and Mingus' composition style.

Stomach full, wrapped up in the comfort of the squashy chair and carried along by the murmuring music and Sanders' low voice, Alice's thoughts wandered. Without any apparent change, she was listening to a story about a bear and a badger and a professor and a journey into the clouds to visit the king of the birds.

She awoke slowly. The record had finished.

"More cake?" said Sanders.

"I couldn't eat another bite," she replied.

This pleased him enormously and he went off to collect the last slice for himself.

Alice went to Sanders' for tea the following Sunday and each Sunday after that through to the new year. She invited him to tea at hers more than once but he politely refused and then insisted she come to his.

Drinking tea, eating cake - plum loaf, pound cake and Victoria sponge – Sanders tried to educate her in the ways of jazz and Alice luxuriated in the reassuring rumble of his voice and the cosy gloom of his cave-like rooms. She often dozed in her chair and eventually stopped being embarrassed by this.

Sleeping, she dreamt of a donkey in search of its tail, of magical adventures with a conjurer's daughter, of a lost orphan left on a railway platform with only a battered suitcase and a label attached to his coat. She hovered above all of them, like an interloper, peering down through the window of Sanders' mind, the cold wind tugging at her yellow hair.

One day she awoke and Sanders was still talking.

"They took us from the forest in chains," he said.

She sat upright.

"They?"

"The men. They chained us and put us in cages."

He described in simple unemotional terms what they did to him and others. He told her of the clearing of their homes by the people from the west. He spoke of hot iron brands and pointless mutilations. He told her that they took his parents from him. He mentioned the Romany and the people in the towns who laughed at him as he was paraded through the streets to coarse, mocking music.

"The Chinese were as bad," he said.

"The Chinese?" she said, confused, a gulf opening between his understanding of history and hers.

"They cut us open," he said, drawing a line across his belly. "They experimented. They wanted medicine."

He looked past Alice's shoulder. She turned to see the pottery pagoda on the bookcase.

"No," he told her. "Tiger Lily was different."

She looked at him.

"I wish I understood you better," she said.

"Why?"

"Why?" she said. "Because you're an interesting person. But strange. I don't have a hold on you."

"A hold on me?"

"How can I tell other people what you are like when I don't understand you or your stories?"

"I don't tell you stories so you can tell them to others," he said with a huff.

"I want to share your stories. Share you."

He began to shake his head as though he had a bad taste in his mouth, suddenly slammed his hairy fists on the arms of his chair and stood up.

"No," he barked. "They were for you and you alone. This was for you. For you and for me."

"Sanders."

"No!" He stomped away from her, to put some space between them and stood with his back to her.

Alice stood.

"I've offended you," she said.

"No," he said. "I made a mistake."

"A mistake?"

He turned on her.

"It's you," he said. "It's always you. You think the world is yours, with your golden hair and your blue eyes."

"I don't."

"You broke in here. You always break in. Here, the door is open. Walk right in! Take what's not yours!"

"I'm not a thief, Sanders," she said.

"Always!" he roared. "My food! My furniture! Take this! Take that! This is too small! This too large! Too hard! Too soft! You find something that is just right and you take it!"

Alice felt her heel touch the skirting board and realised she had been backing away from him.

"Sanders, you're scaring me."

"Not enough!" he growled, his mouth hanging open, his sharp well-spaced teeth exposed. "You've taken everything, haven't you?"

He stepped forward on his huge round feet.

"I'm going," she said.

"What else is there?" he said, coming forward to the bookshelf and sweeping the pottery pagoda up into his paw. "No more mother. No more father. No more hundred-acre wood. The Brown children grown up and gone. What else is there?"

156

Her hand found the door handle. She twisted it and was through. She might have said something, sobbed something, but afterwards she wasn't sure.

Halfway down the stairs, there was an animal roar and then a crash, the shattering of something small, delicate and precious.

Blalk

When it was Sunday, Lesley telephoned and asked if I could go over to play. I told mum.

Mum said, "Take Blalk with you."

Mum was upstairs doing the beds. I was downstairs, already putting my coat on.

I said, "Aww, mum, do I have to?"

Mum said, "She can't spend all day in the house. She wants to go out and play too."

"She can go out with her own friends," I said.

"She doesn't have her own friends, you know that," said mum.

Blalk was in the sitting room watching the test card on television. When she saw me in my coat and holding her shoes, she clapped her hands wetly and waggled her feet at me. I helped her put her shoes on and did up the laces. Blalk has to wear these black shoes with super thick soles. They're big heavy things and she uses them to lash out and break milk bottles on the doorsteps we pass. The milkman knows about Blalk and blames her for milk bottles that get broken even when it isn't her.

Lesley's house is not far but we couldn't go down the old railway line because there is a big patch of nettles growing there and Blalk is terrified of nettles so we had to walk the long way round. When Blalk has got on my wick too much I threaten to push her into a nettle bush or put nettles in her bed but then she wails and mum tells me off.

I took a firm hold of Blalk's hand and led her across Spire View. Her hand is bristly and the purple-green colour of a day old bruise.

Blalk said, "Park?"

I said, "No."

"Park," she said.

"No," I said. "We are going to Lesley's and you are going to be quiet and not make a fuss."

I knocked on Lesley's door and, while we waited, I told Blalk to wipe the drool off her chin. Lesley opened the door and gave Blalk a look.

"What did you bring her for?"

"Mum said I had to." And I did a shrug to show I wasn't happy either.

Lesley said, "She always tries to eat my things," which is true.

Blalk said, "Dollies."

Lesley said, "She's not playing with my things."

We went inside and once we were inside I could smell something I had not noticed before. Blalk had dog poo on her shoes. I grabbed her ankle and lifted her foot up. There was dog poo in the big treads of her shoes and a brown smeary mark of it on Lesley's mum's beige carpet.

Lesley held her nose and said, "Mum's going to go ape."

I made an angry noise at Blalk. With one ankle still held in my hand, I made her hop through the house and out into the back garden. She wobbled and banged against the radiator and knocked over an umbrella stand on the way but didn't break anything.

I said, "Go wipe it off on the grass."

She ran onto the lawn and began dragging her foot along the grass, dragging backwards against the grain, not sideways as she should have done. Lesley's cat, which was a fat ginger tom called Tom, sat on the fence and watched her.

"Cat," said Blalk and pointed.

Tom was a big old fat cat and did not like children. He had scratched me when I tried to stroke him.

I asked, "Do you want to play out here with the cat?"

Blalk said, "Cat."

"Fine," I said.

Me and Lesley went up to her room. Lesley has a tape recorder and she records the top forty off the radio every Sunday. We listened to last Sunday's countdown and sat on her bed so we could watch Blalk out of the bedroom window.

Tom had moved from the fence to the roof of the shed. Blalk was standing by the side of the shed, jumping up and down, trying to reach the cat. Her fat little legs and round veiny body wobbled with every jump. There was no way she was going to reach that cat. We knew she would get bored quickly and then we'd have to do something with her.

Lesley showed me her flower press she got for her birthday. It has screws in the corners to tighten it. She had put some daisies and some dandelion clocks in it the other day. The daisies looked good. The dandelions looked like squashed insects. Lesley tried to make out that they were pretty just in a different way but they still looked like squashed insects.

When I looked out of the window again, the garden was empty. I couldn't see Blalk or Tom. I told Lesley I had better check on her. We went downstairs and into the garden. Lesley's mum's garden has tall fences on either side that smell of creosote and a hedge along the bottom with a gap in it that you can squeeze through if you hold your tummy in and don't mind prickles. There is a small brook which runs behind the hedge and we sometimes go down there to play dens.

We squeezed through.

Blalk was there at the side of the brook. There were three boys there too. They were about mine and Lesley's age but I didn't recognise them so they must go to Cordeaux. We hate Cordeaux boys.

By Blalk's feet at the edge of the brook were several little castles built from mud and twigs and leaves. The boys had trod on one. Blalk was frightened. I could tell by the way she clenched her square yellow teeth and the way she scratched at the scales on her belly.

I said, "Come here, Blalk."

Blalk ran to me and wrapped her arms around me, putting muddy handprints on the Aran cardigan grandma knitted for me. One of the boys trod on another of Blalk's castles, the leaf and twig flag on its battlements crushed beneath his foot. Blalk flinched and her lip wobbled.

I said, "Leave them alone."

The boy said, "You can't make me. This is public land and she's a spaz."

They boy's friends laughed at that.

Lesley said, "You go away now or I will call my mum."

The boys laughed and made pretend-scared noises but they went anyway, along the brook.

Blalk was all muddy and she didn't want to play in the garden by herself anymore so I decided it was time to go home. Lesley gave me one of her pressed daisies and then we left.

Blalk was still shook up because of the boys. Her hand was all slimy in mine. Mum would be annoyed if I took her home and she was upset.

So I said, "Do you want to go to the park?"

"Park!" shouted Blalk and clapped her hands, flicking some of her ooze on my cheek.

At the place where we have to cross the road to get to the park she was so excited she slipped out of my hand and ran out into the road. I leapt forward and grabbed her but a car had been coming along and had to brake suddenly and the man wound down his window to tell us off.

I said, "Sorry."

"It's not your fault," he said. "Does she live at home with you?"

I nodded.

The man shook his head and said, "Well, you're her sister and that but I don't think they should be let out in public."

He wound up his window and drove on. I gave Blalk a glare and we crossed the road properly and went into the park.

We went on the slide, the rocking horse and the swings. Blalk kept wanting me to push her and when I got off my swing to push her a bigger girl took my swing. We went on the witch's hat but Blalk fell off and grazed her knee and started to cry. We sat on a bench and I looked at her knee. It wasn't bleeding properly, not that Blalk bleeds proper blood anyway, just a milky goo like cuckoo spit. There were pieces of black grit in the graze and I tried to pick them out but Blalk squealed.

We went to the ice-cream van to buy ice-creams. I wanted a screwball with the bubble-gum in the bottom of the cup. Blalk wanted a Mr Whippy.

Blalk said, "Flake."

I said, "We can't afford one with a flake."

"Flake!" said Blalk and rubbed her knee and tried to make a sad face although she can't do it properly with her eyes.

I bought a Mr Whippy with a flake for Blalk and because we didn't have much money an Orange Maid lolly for me.

We sat on the bench to eat them. Blalk licked her ice-cream once and then shoved the whole thing in her huge mouth, ice-cream, flake and cone, chomped once and swallowed it.

"You'll make yourself sick," I said and licked my lolly slowly to show her how it is done.

Blalk jumped down and wandered around picking up twigs and stuff. She had calmed down a lot since the thing with the Cordeaux boys. She came back to the bench and, with her fat tongue stuck out, tried to make something out of the things she had picked up.

I asked, "What are you making?"

Blalk held it up. She had shoved some twigs into the side of a pine cone, giving it arms and legs.

Blalk said, "Susan."

I said, "Is it for me?"

Blalk nodded.

I said, "Thank you" and then Blalk threw up on the ground in front of the bench. She made a lot of noise and coughed when she was done.

I looked at the sick on the ground. There was a lot of red in it and I saw a large lump with orange fur.

Blalk said, "Flake" and pointed.

There was the flake, floating in one piece among the chewed up bits of cat.

"Oh, yes," I said and I got up and we went home for tea.

• Eulogy

She possessed the kind of personality that could only be motivated by tight and immovable deadlines and the oncologists had been fiercely specific about the number of weeks her grandfather had left to live. The recent promotion to a diocese in the Midlands also resulted in her being the geographically closest family member to the city where the old man was dying.

She armed herself with a chess set, a book of Sudoku puzzles and a Dictaphone and followed the satnav's instructions to the hospital, a route that seemed elliptically indirect and long-winded. Her grandfather saw the items she carried and immediately understood the rules they were to play by. She set the Dictaphone and chessboard on the bed table and as they played the first of many games, prompted her grandfather to recount his life's story.

Chess and stories; the scene was not new to either of them. Back when her grandmother had been alive and the two of them had lived in the council house on Fairfield Lane, she and her grandfather had played chess on the unlaid dining table. As they played and as the industrious sounds and fat-laden smells of Sunday dinner drifted in from the kitchen, her grandfather would sip stout and tell her stories of people and places she only half knew or did not know at all: the German POW who had worked on their farm and fallen and died on his own pitchfork a week after VE day; the Hillman Minx he and a friend drove into a dyke and then towed out with a tractor borrowed without the owners of either vehicle ever knowing; his cousin's business partner who emptied the company's bank account and fled to Spain with the secretary only for her grandfather and his cousin to track them down and return to England with the money and heavy consciences.

She knew the stories but only as individual tales, told without context. She juggled them in her unconscious and sometimes they slotted together – that this story must follow that if so-and-so were still alive at the time or this story could have only taken place when her grandfather worked at this factory or that workshop – but some random and contradictory detail would force the stories apart again. They were loose pearls, handfuls of them, rolling in her hand without a thread to be strung upon.

Over the course of days (the Bishop's PA had told her to take all the time off she needed) she probed for specifics and questioned vagaries and asked him for details to link one chapter of his life to the next. When he slept or when they wheeled him away for an X-ray or barium meal, she went down to the refectory, played back what they had recorded and made notes in a spiral-bound pad. The stories did not connect together automatically but tendrils and sub-plots reached out from each, ready to be tied off to another event on another page of the grand story.

Like the chess games, the stories were repeated with subtle and not-so-subtle variations and sometimes span off in unexpected directions. They travelled up and down the last seventy years, crossing over stories that she had heard from her parents: the suspicious events surrounding her great aunt's death on a country lane; her grandfather's disastrous six-month stint on a Caribbean drilling rig; the violent and final argument between her grandfather and his cousin at her parent's wedding. He spoke of things that she vaguely recalled from her childhood, episodes that she remembered with a fresh clarity or remembered as being quite different from his version of events.

The story of his life was slowly transformed. The pearls were still rolling in her hand but the thread of history was strung through most of them. She could see the shape of them and made plans to catalogue, order them, and question him about the loose ends. But then he died, as they had predicted he would.

At home, she put the chess set in a drawer and threw the book of Sudoku puzzles in the recycling. She was initially asked to deliver the old man's funeral service but, following terse negotiations between the feuding branches of the family, she suggested that her role be reduced to the reading of the eulogy. This was acceptable – just about bearable – to all and she was grateful for the fresh deadline to spur her into putting her grandfather's life story in order. Without it, the Dictaphone tapes and notepad might have mouldered in a drawer for years.

She copied notes out onto file cards and spread them on the kitchen table and shuffled them round, wrote out fresh notes and shuffled further, a jigsaw of white card and blue ink slowly forming on the table top. There were pieces that simply made no sense, although conversations with her parents and other relatives often brought these pieces into clarity allowing them to be unified with the whole.

She visited an aunt, who now lived in the old family home on Fairfield Lane. Her parents had not spoken to that aunt in years, following some nebulous rift, and she had not been to the place since her childhood visits to her grandparents there. The aunt was garrulous, over affectionate and had the kind of sharp wit possessed by women who grew up in an age when wit was not a desirable quality in women.

The house was smaller than she remembered it, the ceilings lower. After tea, cake and some illuminating answers to questions about her grandfather, she visited the bathroom and, as she climbed the stairs, found herself scrutinising the walls and doors as though expecting secret rooms and fresh spaces to open up before her eyes.

Downstairs, she asked the aunt if she might have a look at the garden and went out through the back door. She looked at it and nodded.

"It seemed bigger when we were children," she said.

With a good deal of clucking, eye-rolling and sighing, the aunt managed to communicate that it was not an uncommon experience.

Leaving her furry-slippered aunt at the back door, she walked down the garden, remembering the places where she and her cousins had played, the places they had hidden. Her grandfather's shed still stood to one side, the old man's workshop she remembered reduced to a tiny shack of rotten rain-soaked boards. There was the tangled bush with the darky thorny space underneath which had been home to monsters and devils and from which none of them had dared retrieve lost balls or frisbees. Too quickly, she reached the end of the garden. She looked back. As a child, she remembered standing at this place, knowing she was far from the house, beyond the dominion and safety of adults.

"I'm not much of a gardener," called the aunt.

"It's very nice," she replied.

Along the bottom of the garden there had been a picket fence. Beyond that, she recalled, there had been a vast scrubby wasteland of brittle cow parsley, hidden brambles and deep water-filled hollows. The children of the family called it the Wilderness and it was where they threatened to send one another to die. When she first encountered the gospels and truly understood them, she imagined Christ being tempted in a wilderness like this. Her aunt had replaced the picket fence with a tall fence of wooden boards and now she had to stand on tiptoes to peer over the top of it.

She instantly wished that she had not looked and yet felt no surprise. There was a strip of nondescript uneven weed-filled land, no more than ten feet deep, then a chicken wire fence and the back gardens of the houses on the next road over. The Wilderness had not been torn up or built over. This was the same landscape, one she had misremembered as something great and mythical and now diminished by experience.

"What can you see?" called the aunt.

"Nothing," she replied. "Nothing."

She went home and imposed her aunt's recollections on the old man's life story. Consumed by the need for completion, seeing the finish line in sight, she scribbled notes and rearranged file cards into the night. With a number of crucial details filled in, a duplication of events removed and the relocation on one key event from one county to another, the entire thing came together quite suddenly and she found herself frozen, poised over her grandfather's biography, looking for the next incongruity to be resolved and seeing none.

She went to bed, tired and confused, and woke with a dreadful suspicion that she had done something unforgivably wrong, had made a profound mistake. She went into the kitchen, inspected the file cards, and saw what she had done. She felt a sudden sickness but she could not undo it and she had a eulogy to write. It was a workman-like effort but it would pass the scrutiny of the wider family.

The funeral service took place at a Methodist chapel near her parent's house. She read the eulogy with a fervour and sincerity she did not feel. It was possible that the family took her hesitations and lengthy pauses as a sign of grief. It was not the case but she rather they thought that than know the truth. She couldn't contemplate telling them, she didn't have the words to articulate her crime.

There had been a man who had been her grandfather. She grew up with his stories and the stories she heard about him. The jack-of-all-trades, the roguish scamp, the fighter, the husband, the father, the man of too many stories to fit into one lifetime. He had been her grandfather and had been a bundle of contradictions, an enigma, something great and mythical. No longer.

With her notes and her questions, she had tied him down to points in space and time. He was still the jack-of-all-trades, the scamp, the fighter but the enigma had vanished, the gaps gone. All the stories fit comfortably into that one lifetime; there had perhaps been room for even more but she had sealed up the empty spaces. The myth of her grandfather was a complete piece, trapped in a pile of file cards small enough to be carried away in a shoebox. The eulogy, the summary of that life, was the bow tied to seal the box up before it was put aside in order to be forgotten.

At the wake, she stood by herself, drink in hand and tried to think of nothing. She found herself thinking of Christ in the wilderness.

The Devil took Jesus to the top of a mountain and showed him the kingdoms of the earth. The Devil showed him all of the world, every detail of it, with all mystery stripped away. He showed Jesus a world without gaps, a world diminished by experience.

"All this I will give you," he said, "If you bow down and worship me."

She drank her drink and did her duty to her family and then went home and burned the file cards.

Two weeks later, on her way home she found by chance a shortcut between the cathedral and the train station. When she emerged from the alleyway and realised where she was, her mental map of this new city turned in on itself, became a clearer, smaller thing. She immediately burst into tears and everyone turned to look.

The Land of Take-What-You-Want

"Of course, you shouldn't really believe any of what you read," she says.

"Sorry, grandma?"

"Pull over here."

"What? Here?"

"Here."

The little car throws up dust in the lay-by. It has been a dry summer in the Chilterns.

Grandma Bessie steps out and stands with her back to the car.

"Are you all right?" I ask and, getting no reply, get out.

She has her head raised to look up at the trees at the roadside. Her hands are on the small of her back as though she is trying to locate her own kidneys.

"Grandma."

She turns to me. I know why they call her a tough old bird at the retirement village. There is a bird-like quality in those ice-blue eyes, in those sharp fleshless fingers.

"This is the place," she says.

"What place?"

"Come on," she says. "I will show you where they found his body."

"Whose body?"

There is a small gap in the fence and then a shallow ditch with two short thick planks to bridge it. The woods beyond are disordered and uninviting, beeches, oaks and ash. The only path I can see is so narrow it might as well have been made for rabbits.

"This could be private land," I say.

She snorts.

"Where's your sense of adventure, child?"

"I'm twenty-two," I say but she has already crossed the little bridge and is picking her way along the path in her sensible flat shoes.

I follow her. The woods are dim and green. The ground is dotted with golden coins of sunlight here and there but I feel cooler under the thick canopy of trees and automatically fold my arms for warmth. Grandma Bessie is a short distance ahead. I have a sudden premonition and imagine the look on dad's face if his mum falls and dies in the woods on my watch.

She said something about a body.

"Grandma!" I call.

She turns with a finger raised.

"I showed you where our old house was," she says. She points carefully. "About half a mile in that direction if I'm not mistaken."

"Uh-huh," I say, catching up with her.

"We didn't want to come to live here, you know."

"No?"

"I liked London. Mrs Pollock had that wrong. And that bit about my father getting a job in the country. Codswallop."

"Oh?"

"My father – your great grandfather – was a member of the cabinet. Stanley Baldwin. Don't suppose you've heard of him. No? Anyway, there was some awful business with a party girl, killed herself I think. Silly thing. And we were all packed off to rural Bucks to shield us from the scandal."

She casts her gaze up and around.

In the silence, the breeze rustles the leaves in the trees and they whisper wordlessly to one another.

"I used to think the trees here were a darker green than usual," she says.

"You used to come and play here," I say.

She nods.

"The three of us. There was the long summer when we arrived and then, in the autumn, the village school was closed by an outbreak of scarletina. No one gets that anymore, do they?"

"I don't think so," I say.

"The tree should be around here somewhere."

"What tree?

She starts to walk on and I fall in beside her, kicking distractedly at the dried mulch on the forest floor.

"My father still took himself up to London most days to petition Mr Baldwin or the bigwigs in Whitehall," she continues. "He was fearful for his position. Mother too. She said she would have to start taking in washing if father lost his post. We never took her seriously. She used to say it only when she'd been at the drink. Have you ever seen your own mother drunk?"

"There was Aunt Lucy's birthday last year."

"Oh, yes. Not a pleasant sight, is it? Maybe that's one reason why we came out here to the woods so often. Jo and I didn't want Fanny seeing our mother that way. Ah!"

Her cry is so sudden that I think she has turned an ankle but she is pointing.

"Do you see it?"

"The tree?"

She makes a noise, a disparaging hiss.

"The hut. See?"

She picks up her pace. The ruin of some sort of shack resolves itself amongst the greens and browns of a broad hollow. Its rotten timbers are darker than the earth, its fallen roof has long been replaced by bramble and creepers.

She hurries towards it as quickly as her stick legs will carry her.

"This is Old Saucepan's place."

Amongst the undergrowth and punk wood, I see the broken cylinder of an old paint tin, so corroded with rust that it will probably crumble in my hand if I try to pick it up.

"Old Saucepan. That's what Jo called him. He was a strange little man. He did jabber on in this weird little voice." She pauses thoughtfully. "He might have been Irish," she says and then gives me a look. "Not that I'm saying all Irish people talk... funny, you know."

"It's okay, grandma."

"Well, I never know what we're allowed or not allowed to say about people these days. You know, 'nigger' wasn't an insult when I was a girl."

"Grandma!"

I look round to see if anyone heard her in this deserted place. She snorts.

"I'm just saying. You can't call them Micks anymore, can you?"

"Who? The Irish? Not really, no."

"I think Old Saucepan was probably a bit backward."

173

"You mean he had learning difficulties," I prompt.

"No," she says blithely. "I mean he was a bit backward. Not sure what he did for money. I suppose he was a tinker. He lived in this hut with all these pots and pans hanging over the door. Always pleased to see us. Always offered us a cup of tea when we dropped by. Not that we ever said yes." She shudders. "Grubby little man."

She scans the woodland around us.

"If this is here then the tree must be..."

She starts off hesitantly in a fresh direction and, after five minutes, stops with her hand on the trunk of an old and twisted beech. She looks up at it with faint dismay in her eyes.

"Everything seemed bigger when you were children," she says sadly.

I look up at its gnarly branches, the vast knots and whorls in its trunk.

"It's a big tree," I say.

She shakes her head.

"It was the tallest, grandest tree in the world. That's how I remember it. It touched the sky." She sighs heavily and says, "I need a sit down."

I guide her to the trunk of a fallen tree and brush the leaves and dirt from it so she can sit. Grandma Bessie is breathing hard and her face is unpleasantly pale. It occurs to me only then that I can't be certain from which general direction we came.

She says something that I can't hear.

"Sorry, Grandma?"

"We tried to climb it," she says. "We couldn't get higher than the lowest branches. Not even Jo, and he was a good climber. We just sat at the bottom of the tree and had to be content with imagining what it would have been like to climb it. We camped out here one night."

"By yourselves?"

She nods.

"It wasn't a happy time at home. Father was staying up at London during the week. I'm guessing that he had a woman cosseted away somewhere. Mother... well, the good days were fewer and farther between. She slept most days. Sometimes didn't even get up in time to cook dinner. I did a lot of the cooking."

174

"You never struck me as the cooking type."

"Had to do too much of it as a child. I never saw it as a pleasurable thing, only something to be done out of necessity. And guilt."

She pats her lap. I'm relieved to see that some colour is slowly returning to her cheeks.

"And so one day we decided, 'To hell with it!' and packed a picnic and a tarpaulin and spent a day and a night out in the woods."

"Was it scary?"

She shakes her head slowly.

"Fear is learned, dear, and there are only so many things one person can learn to fear. When it got dark there was a full moon up in the branches of the tree. We made a small fire just there, laid back on our blankets and watched the man in the moon looking down at us. His bright round face. And Fanny, poor Fanny, said 'Does the moon live in that tree?' and, of course, Jo and I immediately replied, 'He certainly does,' and told each other stories of the moon-faced man and his little house in the trees." Her lips twitch. Grandma Bessie rarely smiles. "And when the clouds came over and covered the moon, we said that he had gone to visit the lands about the clouds and we told Fanny stories of his adventures there until we were too tired to talk and we slept."

"It sounds wonderful," I say cautiously.

She goes quiet, goes away for a time. She gestures generally towards the branches halfway up.

"That's where they found your great uncle Jo's body."

There's nothing I can say. Incongruous and tragic. It's too large a thing for me to sensibly respond to.

"He was hanging there," she says. "Amongst all these ropes. Tangled. Strangled."

"I am so sorry."

She shrugs.

"We move on. There's been a world war since then. Men on the moon."

"How did it happen?" I ask. "This was when you went camping in the woods?"

"No," she says irascibly. "He died a couple of years later, shortly after Fanny disappeared. No, that night we camped was... it *was* wonderful. I don't think the three of us were ever happier. When we woke, I remember feeling thick-headed – one can never sleep deeply in the woods – and we were hungry. But we hadn't the foresight to bring breakfast things with us. We gathered ourselves together and set off."

Grandma Bessie suddenly stands and walks off, retracing the footsteps she had taken over seventy years before.

"Was your mother worried when she realised you weren't in your beds at home?" I say.

She scoffs.

"She didn't know, did she? Not that we went home straight away anyway. We got lost."

"I thought you knew these woods?"

"We were children!" she snaps. She glares at me. "It seemed like a jolly old adventure but we were children. Alone in the woods when we should have been in the care and protection of loving parents. Can't you see how wrong that was?"

"I'm sorry," I say, taken aback.

Her eyes are burning with a cold blue fire.

"The Pollock woman couldn't see what was wrong with it. She just couldn't."

"Who?"

"She had her house somewhere over there. Come on." She sets off again. "It was a huge mock Tudor thing. Far grander than our squalid little house. Wandering and lost, we pushed through some bushes and came out on the green-striped lawn at the back of her mansion house. She was eating breakfast on the back porch and saw us at once. I'm not sure she knew what to make of us at first. I imagine we looked quite a sight, with dirt on our clothes and our hair all tangled."

A small laugh bubbles in her throat but does not quite make it past her lips.

"She said, 'You will need to brush that a hundred times before you go to bed tonight.' Those were her first words to us. Incredible. And she pointed to my torn petticoat and said, 'And that will need darning.' Peculiar woman. Quite severe too. I gather she had children of her own. The younger daughter could have only been a baby back then. Neither of them were on the porch with her. For all the books she wrote, she didn't like children very much. They fascinated her but I don't think she actually liked them."

"She was a writer?"

"Yes. You've not been listening, child. She published under her maiden name. Her poor husband. She was making a cuckold of him all over London town in those days. He was one of her first publishers and helped make her a success but, in the end, she drove him to drink and bankruptcy, forced him to take the blame for their divorce and then barred him from seeing his children ever again."

She comes to a sudden stop.

"I think I would like to go back to the car now."

"Sure, Grandma," I say.

She nods.

"Which direction is it in?"

"Don't you know?"

I gaze around and settle on a direction in which the trees look well spaced, where the sun has broken through the canopy, the kind of direction that looks like it ought to lead somewhere. She threads her arm through mine and we take it slowly.

"I never liked her books," says Grandma Bessie. "Your mum used to read them to you when you were younger. *The Wishing Chair. The Secret Seven.* She seemed obsessed with children flying off to have adventures, far from the world of adults."

"Wish fulfilment stuff," I say.

We reach a T junction of sorts and she steers us left.

"You think?" I say.

"Looks familiar," she says. "Well, you can imagine Mrs Pollock's secret joy at seeing us appear on her lawn. Three children, running away from home to camp alone in the wood. She had us sit down with her, told the maid to fetch tea and toast for us – we were ravenous – and had us recount our story. When we were fed and she had had enough of our company, she called a driver to take us home. Ah!"

We can see the edge of the woods, a doorway of afternoon sunlight opening up before us. It brings us out at a gateway in a three bar fence.

"This is not where we came in," I say.

"No," says my grandma. "This is Knotty Green."

We had driven through here earlier. We are several miles from the car. I groan.

Wearily, we follow a residential road down to the village centre and the Red Lion pub. Although she isn't complaining or taking a turn for the worse, Grandma Bessie walks slowly and I can hear her slightly laboured breathing. I sit her down as soon as we get inside and order her a glass of water from the bar.

"The barman says they have their own little library of Enid Blyton books in the pub," I say.

She drinks her water and says nothing.

"If you're all right, I'll walk to the car and bring it back to pick you up."

"Okay, dear."

I prepare to go but can't. I sit down.

"But what happened?" I say.

"When?"

"After the driver brought you home."

"Oh. Mum hadn't realised, not until the car pulled up outside the house. She came out in her night dress, full of overblown apologies to a chauffeur who... well, he couldn't give a fig how sorry she was. He just wanted to get away again. And when she had us alone, our own mother couldn't decide whether to scold us or apologise to us. She knew exactly what kind of mother she was. She said – hah! – she said, 'wait until your father gets home,' and immediately burst into tears, ran upstairs and we didn't see her for the rest of the day. After that? Everything. Nothing."

"Didn't Mrs Pollock call the police?"

She puts her glass down and puts her hands flat on the table.

"The police only came to our house a couple of years later when, one day, Fanny went off into the woods and never came back. They searched the woods and found nothing. They went to Old Saucepan's house. He had nothing to do with it but something must have been said, something must have happened because he vanished too not long after. The police even questioned our father. They could see something was horribly wrong in our household but..." She bows her head slightly. "You know *your* parents are lovely people, don't you?"

"I know."

She sniffs.

"You've no idea how lucky you are."

I put my hand on hers.

"I do, Grandma."

I find a tissue and push it into her hands. She dabs at her tears.

"For Jo, they recorded death by misadventure. He was trying to climb the tree for some reason. I wonder how much attention he paid to the stories she wrote about us."

She sits back, looks off to one side and blinks to clear her eyes.

"She took it all in. She even produced a notebook to write it down. The three children in the woods and the moon who lived in a tree. Even Old Saucepan. She took it all down, wrung every detail from us. And, when she was done, she just... she just sent us on our way."

"You blame her?" I ask.

"No," she says. "It doesn't quite work like that, does it? You need to get your car."

"I do."

I stand and kiss her on the forehead. I get her another glass of water and speak briefly to the barman.

I stop at the door and look back at her. She is gazing blankly at her glass of water.

When I return, dusk has fallen. Grandma Bessie sits in her seat, eyes closed, body perfectly erect. I touch her hand. Her eyes fly open and she looks at her surroundings in panic.

"It's okay, Grandma," I say.

She focuses on me and I can see the fear ebb away.

"You were asleep," I say.

"Dreaming," she replies.

I help her to the car and guide her seatbelt into the slot. On the journey back to Oxford, the moon, pale in the not-yet-dark sky, follows us, skimming across shadowy Chiltern woodlands.

I make to point it out to Grandma Bessie but I realise she is asleep again and then the clouds come in and take it from us.

Hrönir Malin

"I used to like listening to the Shipping Forecast," he says to her.

"You don't anymore?" she replies and turns in her seat so that she is half-turned across the aisle to face him. She puts the novel she's reading down in her lap.

"I can't," says Gary. "The baby monitor interferes with the radio signal. They interfere with each other. The noise they make, it's like the baby's weird alien language. Burble burble Cromarty Forth. Fizz crackle Dogger and Fisher."

The woman – Gary doesn't know her name – puts her tongue in her cheek in thought. Is she thinking about the fact that he's mentioned the baby monitor, which implies a baby, which implies a baby's mother, a girlfriend, a wife? Is she taking it as a sign of honesty, the declaration that he is taken and therefore harmless, that he's not hitting on her? Or is he only imposing those thoughts on her because, although he isn't consciously hitting on her, she's a young woman with sharp grey eyes and curls of wine red hair and his subconscious mind has far less honest intentions?

The train slows for Moor Street Station. They are in the city now, touching it, partly beneath it.

"You're a bit far inland for a sailing man," she says.

"Never sailed. One ferry journey to Ireland doesn't count, I guess. I just like the Shipping Forecast. It's a... a poem, a map of the sea, like one of those maps you get in the front of big fantasy novels."

He naturally looks at the book in her lap. She turns it over so he can see it. *The Multiplying of the Hrönir* by Ezra Buckley.

"Can't say I've heard of it," he says.

"It's a pretty niche title. I got it from this bookshop I work at. And, yes, we stock our fair share of books with fantastical maps."

The train pulls out of the station and into a tunnel that runs for more than a mile directly under the heart of the city.

"I got into a taxi the other day and asked to be taken to an address in Erdington," Gary hears himself say. "The cabbie asked me for the postcode. I didn't know it. He said he couldn't take me unless I could give him the postcode to type into his satnav."

She frowns at him, confused but mildly amused.

"Sorry," he says. "I was thinking of maps. Maps and books. Back in my day, a taxi driver knew the entire city. The Knowledge. Or does that name just apply to London? This one, he didn't even have an A to Z."

"You know when you say 'back in my day' it makes you sound very, very old," says the woman.

And Gary suddenly feels very old. He's felt old for a while now. Maybe that's parenthood. He's certainly tired, always tired.

"Surely though," he says, "the skill of the cabbie is knowing how to get to places. That this cut-through gets you from road X to road Y, that this route is faster than that. If you drive enough, are willing to learn the map, explore a little, get lost a bit, you can close up the gaps in the map."

"I know what you mean," she says. "You have your set routes between places. You stick to the main roads, the dual carriageways and then, one day, you take a wrong turning, perhaps a deliberately wrong turning and two bits of the world fold in together and you discover that this point joins with that."

"Right," he says. "And you understand the world better."

"And you make it a little smaller," she says. "And stranger."

"Stranger?"

"Can you imagine what it must have been like for that first man – almost certainly a man, sadly – who circumnavigated the globe and found himself coming into a familiar port or to a stretch of coast from the east instead of the west or whatever? Seeing the familiar made new by a fresh perspective."

Gary laughs and, although he knows exactly why he's laughing – it's a laugh of recognition, the realisation that someone else has thought something he previously thought private – he cannot tell her.

Instead, he says, "There was this time once when I was maybe eight or nine years old and I was alone in my classroom at school and, I don't why but I wanted to see the room from a new angle, a fresh perspective. I put a chair on my desk and climbed up and it was just like you said. A different viewpoint and it was made new. It was like... it was like I had never seen the room before."

"Jamais vu," she says.

"Yes," he says. "And then I fell off the chair, cracked my head on a table and had to be sent home. I don't remember but apparently there was blood everywhere. There were dried splashes of it on the pasta shell artwork on the wall for the rest of term. I've still got the scar. Here."

He leans over, a finger on the line in his crown where the hair still does not grow nearly thirty years on. He feels her fingertips on that tiny ridge of flesh.

"Shannon," she says.

"What?"

"You think you should let a woman touch your scars without knowing her name first?"

Her touch, not just a polite acknowledgement of his scar, but an exploration of its length, shape and contours, makes him picture it as a geographical feature, a mountain range and she the cartographer sent to map it.

An increase in the train's speed makes him sit up. They are pulling out of the Jewellery Quarter station, his stop.

"What the...?"

Gary stands. What happened to Snow Hill, the station before his stop? What had happened to the last ten minutes?

"I'm a dead man," he says.

"You missed your stop," says Shannon, neither mocking nor sympathetic.

"I'm going to miss bedtime again."

He gathers his things and hovers by the door just behind their seats. He wants to press the door button as though that will somehow make the next station come all the quicker. He exhales sharply, angry with himself.

Shannon watches him and he sees the humour in his situation and the futility of anger.

"This bookshop where you work," he says.

"Mmmm?"

"What's it called?"

She stares intently at nothing.

"Do you know," she says, "I don't think it has a name. I really don't."

"Well, where is it?"

"In the city."

The train is slowing already. Gary looks ahead.

"Drop by sometime," she says. "It's only open nights, mind."

"Oh," he says archly. "It's one of *those* bookshops."

"Yes, it is," she says. "And, no, it's not. What kind of woman do you think I am, Gary?"

It's a question that invites a certain answer and Gary, despite his conscious honest intentions, can feel himself crossing a line which is not really a line but a gradation from one thing to another.

"So how do I find it?" he asks.

"Do you need a postcode?" she replies.

It is exactly as he fears. He arrives home nearly an hour late and Jessica is furious. He's missed bedtime for the fifth night in a row and she accuses him doing it on purpose. The questions she flings at him are all about pulling his weight and the fact that parenthood is a partnership but the questions that both of them can hear are about Gary's commitment, about whether he really wants to be a dad because he sure doesn't act like one.

And, naturally, effect following cause, this angers Gary because he does want to be a dad. He *is* a dad. This *is* what he wants and if she is accusing him of otherwise then it's a sign that she doesn't understand him, doesn't deserve to understand him. Does she think she's the special one because she carried Daniel inside her for nine months? Daniel is his son as well as hers and the fact that he's working all hours is an expression of his love for them, the casting of a protective bubble of wealth around the pair of them.

And Jessica cries, because she's angry and because she's tired and because she's all alone in a flat on the wrong side of the Great Hampton Road and she's lonely and she just wants him to help her and reassure her. But Gary's angry too because he feels increasingly rejected and unappreciated. And he's tired too.

And he does the easy thing, which is the wrong thing but the easy thing. He goes out again, not slamming the door and waking the baby because he does love them so very much. Silently he goes and walks into the city.

Night settles over the city as he walks down the Great Hampton Road. The shops of insurance companies, travel agents and hairdressers are already closed. Taxicab offices and mobile phone shops are lit up but there's no sign of life within. The restaurants are getting busier: the Indian, the Egyptian, the Caribbean.

Gary, stewing over arguments real and imaginary, lets his feet take him where they will. Before getting to St Chad's cathedral, he takes a slip road down by an old silverworks and follows the line of the railway arches. Passing by one arch, he looks down to see the canal in a cavernous tunnel. Railway lines above, canal below and Gary floating in between.

He takes a turning down a fresh street, putting the tunnel behind him, imagining that same canal running beneath his feet, the strata of tarmac, stone, air and water and the silt, clay and stone further down. The street sign is obscured by layer upon layer of graffiti tags. He finds an inexplicable satisfaction in that and walks on with purpose, eyes on the pavement, not on the way ahead.

He vaguely grasps where he is. The BT tower looms up to his left and anchors him in a certain section of the city centre. He imagines that over *there* is Newhall Street and the Queen's Arms pub and over *there* is St Paul's Square, but the specifics fail him. He knows that if he walks in this direction long enough he will run into the dual carriageway or the ring road. In a city girdled by motorway, it's only possible to be lost for so long.

Hocbley Street. He looks at the sign, thrown by the un-English word, and then shrugs and continues onward.

He does not meet the dual carriageway or the ring road and night has fallen fully. Down an alley lined with industrial units, a fire burns in a petrol drum. Across the way, a doorway is outlined in purple neon and there is the sound of a saxophone, soft and mournful, but there's no indication whether the place is a nightclub, massage parlour or private house.

Rlaƀy Road. He recognises the word but cannot remember from where. He has been walking for an hour or more since leaving Jessica alone with their boy. He has no idea which side of the city he's on. He looks up for a sign of the BT tower or other landmark. There are lights on the invisible heights of the buildings around him. Something distant and massive passes between the lights and Gary.

Stunned, he steps back and his hand touches the stonework of an archway. There's an open wrought iron gate set into the archway and this he definitely recognises. This is the gateway and the gate that stood next to his grandmother's house, two hundred miles away in a different city. This gateway cannot be here but it is and Gary is put in mind of the virtual worlds of on-line adventure games in which the same building layouts are used again and again in different locations. This gateway is lazy repetition of an unimaginative world.

He steps through into Ħqbℋri Suąrn. It's a small courtyard, cobbled and surrounded on all sides by identical windowed walls as though the square is a single stone house turned outside-in. There are doors and short flights of stone steps and other doors. A wrinkle-faced man sits in a doorway, slowly and tunelessly squeezing a concertina as though simply doing enough to keep it alive.

There is a shop window, too grimy for Gary to see what's inside but he automatically knows, as one knows in a dream, that this is a bookshop. The bookshop. Shannon's bookshop. The light from within is soft, as though filtered through cloth.

Gary looks to the old man pumping the concertina lungs and the man gives him a nod of consent.

Gary enters the shop.

The bookshelves are all wooden but no two are alike. Most of the books are stern-looking tomes, bound in leather. He sees titles that suggest dusty memoirs and travelogues for countries that might no longer exist. Many of the authors' names are preceded by military ranks and feature strings of initials. But there are newer books too, much-creased paperbacks with artlessly photographed covers. Cheap railway thrillers and collections of suspense and horror stories by forgotten authors.

Gary doesn't look at any of the books. He knows that he will not be able to read any of them and any he does manage to read will only leave the faintest impression on him, a distorted variation on a memory a book he had read years before.

There is no one about in the shop but there is a bead curtain and a dark doorway. The beads rattle as he parts them, a dozen clicking rosary beads. Whether it is born from the thought of rosary beads or mere coincidence, Gary can smell incense as he descends the stairs. There is light but not enough to even clearly illuminate the wall next to him. It glistens faintly and he suspects that, if he reaches out to it, he will find it soft, yielding and warm, like the lining wall of an intestine.

He is not frightened by this thought. He is descending into warmth and comfort. He is drawn down, by a gravity that has nothing to do with direction.

At the base of stairs is a chamber, candlelit and prepared for his arrival. The chamber is a regular polygon, pillars at each corner, arches on every side, but he cannot count the number of sides. Six, seven or eight, the number of walls is small but entirely innumerable.

In the centre of the chamber is an altar, a woman, a book. The altar is dressed in a blood-coloured cloth, a chalice of red wine at its centre. The woman smiles, open-mouthed as he approaches. The book is open, the pages spread for him.

Gary reaches for the chalice and presses himself against the pages. The woman puts her mouth to his ear and speaks to him. The book contains a poem, a map for a place he knows but does not recognise. Her fingers run across the scar on his head and he does not lie to her. It is a birthing scar, the mark of something that has passed through into life. It is the folding together of the world and all is made strange.

He does not miss his stop.

Gary gets off at the Jewellery Quarter and climbs the stairs to street level. The sun has dipped below the roofs of the buildings but it is still light.

He walks along Vyse Street and then across the Great Hampton Road to their apartment block.

Jessica gives him a look as he enters the flat.

"Am I too late?" he asks.

She shakes her head tiredly.

"Sat in his cot. You can put him down. Read to him."

Gary nods, kisses her on the cheek and goes into their bedroom to shuck off his tie and jacket. The baby monitor by the bedside fizzes.

"Ħqb)Ҟri Shannon."

Gary pauses in removing his tie. The monitor shushes like the sea, like a train passing through a tunnel, the sound of Daniel breathing.

"Rockall ... Rlaþy."

Interference from a radio, he realises, kicks off his shoes and makes his way along the hallway to his son's room. The boy, his little man, sits up in his cot in his blue babygrow.

"Hey, you," says Gary.

Daniel looks at him with sharp grey eyes and speaks.

"Feʹbrç... Hrönir Malin."

The world folds.

• The Token

It has been announced this week that Ellen Shipton's grisly fairy tale for children, *The Token*, is to be adapted for the screen by Tim Selleck, acclaimed director of juvenile stop-motion nasties such as *Halloween Dreams* and *Mr Rumbleshanks*. It has sparked renewed interest in Shipton's 1968 book and reinvigorated the debate on what children's fiction should *do*. Children's literature, more so than its adult counterparts, continues to generate outrage, denunciations and calls for certain titles to be suppressed. From JK Rowling's perceived celebration of witchcraft and Pullman's *His Dark Materials* trilogy's anti-Catholicism to the debatable racism of Enid Blyton's Toy Town stories, modern children's literature stirs up strong feelings in those who would seek to protect the vulnerable minds of the young.

That Shipton's story of forced marriage and body parts should be targeted by such vitriolists is farcical for any number of reasons but foremost should be the fact that the central story of *The Token* is not original to her. Ellen Shipton borrows her plot from a play by the dramatist and the original bowdleriser, Nahum Tate. Tate, poet Laureate to King William III, is most famous to us as the man who rewrote much of Shakespeare and gave tritely happy endings to the likes of *King Lear* and *Romeo and Juliet*. Most of his works survive but are rarely performed. The only significant production of his works in recent years was the Farshore Theatre production of *King Lear* in 1997 but even then the players felt the need to insulate themselves from Tate's work by presenting the piece as an ironic play within a play.

Tate's, *The Token of Love Eternal*, is a one-act comedy, a morality play of sorts written long after the genre had ceased to be popular. In it, Gisbert, a wealthy merchant, marries Sybillia, a woman whose beauty is only matched by her avarice. There are various shenanigans involving pirates, a scotophobic clown, a court physician with three unmarried daughters and a heroic soldier masquerading as a shepherd but the nub of the story is the business with the eponymous token. On the day of their marriage, Sybillia enquires of Gisbert what gift he has for her. Gisbert, either affecting ignorance or perhaps genuinely so, asks her what she means.

189

Sybillia puts it to him that, on such a momentous day there must be a gift, a token of love, to celebrate their union. Gisbert then launches into a long and tedious speech, delivered partly to Sybillia and partly as a clumsy aside to the audience, explaining that by giving her his hand in marriage he has also given to her his heart, his soul, his very being. Rings and necklaces and jewels, he argues, are nothing in comparison to the gift of love itself. Sybillia scoffs at his words and jokingly asks if he could cut out his heart and present it to her there and then. She demands a token of his affections, that she might hold, that might offer her comfort in times of loneliness, a thing whose value demonstrates the esteem in which Gisbert holds their love. Gisbert goes off, in search of a suitable token.

In the final scene (after the pirates have been hung, the clown entombed alive and the soldier revealed and married off to the doctor's youngest daughter), Gisbert returns to his wife, hunched over and pale, with a box containing the token of his love. Apparently weak and on the verge of collapse, he gives the gift to Sybillia. She opens it and discovers a severed hand. It is, Gisbert points out, something that she might hold and seek comfort from in times of loneliness; and its value to Gisbert was without measure. Sybillia screams and faints away. Only then is it revealed that Gisbert has tricked her and that the hand is, in fact, that of the pirate chief, taken from his body by the court physician. In the closing lines, as the good folk of the tale crowd the stage, the physician assures Gisbert that his wife will recover from her swoon having found a humility more befitting a woman.

As with his edited Shakespeares, Nahum Tate's *Token* is a sanitised version of earlier works, in this instance taking its central idea from Robert Daborne's *The Fair Maid Lost to Lust* (c. 1608). Daborne's play received a recent reading at the Shakespeare Institute, Warwick, as part of a season of 'Turk Plays' that also included George Peele's *Soliman and Perside* and Thomas Goffe's *The Courageous Turk*. These overtly racist and anti-Turkish pieces are being subjected to renewed interest as Anglo-Islamic relations rise once again in the public consciousness.

In *The Fair Maid Lost to Lust*, a Christian woman, Beaumelle, is betrothed to the sinister and alien, Abdelazar, a Turkish merchant. The tale that follows could be mistaken for a strange inversion of the Bluebeard story. The newlyweds live in a many-roomed mansion and there are hints of a dark secret from Abdelazar's past hidden away in the house. When the secret is uncovered, Abdelazar offers to make amends to Beaumelle by offering her a valuable token of his love for her and cuts off his hand and presents it to her. She is horrified but not so horrified as when Abdelazar, seemingly motivated by his desire for the luscious Christian woman, offers her a fresh token of his love at the rising of each new moon. Beaumelle is presented with eyes, ears, a nose, feet and more besides until Abdelazar is dead and Beaumelle, driven mad, throws herself from the roof of their home. The moral of the tale is clear, even if the narrative is not: Turks are mad and dangerous and good Christian women are best protected from them.

As said, this tale could be mistaken for a strange inversion of the Bluebeard story. But it is not. There is a far more likely, if less well known source, in the medieval myths of the Sibyl of Cumae, the pagan prophetess reported to dwell in the highest reaches of the Apennine Mountains of Italy, in a cave guarded by bears and poisonous streams. For centuries, she was sought by Christian knights (who wished to slay this whore of Babylon) and various wizards, warlocks and necromancers (who sought her wisdom and patronage). Whether she existed on not, such was the stream of foolish or unholy pilgrims to her domain that a local noble had the pathways to her cave destroyed with explosives in the mid-seventeenth century to prevent any further incursions.

Various stories connected to the Sibyl of Cumae detail how those men who managed to pass the tests and trials in the cave then proceeded to discover an underground realm of carnal pleasures in which the Sibyl and her winsome female companions cavorted with male visitors in clear pools and shady bowers. Most stories then relate that this unholy paradise revealed its true nature on every seventh day, when the Sibyl and her companions took on their true form of writhing demonic serpents. In some tales, this revelation causes men to flee, repenting their sinful sojourn. In others, men accept that there is a price to be paid for pleasure and remain.

One specific version, related in Antoine de la Sale's *Salade*, concerns the knight Gascon who not only discovers that his lady love Sibyl is a demon but must give her a token of his love for each week that he remains in her cave. Such is Gascon's desire that he does not hesitate in paying up. However, once he has exhausted his supply of rings and trinkets, Gascon begins to offer up his body parts as payment. His hand, his eye and his ears are willingly sacrificed in the name of sexual fulfilment. Only after he has cut off his own manhood and presented it to the Sibyl does this cycle of sex and violence come to an end. With Gascon's penis and testicles in her grasp, Sibyl no longer needs her knightly lover and he is flung down, pleading and wailing, into that circle of hell reserved for fornicators.

How light and innocent Ellen Shipton's book appears in comparison! And yet, it bears more similarities to the original tale than some might like. In *The Token*, our teenage heroine, Kat, is kidnapped by and forced to marry the Undertroll. In an attempt to forestall their wedding day Kat, like Tate's Sybillia, demands a token of her betrothed's affection and, like Tate's Sybillia, is presented with a fake hand (the finger-like roots of a mangrove in Shipton's tale) in the hope that this will shock her out of such presumptuousness. However, the modern heroine is cleverer than her deceiver and Kat pretends to be delighted with the Undertroll's present and demands more. Now, not only does the Undertroll have to pretend to be minus a hand but he must deliver other cunningly disguised anatomical gifts in order to secure her love. Throughout Shipton's cavalcade of squeamish mock-dismemberments, Kat is always one step ahead of her would-be husband.

The cycle of stories comes full circle. Like the Sibyl of Cumae, Kat is in total control of the relationship and the man, be it Gascon or the Undertroll, is forced to continually and increasingly humiliate himself in pursuit of his desire. And whereas the Sibyl's power is demonic in nature, Kat, a twenty-first century embodiment of female power, wields a more insidious witchcraft of her own.

• The People Factory

It isn't a ritual as such. It is a pattern they have fallen into, a tiny but inescapable loop to be played out every day.

The boy, Anatoly, opens the rear door and gets in. Oven-hot air and piercing sunlight enter the car for a second.

"Hello, Vladimir," says Anatoly and, with a small grunt, pulls the heavy door shut. The air-conditioner becomes louder for a few seconds.

"Seatbelt," says Vladimir. He listens for the click.

"Seatbelt," says Anatoly.

Vladimir puts the car in gear and slips out from the parked rank of cars. Other drivers waiting for other children.

"So, what did you learn today?" he asks.

This is the routine. It is learned behaviour. But they are men – the nine year old boy and his driver – and they like routine. Vladimir has said so in the past and the boy, Anatoly, does not disagree with him.

Vladimir pulls out of the Palm Ridge School compound and onto the Rue d'Égalité. The road runs from the promontory down through Ducos, to the coast road and the hotel complexes that huddle jealously against their own slice of beachfront.

"History," says Anatoly.

"Pfff. History. The past is the past," says Vladimir.

He knows the boy is smiling even though he doesn't look back. They know each other and Anatoly finds Vladimir funny. Vladimir doesn't mind. It means the boy thinks he's interesting, different, and this is good.

"We learned about Queen Honore," says Anatoly.

"Who?"

"Queen Honore. She was queen of Saint-Cyr a hundred years ago. She was the most important queen."

"Most important," says Vladimir, unimpressed. "Is she the one on the banknotes with all the flowers around her?"

An old man with dreadlocks and no shoes is shuffling into the road ahead of them, waving at them. Vladimir is not sure if he is a beggar, a street vendor or is just intent on crossing the road. It does not matter; Vladimir is not going to stop for him. He will hit the man if he doesn't get out of the way. There is no malice in this. Vladimir knows his job and the old man should know better.

"They're not flowers. They're birds," says Anatoly. "Cuckoos. They are the national bird," he says, in a manner which suggests this is one of the facts he has learned today.

"Birds?"

Vladimir simultaneously takes his wallet from his pocket and makes a minor course correction to drive round the old man. In his wing mirror, Vladimir sees the old man spinning and hopping angrily in the dusty street. Maybe he had run over the man's toes. Maybe the old man has a misplaced sense of his own importance. Vladimir takes a twenty franc note from his wallet and places it against the steering wheel to look at it.

"Huh. Birds. Cuckoo. *Kukushka*? It lays eggs in other birds' nests?"

"That's right," said Anatoly.

Vladimir is, at once, put in mind of the boy's mother. This strikes him as odd as she is not the one who has put her own child in someone else's care. Perhaps it is because she seems so out of place, the one who does not belong. This is also odd. None of them belong here; Russian ex-pats abandoned in the Caribbean.

"I have not seen these birds on the island," says Vladimir.

"They're extinct now, apart from in zoos. The queen brought jays here from America to drive away the amazons."

"She did not like parrots?"

"They were eating all the food in the fields. But the jays ate all the cuckoo eggs."

Vladimir grunts.

"Some queen."

"Queen Honore believed that the people of Saint-Cyr deserved the best. She was brave. She took risks."

"Risks. You learned this word today?"

"No."

"She started a programme of eugenics on Saint-Cyr. I learned *that* word today."

Vladimir turns onto the coast road, heading north.

"This eugenics, what is it?"

"It was where they stopped people having babies," says Anatoly. "Not everyone. Just people who shouldn't have babies."

"Oh-ho, who shouldn't have babies?"

Vladimir hears the boy's back rub against the seat covers. A shrug.

"People with diseases. People who will have children who are weak or poorly or..."

"Stupid?" suggests Vladimir.

"Yes," says the boy.

"They do this back home in Russia. They sterilise disabled women, make sure they don't have little disabled children."

"Well, they were doing it on Saint-Cyr a hundred years ago," says Anatoly, competitively. "What does 'sterilised' mean?"

"Make them stop having babies. Cut out their –" He makes a whistling, cutting sound and then stops, realising this is probably not the sort of conversation he should be having with the boy.

Already the sun is beginning to set over the hill. Ducos begins its slow change from day to night. Everything looks different in sunlight, looks better. When night comes, Saint-Cyr's other face is visible. At night, away from the big hotels and grand residences, night shines its harsh light on the cheap concrete storefronts, on the web of overhead wires, looped around palm tree and pylon alike, carrying over-priced electricity and stolen cable television, on the people who are out on the street because they have no home to go to or the home they have is worse than the street.

Vladimir does not quite hate Saint-Cyr. There are a small number of things he values. The boy, the money, the privacy. He wonders if he would miss Monique if he left or if he would find a replacement in another bed above another bar in whatever city in which he next found himself. He doesn't necessarily hate the rampant corruption or the violence. Corruption and violence are a sea that he can swim in.

"I believe in evolution," says Vladimir.

"What is that?" says the boy.

"Chance," says Vladimir. "Let the people have babies with whoever they want. Well, maybe not whoever they want but if they are sick they will die. The strong will survive. Like you and me."

The boy grunts approvingly.

195

"But if we stop weak people having babies then all the babies will be strong," says Anatoly.

"Strong babies. Like breeding up fat pigs, eh? I bet President Villaplane would love that idea. This country..."

He says no more and the boy doesn't question him. It is how many of their conversations end.

Vladimir slows to turn into the gate of the Yurevich family compound. The wall is high, white and topped with shards of glass and CCTV cameras. The steel gates have a composite material core and are held in place by fat rods rising out of the concrete driveway. The man on the gate with a machine-pistol at his side is the weakest link of the security. Jean-Marie is a local and Vladimir does not trust the locals.

Jean-Marie waves them through and Vladimir drives up to the fountain outside the main house. Vladimir gets out first. Anatoly waits until Vladimir is happy. Vladimir hears splashing from the swimming pool and a laugh. The laugh is Milla, the boy's mother. Vladimir sees one of the maids, Beatrice, mopping the hallway floor. Beatrice smiles at him.

Vladimir is satisfied and opens the door for Anatoly.

"It is okay. Do your homework and be good," he says.

"See you tomorrow," says Anatoly.

This is the accepted farewell between them. The boy will go inside, be fed, do his school work, play with his puppets and trains, read his books and be put to bed. His mother may or may not have a hand in any of this. Vladimir suspects that there are nights where the words of Vladimir's farewell are the last words spoken to the boy before Vladimir's greeting to him the following morning. He suspects this but he does not know.

Vladimir goes around the house, down the steps that go past the tiered garden and alongside the swimming pool. Milla Yurevich lies on one of the poolside loungers, dressed in a bikini and a wide-brimmed sunhat. She dips her toes in the pool and flicks water at Beatrice. Milla is Lithuanian by birth, slim and not yet thirty, and beautiful only because she is slim and not yet thirty. She is the widow of a Russian millionaire and wants for nothing. Vladimir knows she is desperately unhappy, caught in a trap quite different to the one that holds him – his trap is made of loyalty and inertia, hers of roubles and apathy – but he cannot bring himself to feel any sympathy for her. Vladimir has no idea what Pavel Yurevich saw in the girl, apart from the tediously obvious. There is none of her in the boy. It is as though she was merely the receptacle that carried the boy for nine months, carried him in a vacuum and gave nothing to him. Anatoly is entirely his father's son.

Milla looks in Vladimir's direction just before the steps take him down and out of sight. He nods brusquely to her and continues.

Vladimir lives in one of the stone chalets by the rear wall of the compound. He lives alone. Some evenings, he stops by the security office and checks the log. Sergei, fat and old Sergei, will moan about his day, pass comment about one of the girls in the pornographic magazine he will have open on the desk and, perhaps, begin to reminisce about some person or other he used to know in Lvov. Most of the time, Sergei talks about people Vladimir didn't know or cannot remember. Those he does recall are invariably dead.

Vladimir only goes up the main house in the evening to collect his dinner from the kitchens. On nights when he does not then go out, he sits on his bed in his underwear and deals out cards on the white sheets. Poker hand after poker hand. He looks without expectation for high hands. He grunts at threes of a kind and makes soft exclamations when better hands fall from his fingertips. He waits for a straight flush or four of a kind to appear from the deck. He knows that miracles are only a matter of patience and vigilance.

"Hello, Vladimir."

"Seatbelt," says Vladimir.

"Seatbelt," the boy replies.

Vladimir pulls away smoothly away from the school.

"So, what did you learn today?" he asks.

"We learned about octopuses," says Anatoly.

"Octopuses?"

"Octopuses. It's an important animal to the people of Saint-Cyr. There's this myth –"

"Octopuses?" says Vladimir a second time. "Tentacles and suckers and everything?"

"Yes, Vladimir," says Anatoly, laughing.

"I thought it was all bird, birds, birds on this island."

"And octopuses. Do you want to know what I learned or not?"

"Of course," says Vladimir and then, muttering, "Horrible things."

"There's this myth that octopuses are survivors of a previous universe," says the boy. "On the island Queen Honore's mother came from they believe that when the universe comes to an end, one animal is chosen to continue into the next world. Octopuses lived in the last universe and the creator god, when he made this world, chose the octopus."

"This is a stupid idea," says Vladimir.

"Well, I like it," says the boy defensively. "It's nice. Isn't it nice that when all this is gone, something might survive? It's like those... those bald people who think that when we die we come back as a tiger or a bird or a bat."

Vladimir shakes his head.

"The past is the past. The future is the future. When we are dead, we are dead. One day, the world will be ended and I will be glad."

The boy does not speak again until they reach the coast road. Vladimir does not know if he has offended Anatoly or if the boy is deep in thought.

"What do you think happens afterwards?" says the boy.

"Afterwards?" says Vladimir.

"After we die."

"Nothing," says Vladimir simply. "When we are dead, we are dead. Life comes and is gone. In Chechnya..."

Vladimir can hear the boy shift forward in his seat. Vladimir rarely talks about Chechnya or about the boy's father, Pavel. The two are things are frequently linked.

"In Chechnya, the night before an attack against the village of Komsomolskoye, I could not sleep and I went outside. Supply trucks would come up the road, through the darkness. I saw their lights, come out of the night and then go past and be gone. I had, er, I awoke. I understood. Eureka. I thought, 'This is life. A little light in the darkness.' I saw each truck as a soldier, a life, going to the front to be killed, a light to be put out."

"Were you drunk?" asks the boy.

"I do not drink," says Vladimir and laughs because he knows the boy is joking. "You know I don't drink."

"And what did my dad think?"

"Hmmm? Your dad, my commanding officer, he was fast asleep on his bed. He had no problems with sleeping. And he did not drink either." He catches himself lying. "Much."

"Did my dad tell you to work for him after you left the army?"

"Tell me?" says Vladimir and then thinks.

Cars and egg-shaped cocotaxis bunch together in the road ahead. Vladimir slows, leaving plenty of manoeuvring space between him and the car in front.

"Your dad found me a job, afterwards. It was not *his* business but the man who owned it owed him money so..."

Stuck in traffic, Vladimir's eyes flick between the road ahead, the rear-view mirror and the wing mirrors. There are lots of mopeds on the island but few cars and traffic jams are few and fleeting. Vladimir does not like it when they are stationary. The potential dangers around seem closer, more imminent.

"What business was it?" says Anatoly.

"A bear farm. It was not legal and I did security, made sure the local police did not find it or did not care if they did."

The cause of the traffic jam ahead is revealed. A food vendor's stall has tipped off the pavement. Chunks of something – maybe chicken, maybe goat – are strewn across the dusty road. The metal stall, stove and cooking pot within, looks heavy but, regardless, no one is attempting to right it or get it out of the road. Three men and one woman are arguing. Vladimir notes, with professional interest, that one of the men keeps putting his hand to his belt where the bulge of a knife can clearly be seen.

"What's a bear farm?" asks the boy.

"They kept them for Chinese medicine, plugged tubes into them and took their... *zhelch*? Juices? From their stomachs. Your dad thought it was an interesting business. He was always interested in medicine, in science. That's why he invested in the companies in Lvov. That's why he invested in your school. He took me with him when he went to Lvov."

Two vehicles up ahead attempt to circumnavigate the traffic jam via a narrow road to the left between the Caribbean Bookshop and a boat rental office. Vladimir edges forward and considers whether to follow them.

"Did you miss the bear farm?" says the boy.

Vladimir shakes his head slowly.

"It was a sad place."

In the rear view mirror, Vladimir spots an open top jeep, the colour of sand, a short distance behind them. For reasons he cannot articulate, Vladimir does not like the look of it and decides to take the road to the left.

"Why?"

"They brought the bears out of the forests and put them in cages. All together, side by side. They hurt them." He shrugs. "We all get hurt. But they brought them all together and bears prefer to be in the forests. Alone. Solitary." He tastes the word as he says it.

Vladimir accelerates up the side road. It is dusty and heavily pitted. As he reaches a crossroads made by the gaps between concrete houses, he sees the sand-coloured jeep appear in the road behind him. Vladimir turns right into an alleyway that is not much wider than the car. A cat runs ahead of the car for maybe five metres and then leaps to the safety of an open window.

"I think I am like a bear," says Vladimir. "I like to be alone most of the time."

"In your bear cave at the bottom of the garden," says Anatoly.

"Yes," says Vladimir, liking the notion.

"Don't you like being around people?"

"No," says Vladimir firmly and then, out of nowhere, finds himself thinking of Monique. "Most of the time."

"And me?" says the boy.

"I like you," says Vladimir instantly.

"Like a bear cub."

Vladimir wants to agree but finds himself saying, "Male bears do not look after their cubs. They go off into the forest and the female looks after the little ones."

The jeep has followed them into the alley. It is possible that they are following them in the belief that Vladimir knows a legitimate shortcut. It is possible. Vladimir reaches under the newspaper on the passenger seat and flicks off the safety of the Makarov pistol that sits there.

"My mum was crying this morning."

Vladimir says nothing.

"Someone had phoned her. I don't know who," says the boy.

"No," says Vladimir. "Me neither."

"Did you know that octopuses only have babies once and then they die?"

"I did not know that."

"The mother lays the eggs in her nest."

"She has a nest?"

"In her hole on the sea bed and doesn't leave them once. Not to eat or anything. And when they are born, she dies," says Anatoly flatly.

"I approve," says Vladimir.

"You do?"

"It is like I said, you are born and you die. Nothing else. The octopus has no silly dreams about living forever."

The setting sun does not reach this narrow thoroughfare and it is dark here. Up ahead is a road, a proper road. Rue des Amours, he guesses. Vladimir accelerates to sixty kilometres an hour and judges the weight of the traffic passing ahead. It is worth the risk.

"Lie down," he says.

Without a word, Anatoly does as he is told.

Vladimir pulls out onto the road at speed, already throwing the car sharply to the right. He hits nothing. A horn sounds and there are shouts but he has hit nothing; a minor miracle. He drives back down towards the coast road, quickly but cautiously, his eyes flicking between the road ahead and the rear view mirror. As he reaches the junction with the coast road, he sees the jeep nudging out of the alleyway. Vladimir slows to a halt at the junction and watches. He unclips his seatbelt and takes hold of the Makarov.

"Stay down," he tells the boy, although the boy does not need telling.

The jeep turns left, up the hill. Vladimir sniffs. People cross the street in front of him. A woman stops and looks at him through the windscreen: Monique. She wears denim hot pants and a ripped T-shirt that doesn't reach down to her midriff. She carries a string shopping bag containing cartons of milk and some leafy vegetable. Deciding it is him and not some lookalike, she smiles and gives him a questioning look. Vladimir gives a small shake of the head and does his seatbelt up once more.

Monique gives him another look, this one less decipherable, and walks on. Vladimir pulls out onto the coast road.

"You can sit up now," he says.

"Also," says the boy, as though nothing has happened, "octopuses have parts of their brains in their tentacles."

"Do they?" says Vladimir.

"Each tentacle has a sort of mini-brain of its own. One tentacle might go looking for food while another fights off... off... a shark."

"One tentacle does not know what the other is doing," says Vladimir, amused.

"They act independently," says Anatoly.

"Sounds like the Bratva."

The boy goes quiet.

"Was my dad part of the mafia?" he asks.

"Who told you that?"

"Sergei."

"You are not your father," says Vladimir.

"What do you mean?"

"We are nearly home now."

Vladimir double-checks the log book in the security office and has a quiet but insistent word in Sergei's ear. As he heads up the steps toward the front gate, Vladimir looks up to the boy's bedroom window. The light is on, a peach glow against the thin curtains.

The night air is hot but there is a cooling breeze from the sea. Vladimir walks from the Yurevich compound and towards the lights and noise of the capital's bars and clubs. The beachfront bars are expensive and purely for the tourists who have ventured beyond their hotel complexes. Vladimir makes towards a bar several streets back from the beaches, not exactly a local's bar but one where islanders and foreigners can be found in equal measure.

Up the hill, Vladimir can see concrete roadblocks and two police officers slouching at their posts, one using his assault rifle to lean on like an old man with a stick. The barricades form a loose circle around the presidential palace. Villaplane is an outsider on the international stage and is losing popularity with his own people. The man is becoming defensive and isolated but, perhaps, his only friends are the resident foreign nationals who fund his regime.

Vladimir enters the Café Savane and takes a stool at the bar. He takes a deck of cards from his pocket and deals out poker hands on the bar, watching for miracles. The young barman, whose name Vladimir has never bothered to remember, brings him a bottle beer and uncaps it without a word passing between them. Vladimir sips and then puts the bottle to his brow. He will nurse the beer until Monique finds him. He is, as he told Anatoly, not much of a drinker.

Pavel Yurevich did like a drink but never let it be the master of him. In a sense, this was a shame. Vladimir would perhaps think better of the man if his violent excesses could be blamed on alcohol or another demon. Pavel had a gift for torture; yes, the anatomy of pain but also the theatre of it. When he cut and boned Viktor Mikhailov, stripped the flesh from his arms and legs, not letting the man die until the job was done, it was not the act itself that stayed with Vladimir. Pavel tortured Mikhailov to death in the street outside the house where he lived in Lvov – not where Mikhailov lived; outside his own home. What message did that send? What lessons did the people of Lvov take away from that?

In this way, a legend and a fortune were made. Pavel took the city for what he could. Pavel bought businesses and cultivated just the right level of legitimacy. He transcended the border from gangster to businessman with such subtlety that even Vladimir did not notice it. And, most astutely of all, Pavel got out before it was too late. Pavel left Lvov, left Russia too, cutting all ties, selling all assets and leaving everything behind but for a trophy wife, the most trusted of his underlings and more money than God. Pavel got away clean, apart from (as the man himself said) the stains on his soul.

The perfect execution of Pavel's life of crime made his death all the more incomprehensible. He had made Saint-Cyr his home, built his fortified palace and invested in the founding of the international school even before Anatoly's birth. Vladimir could see the setting down of roots, the foundations of something permanent. Milla fell pregnant. There were almost daily visits to the clinic attached to the school, both before and after the birth. Then, when Anatoly was three months old, Pavel hired a boat from the marina and took it out toward the coral reefs.

The boat was found five days later, floating hundreds of miles to the east. The throttle had been tied open with mooring line and duct tape. There was no sign of Pavel. A search was conducted but the search area was unfeasibly large. Milla, dutifully bereft, insisted that he might still be alive, somehow. It would take a miracle for Pavel to survive his own suicide, a cruel miracle. Vladimir had loved him more dearly than a brother. Nonetheless, Vladimir hopes that there is some justice in the world and that Pavel's death was not a quick one.

Vladimir raises his beer to drink but stops as a man slides onto the stool next to him. It is the man's white bright smile that makes Vladimir stop.

"It's Mr Medvedev, isn't it?" he says; an American accent. "Can I get you another drink?"

"I am fine," says Vladimir.

He swiftly takes in the man's attire. He's dressed like a student traveller. Faded designer T-shirt, khaki shorts, Converse trainers, a canvas satchel slung across from shoulder to hip. The man is too old to be a student backpacker. Vladimir's first thought is spook, CIA or somesuch.

"You drive for the Yurevich family, don't you?"

"Go away," says Vladimir.

"I wonder if I could ask you some questions about the Palm Ridge School."

The man puts a business card on the counter. Vladimir only glances at it. The masthead of the Toronto Star is printed large in the centre. Canadian then, a journalist, thinks Vladimir. Or at least pretending to be.

"Are you aware of the international condemnation that surrounds President Villaplane's pet science project, his little people factory?"

"Is this man bothering you?" says Monique, appearing from nowhere and slipping a hand across Vladimir's shoulder.

Vladimir makes a noise, a gentle moan, both an answer and a greeting.

"We were just talking," says the Canadian.

"I don't think so," says Monique.

"I wondered what your thoughts were on the United Nations declaration, supported now by the United States, to ban all forms of human –"

Monique grabs a handful of the man's exquisitely weathered shirt and twists.

"Someone is going to get hurt if you don't shut up and leave," she says.

"Who are you to tell me –"

The stool scrapes on the wooden floor as Vladimir stands. The man takes the hint, backs away and turns to leave only when at a safe distance.

"I wouldn't have hurt him," says Vladimir.

Monique takes the beer from his hand and, running her fingers down his chest, drinks.

"Who says it would be you doing the hurting?"

The bedroom upstairs is not Monique's and the flock of pottery angels on the table are not hers. Monique lives with her mother but Vladimir does not know where. Vladimir lies on the bed, holding but not drinking the beer, and watches Monique undress.

"You think there will be revolution?" she says.

Vladimir laughs.

"Revolution?"

"I hear the Americans are offering General Lucroy ten million dollars to stage a coup?"

"And who did you hear that from?"

Monique pulls her T-shirt over her head and runs her fingers through her hair.

"You think I am making it up?" she says.

Vladimir closes his eyes for a second or two.

"Why would there be a revolution? Why would anyone bother?"

"I hear that Villaplane is being paid to take and scrap ships full of toxic waste, chemical waste, that no other country will touch."

"You do hear a lot of things," says Vladimir and pats the bed.

Monique comes over and straddles him.

"Journalists, like that one downstairs. They're gathering like seagulls. Something is happening."

"He was not a journalist."

"Whatever," she says. "The people have had enough. Villaplane will permit any outrage if the numbers are right."

"Oh, you can do anything if the numbers are right," he agrees.

Vladimir reaches for the condom on the bedside cabinet.

"You think I'm not clean," she says. "You are the only man for me, you know."

She leans forward and pecks him on the lips. He rests his hands on her hips.

"It is just protection," he says.

"You think I'm not fit to bear your children?" she says, smiling. "You don't want any little mulatto babies, hmmm?"

"I don't want children at all," he says, perhaps too seriously. "Some men – evil men – should never have children."

"I think your children would be very beautiful."

He does not mean to say what he next says but it comes out anyway, like a bubble rising from the deep.

"Any children of mine, I would strangle at birth."

Anatoly pulls the car door shut. There is no greeting for Vladimir.

"Seatbelt," says Vladimir.

"Seatbelt," says Anatoly sullenly.

Vladimir puts the car in gear.

"So, what did you learn today?" he asks.

"Don't want to talk about it," says the boy.

"Oh," says Vladimir. "What happened?"

"I got called to Dr Aubert's office today."

"Did you misbehave?" says Vladimir.

"He had to be taught a lesson," says the boy. Vladimir can tell it is a line from an argument the boy has been having with himself all day. "Everyone needed to see that he was wrong."

Vladimir is about to ask the boy to explain when he sees the vehicles coming up the driveway. There are police cars and also an APC on which a soldier mans the machine gun turret. While part of him wonders if these are General Lucroy's men, he simultaneously shifts the car into reverse and pulls back up the driveway at speed. By chance, there are no other cars to block him.

He drives past the main entrance and pulls a bootlegger turn that leaves the front end of the car partway up a grassy slope.

"Move!" he commands and is out and dragging Anatoly with him before the boy has the opportunity to speak.

The school's own security guards are on the driveway and someone opens fire. Whoever it is, there is return fire. Glass smashes. An alarm starts. Something ricochets off the wall near Vladimir and something slices across the top of Vladimir's hand. He does not drop the gun he is holding, the gun he automatically picked up as he left the car.

Vladimir finds a side door, a fire exit. He shoots the glass, reaches through and pulls the release bar.

"In!"

Vladimir realises that his phone is ringing. He also realises that Anatoly is not crying or screaming. The boy's face is pale but set in a tersely determined expression. Vladimir has seen that face before but not on the boy. Beneath that golden blond hair, from those brown eyes. It is like looking at a ghost.

They are near the clinic, the medical centre attached to the side of the school. There is a woman in a lab coat in the corridor. She cannot decide which way to run. For just an instant, Vladimir can smell smoke.

He starts trying doors. The third door is not locked. He pushes Anatoly into the dark room. It's an examination room with a desk, a bed and a screen curtain. Vladimir tells the boy to hide under the bed. He goes to lock the door but there is no bolt or catch. He swings the office chair round to wedge under the door handle but the chair is too short. Vladimir pulls the curtain across to hide them both and crouches down, gun ready.

He takes out his still ringing phone to turn it off. It is Milla's number. He answers it.

"Tell them to lock the gate," he says. "Find a safe place to hide."

"They're here!" she weeps. "They're here. They say they want Anatoly. They say they want all the children. Why? Vladimir!"

Vladimir knows why. He has probably known why for some time. Part of him knew while other parts didn't.

"Hide," he says, simply, and then turns the phone off.

Elsewhere in the building there is more gunfire and there are screams. Blood is pouring freely from the back of Vladimir's hand. The antiseptic smell of the room and the sharp pain in his hand give Vladimir a sense of disembodiment as though, moment by moment, he is not really here.

There are shouts in the corridor.

Vladimir looks at the boy. Anatoly looks out from between the hydraulic struts of the bed. He is not afraid. The uncanny resemblance strikes Vladimir as the cruellest of all miracles. Fleetingly light-headed, he wonders if this was Pavel's plan, to escape without even those stains on his soul. He loves the boy but he also believes in justice.

Someone shouts in French. There is the rattle of a door handle, not this door handle. Not yet.

He raises the gun without thinking about it, as though the hand is thinking for itself.

"Some men – evil men..." he begins to say.

• The Mumblies

You want to know about the Mumblies? What for? Writing your thesis. Uh-huh. Good for you. Media studies student? No? Memetic toxicology? What's that? Flaming heck, I swear they just make these things up.

You found my name through the Mumblies Parents Support Group, yeah? Um, Freda and I went along a few times, what, forty years ago. But what's the point? It was like staring into a mirror for an hour. All that pain, that loss, clear as day on the other parents' faces. Nah, we thought it just best to try to forget it and move on. I don't think that's callous. Pragmatic. It's pragmatic.

Well, most of us parents *have* kicked the bucket since then. Freda died six years ago. No, we didn't have any more children after Ellie. I guess that there aren't many of us left who do remember the original Mumblies TV series. I hear the government has the whole series recorded on disc somewhere. You know, in some secret military bunker where men in white coats do strange and unspeakable experiments. Conspiracy theory crap, if you ask me.

I don't remember when I first saw the Mumblies. One day, flicking through on the remote, this nameless TV channel popped up somewhere between home shopping and the music stations. I can't even remember which of us found it first. I don't think anyone told us about it so I guess we must have come across it by accident. They were the only ways that households tuned in to the Mumblies: by random flicking or by word of mouth. There were no adverts for the Mumblies channel and it certainly never appeared in the TV listings.

Well, that was part of the weirdness of the Mumblies. Nobody came forward to claim ownership or responsibility for them. The Mumblies programmes had no credits, at least not in English. There was no indication of who actually made the programme. The companies who ran the transmitter stations said it had nothing to do with them. They merely received the data stream of information from the broadcast operators and relayed it to British homes. And the broadcasters? They said it wasn't part of their output. I don't know who you believe. Maybe they were all telling the truth.

It created a buzz of media interest. God, yes! For a start, you had a cult hit children's TV programme. And when you've got kids interested, you've got parents interested. Then there was the issue of who made the damned programme. That gave the hacks something to get their journalistic teeth into, something to investigate and speculate upon. It was in the papers for weeks. Never front page. Never headline news. It wasn't that slow a news month but it soon got that everyone in the country had heard of the Mumblies. I suppose it was around then that I came to believe that this whole 'we don't know who makes it' story was just a gimmick, a publicity stunt devised by the true programme makers. I wasn't alone.

What happened in the show? Of course, I forget. You've not watched it. The last time anyone saw the Mumblies must have been twenty years before you were even born. You've read descriptions. I understand. Let's see. The programme always started the same way, with an image of the land that the Mumblies lived in. I don't know, it looked like the Sussex Downs except the grass was blue and there were these cactus plant things with leaves, blue again, that looked like ostrich feathers. And then the symbols started to appear on the screen. There was a row of them but they kept rolling round, sort of like the pictures on a fruit machine. You don't know what a fruit machine is? Before your time as well, huh? Go look it up on the internet.

As the symbols moved, the music began to play. No, I couldn't hum it for you. No more than I could draw you one of the symbols. I remember them but I can't express them. Some people said the music sounded Japanese or Indian but what they really meant was it sounded like nothing they'd heard before. Ellie used to sing snatches of that music from time to time, even years after they stopped the broadcasts. That used to make Freda cry when she heard it. Guess it reminded her of the old Ellie. Our little baby how she used to be.

Anyway, then the Mumblies appeared out of their holes in the ground and they'd have their little adventure for thirty-seven minutes. Thirty-seven minutes and eight seconds. Every episode exactly thirty-seven minutes and eight seconds. Don't ask me what the stories were about. I could never work it out. They'd jump up, run around, fetch this, drop that, bump into each, fall over, get up again. Really mindless stuff. It's the kind of TV that makes adults just switch off. But Ellie... oh, she lapped it up. I mean, even from three months old she'd sit and watch it for as long as we'd leave the TV on. And, in the end, she'd cry as soon as we turned it off. So it was episode after episode after episode. One thirty-seven minute and eight second adventure and then another. The programmes went on broadcasting through the night. No, we weren't the world's best parents but the TV was switched off at bedtime. We put up with the screams and the tantrums. We weren't negligent. The Sleepless? Yeah, I heard about those cases. Very sad.

The name? Well, there was no English, no recognisable language at all in any of the programmes. There were no titles or credits. The TV programme didn't have a name of its own. Someone, I don't know who, probably a journalist or commentator, came up with the name Mumblies. The creatures spoke to each other in this invented language and it did sound like a mumbo-jumbo of words so... yeah, Mumblies.

There was a national debate, well, maybe it was just pub talk, about the language of the Mumblies and what it was doing to our children. A bunch of linguistic pedants said it was positively damaging. The type of people who told us we shouldn't say 'cootchie-coo' to babies. They said babies need to hear proper grown-up talk in order to learn. They said the same thing about Bill and Ben seventy years ago. Bill and Ben. Not heard of them? The Flowerpot Men. 'Flobba-dob.' No? Well, they were before my time too actually but.... never mind. Look it up.

Then there were those who said that what the Mumblies were saying or doing didn't matter. It helped children with numeracy, shape recognition and basic social skills. Of course, all of us parents immediately went 'that's all right then' and plonked our kids in front of the box for an extra hour a day. We didn't need encouragement. If someone says it's educational and it makes our

211

lives easier, we'll do it. People don't want to admit it but the TV is like a free babysitter. The third parent.

About six months later the first Mumblies toys came out in the shops and, God, there were a lot of them. Cuddly toys, jigsaws, books, computer games. Since no one had claimed ownership of the TV series, dozens of toy manufacturers interpreted that as there being no copyright on the Mumblies characters or their catchphrases. There were no court cases that I heard of.

We bought Ellie a talking Mumblie for her first Christmas. They were there on the shelf between the talking Winnie the Pooh and the little robot babies. How old? Erm, six months. It was the character that everyone called Mumbo. He, or maybe she, was the Mumblie with thick green fur running down his cheeks. Made him appear to be sporting enormous bristly sideburns like some Victorian patriarch. If you squeezed Mumbo's tummy a little voice box would repeat one of a dozen phrases that the toy company had sampled straight from the TV programme.

When she was eight months old, Ellie said her first word. 'Ranu'. Yes. R-A-N-U. It was a Mumblie word, something that the one called Booboo used to say. By her first birthday, she could clearly say eight different words. Mumblie words, the lot of them. Nothing else though. No 'mama' or 'dada'. She didn't really communicate with us at all. She would scream for the Mumblies as soon as she woke up and scream for them some more when we put her to bed. I swear, she only ate or drank because we put the stuff right in front of her. There was just no... interaction between us. Do you know what I mean?

Freda had friends with children of the same age. And, yeah, they were the same. Mumblies addicts. Heck, we'd told them about the TV programme. Got their kids hooked. The strange thing was when the babies were brought together, they didn't cry out for the Mumblies. You could sit them down – I guess we knew three or four couples with young uns – you could sit the three or four of them down together and they would play together, quiet as anything. They'd do their Mumblies jigsaws together, build a tower with their Mumblies blocks. Every so often they'd say something to each other, seemingly at random. Mumblie words. It wasn't conversation. It was... I dunno.

You may give me that funny look but it was only around that time that we started to worry. As parents, you find yourself worrying about everything, so you tell yourself not to worry about anything. Ellie was healthy, she was happy, looking after her was a doddle. It was only when things got really weird, maybe when she was eighteen months old, that we became really concerned.

We thought she might be autistic. She was clever, a real problem solver, good with her hands. But she was insular and withdrawn. We loved her, fed her and cared for her. And she let us feed her and care for her. But she showed us no love in return, no affection. We took her to the doctor. We sat down and explained our concerns to him. And do you know what the doctor's first question to us was? Right. "Does she watch the Mumblies?" The doctor had seen a hell of a lot of children with the same symptoms. Dozens.

Mumblies Syndrome they called it. Unoriginal, I know. Very quickly, the Mumblies went off-air. The government had stepped in. The TV signal, wherever it had come from, was stopped. By the end of the year, it was made illegal to show, sell or distribute any Mumblies products. Ellie's toy Mumbo was thrown in the bin. One night, I came downstairs for a drink and found Ellie in the front room. She was sat on the floor, the TV remote in her hand and she was flicking through the channels, from one through to nine hundred. Running up and down through them again and again, looking for a channel that was no longer there. She had turned the sound down so as not to wake us. And she was crying. Not a peep from her but her cheeks were wet with tears.

We were back and forth to the doctors every month from then on, part of a national medical study into Mumblies Syndrome. We were kept in the dark, mind. Each month, a load of questions from the doctor but no answers for us. On it went. She started school, unable to read, write, even speak. I don't know how the schools coped. Whole classes of children with Mumblies Syndrome. Nearly every child in Britain who had been under one year old when the TV series first aired was affected. Over half a million kids. One percent of the national population.

You tell me what else the government could have done with them? I say the Mumblies schools were a great idea. Boarding schools, yes. Ellie had teachers and carers who were attuned to her needs. She was with... with her own kind.

Unhappy? Was she unhappy to be apart from us? I don't think you understand what had happened to her. By the time she was five, Ellie had become entirely disconnected from the world we inhabited. She didn't smile when she was happy. She didn't get angry. There was nothing there. All of the Mumblies kids. They had become unearthly, entirely other. They congregated together but even then there weren't smiles or laughter, no sense of social structure or order. Whatever they did, their strange little games and projects, we were simply unable to understand them.

Cognitive repatterning? I heard that phrase bandied about a lot at one time. It's just scientists hiding their ignorance behind big words. All it means is we don't know how they think or why they think the things they do. Those children, not children anymore, are like computers infected with viruses. Like trying to play CDs on a gramophone turntable. They are alien to us now.

Last time I saw her? It was Ellie's twenty-first birthday. Decades ago. After school, she had moved into one of the Mumblies communes. On some Hebridean island. They have their own community there. Just Mumblies people. Not a word of English amongst them. They've built their homes underground, just like the creatures on the TV show.

I had to apply for a visitors pass. The army keep the Mumblies communes under close guard. They don't like people visiting. They don't like the Mumblies leaving either. Yeah, the government's scared of them. We're all scared of things we don't understand.

She didn't recognise me. The Mumblies tolerated my presence, nothing more. I followed her round, trying to catch her eye, see that smile of hers that we knew so briefly. I had a week long pass. I left at the end of the first day, got the ferry back to the mainland and came home to Freda. We didn't talk about it. Not a word.

Yes. Yes. I've heard the rumours. The radio telescope that a commune built in Anglesey. The constellation that they have been studying. I heard about the secret sterilization programme too. As I say, the government are scared. They don't want any more Mumblies children. What was that? A Mumblies commune

214

managed to build a rocket? What, a spacecraft? Where's it going to go? Excuse me, sunshine. It may have been on the news but I didn't see that. No. I don't watch TV much anymore.

•   Made To Love

They were an ideal couple and, before that, they were ideal individuals. Their lives were painted in sweeping brushstrokes of superlatives that others could only aspire to. He, Dr Truman Gernsback, physicist and engineer, founder of Universal Electric and holder of over two hundred patents, including the T-valve calculator and the prosthetic eye. She, Mrs Eleanor Gernsback, letter-writer and novelist, heiress to the immeasurable Quincannon fortune and hostess of the finest literary salons along the coast. They were colossi, with enough self-belief to sway doubting crowds, buoy ailing companies and shine a light on the golden future that the present did not always promise. And perhaps it was their confidence in themselves that destroyed them as a couple, as self-belief became blind faith became blind recklessness... perhaps that both had put such faith in the ship of their marriage that neither had bothered to observe where it was heading.

The lawyer, Lowell, made a great show of the photographs, laying them out in a precise three by four grid across the polished surface of his desk. Twelve colourised images of Eleanor Gernsback and Mr Arthur Sidler at the Gernsback's summerhouse. Truman Gernsback had been shown them once before at a less formal meeting with his lawyer and had immediately driven the seventy miles south to the house by the waterside and burned it to the ground. Now, with his wife beside him, Truman found himself sniffing at his fingertips and the lingering smell of turpentine and wood smoke.

"It's so sordid," said Eleanor, wanting to sweep the photographs from the desk but loath to even touch them. "You hired a peeper to follow me?"

"I hired the detective," said Lowell.

She turned her head to her husband but did not look at him.

"You knew nothing of this?"

"I have an obligation to look after the family's interests," said Lowell. "I take it very seriously."

Truman sighed and looked to the window. Lowell's offices were on the thirtieth floor and offered an impressive view of the city, its gleaming steel spires, the ribbons of its elevated roadways.

"Put them away," he said quietly.

Lowell collected the photographs together and tapped them against the table edge to make the pile square.

"What do you want me to say?" asked Eleanor.

"I don't know," said Truman.

"I could tell you how sorry I am."

He shook his head.

"It's over now," she said.

"Yes," he agreed. "It is."

"Rudi will be back from school soon."

"Yes," said Truman. "There is that too."

They met their son from school together and together they drove to the bay. Eleanor helped Rudi unpack, running her finger over the brass buttons of his blazer before putting it away. The remains of the summerhouse could be distantly seen from the rear of the mansion, black against the blue of the water. Naturally, he asked about what had happened. Naturally, she lied.

The Richmonds came over for drinks. Truman and Eleanor effortlessly played the happy couple, feeling a shadow of their old bonds in the charade. Rudi went to bed and the Richmonds went home, all of them ignorant of the truth.

Truman and Eleanor stood on the rear terrace and finished their drinks in the chill autumn air. The distant silhouette of a zeppelin was crossing the evening sun.

"He'll have to be told," he said.

"It would be a terrible shock to him," she said.

"I'm sure everyone thought we were the very picture of contentment."

"We were content."

Eleanor carefully set her tall glass on a wrought-iron table and then burst into tears. Truman tried to maintain his distance but could not bear to see her crying and put his arm around her.

"We will each survive this," he said. "We're strong enough."

She turned her body to face his. She sniffed a little, laid her wet cheek against his shoulder and placed a small kiss against the soft skin beneath his cheek.

"We were happy, Truman," she said.

He breathed in the smell of her hair, determined to cling to the memory of it.

"Yes," he agreed. "We were."

She kissed him again. He lowered his head and kissed her back.

"I am flying to Europe tomorrow," he said.

"Tomorrow," she said.

His six week trip to Europe extended to eight before he returned to the house on the bay. Eleanor and Rudi came out into the snow to greet him. Rudi hugged him tightly. Eleanor wore a smile of unrestrained delight.

"You were missed," she said.

"I'm glad to hear it," said Truman and presented his son with a large brown parcel.

Rudi stared at the sheer size of it.

"Toy circus," said Truman. "The high-wire artist has a gyroscopic heart. The man in the shop promised me that he would never fall."

Rudi gave an inarticulate hoot of joy and ran inside with it.

"I have some wonderful news," said Eleanor.

"It took me ages to find it," said Truman. "I knew just what I wanted. I found it down a back street in Geneva. The tiniest of places."

He stopped and looked at her. Eleanor had a hand laid across her lower abdomen.

"Really?" he said.

"Dr Brinkman confirmed it," she said. "Due in July."

Truman blinked.

"I *had* always wanted a second child. A brother for Rudi. Or a sister, I suppose."

"Had?"

He looked at her and, with a sickening twist inside him, saw how much their perception of things, of themselves, had drifted apart.

"I've not come back to you, Eleanor," he said. "I've come for Rudi. He can come to my apartment in the city for the week. I'm happy for him to spend Christmas itself with you. Of course."

Eleanor was shaking her head, an action she could not control.

"No, Truman," she heard herself say.

"And when the baby arrives, we'll sort something out. We'll be able to care for both our children."

"You forgave me," she said.

"I did," he replied.

"The night before you left? You took me..."

"I was trying to comfort you," he said.

"Comfort me? No."

She could feel her lower jaw trembling, her lips melting like candle wax. Truman came towards her with arms held out but she shied away. His arms dropped to his side.

"I'm sorry," he said. "We *were* happy. But it *is* over now, Eleanor. There are certain things that cannot be undone. I'm sorry but it is over."

He walked past her, into the house, leaving Eleanor standing in the cold. Up the curving stairs, Truman followed a trail of ripped brown wrapping paper to the boy's playroom. Truman found Rudi sat cross-legged on the floor, holding in his hand a tin figure on a unicycle. Rudi was frowning at it intently and did not notice his father for some time. When he did, he looked up.

"His heart doesn't work," he said.

"Let me see," said Truman and crouched down beside him.

Truman maintained a fifteen room penthouse apartment in the building across the street from the Universal Electric offices. During the day, Rudi was taken to Truman's place of work where he was alternately fussed over by the typing pool ladies and patronised by the laboratory men. At bedtime, Truman took Rudi to bed and read him James Fenimore Cooper adventure stories and, as he drifted off, told him about the baby brother or sister he would soon have. Then he retreated to his study, the drawer of fine-headed screwdrivers open next to him, each screwdriver with its own felt-lined recess, and tinkered with the mechanical high-wire artist's broken heart.

That week, Dr Brinkman visited the house on the bay and Eleanor told him what she wanted. Dr Brinkman blanched and told her that what she asked was both illegal and immoral.

"But you know people who can help me," she said.

"Of course," replied Dr Brinkman smoothly. "I know people."

Eleanor told Truman of the abortion in a short telegram in the spring. Truman reeled from the five-word message as though struck. The first person he spoke to about it was his lawyer. The Gernsbacks had employed the Lowells for generations and Truman had no better confidante.

"There are legal recourses," suggested Lowell, passing Truman a tumbler of scotch.

Truman looked at him, dead-eyed.

"Procuring an abortion is an indictable crime," said Lowell.

Truman let the scotch touch his lips, felt his mucous membranes recoil from the alcohol.

It's not going to bring the baby back," he said.

"No," said Lowell.

"I don't know if it... if the baby is a boy or a girl."

"I could find out."

"Could you?" said Truman.

"If you wish..."

Lowell downed his drink and refilled his glass.

"The abortionist," said Truman.

"Will stand trial."

"Good."

"After a conviction, the courts could declare your estranged wife to be an unfit mother."

"What did you say?"

"You could have sole custody of your son."

"Rudi..."

Rudi was with Eleanor until Easter. Lowell and Eleanor's lawyer (a man she had taken on Lowell's honest recommendation) had already agreed a week-to-week custody arrangement for the Gernsback's son. No one had mentioned divorce yet. In the background, wills were being rewritten and the title deeds of various businesses and properties were being examined.

Truman shook his head.

He took a cab back to his empty apartment, dismissed the housekeeper for the evening and sat in his study. He turned on the green Tiffany lamp above his drawing board and sharpened a pencil and considered the drawer of fine-headed screwdrivers.

When Rudi next came to visit, Truman showed him the work in progress at the Universal Electrics workshop. Truman had used photographs from the family album in the design process although, of course, he had to wait for Lowell's telephone call before producing a finalised version. Truman invited Rudi to select a shade of plasti-sheen for the hair. In the months that followed, there were issues with the fine motor controls and, in constructing the miniscule thermionic calculators, Truman made almost impossible demands of his engineers but such obstacles were overcome and, as promised, it was all completed by Rudi's ninth birthday.

Truman returned the boy to his mother, the day after his birthday. Eleanor stood on the steps as the car drew up. She was wearing a dress Truman had not seen before. As soon as the car stopped, Rudi jumped out onto the driveway. A blonde haired girl, an inch shorter than Rudi, followed him out.

Eleanor, frowning, walked down towards the car.

Rudi grabbed his mother's hand and, grinning, swung his arm round to indicate the girl.

"Mother, this is Greta."

The girl hung back demurely. She wore a pale blue dress with lace cuffs and patent leather shoes over white ankle socks.

"Greta?" said Eleanor.

"Do you remember?" said Truman. "When you were pregnant with Rudi? You said, if it was a girl..."

Eleanor shook her head, failing to understand. There was something wrong about the girl, although the specifics momentarily eluded her.

"Who is she?"

"She's Rudi's sister." Truman said it as though it was obvious and that Eleanor only needed reminding. "She's our daughter."

And then Eleanor saw it. The too-perfect symmetry of the girl's stance. The utterly uniform tone of her skin, like the subject of a Norman Rockwell painting. The movements of her arms, too graceful to be human.

"It's a machine," said Eleanor, her voice reduced to a shocked whisper.

Rudi ran back to the thing, Greta. He touched her forearm momentarily and then stepped back, as though amazed that she should be standing here and in front of him. He laughed.

"She's amazing, isn't she?" he said.

"She has your eyes," said Truman.

He was proud, noted Eleanor, in some mad, aloof corner of her mind. He was proud of what he had done.

"Can Greta stay with us for the week?" asked Rudi.

"What?" said Eleanor, feeling a sudden nausea.

"She doesn't go to school but she can stay here with you. She's very quiet."

The robot girl smiled bashfully. Eleanor had seen that smile before, caught in glimpses in car windows, studied closely in dressing-table mirrors.

"Go inside, Rudi," said Eleanor

"But she's..."

Eleanor cut him dead with a glare of desperate anger. Rudi bowed his head, turned briefly to Greta, squeezed her hand and entered the house.

The robot remained where it was, eyes on Eleanor but modestly avoiding meeting her gaze. Eleanor looked past it to Truman, standing against the long black hood of his car.

"Greta," he said. "In the car."

Greta silently obeyed. Truman approached Eleanor slowly, hat in hand, footstep after deliberate and solemn footstep across the gravel.

"Rudi is very fond of her," he said.

"Are you trying to hurt me, Truman?"

"No," he said with apparent earnestness. "We wanted a second child."

"I don't want another child with you," she spat.

"You did, that night."

Her eyes blazed in fury. A strand of hair hung between them like a lightning bolt from a thunderous cloud.

"Don't mention that night, Truman."

He fiddled with the brim of his hat awkwardly.

"You are not the wounded party here, Eleanor."

He used her full name as though he were talking to a child. This was him playing Truman the Adult.

"We were a family once," he said.

"And this... thing is your revenge?"

"No. God, no. I'm sorry you see it that way," said Truman. "But we do have a second child now. Greta. And perhaps you and I could reconsider what we have both done."

Eleanor regarded Truman and wondered what had happened to him, why his mind had become incomprehensible to her. Finding no answers, understanding nothing, she turned away and looked across the long lawns that stretched to the road. When she had calmed she turned to him once more.

"Truman, did you not think to consult me before creating this thing?" she asked.

His eyes became colder.

"So, you're the one who decides whether we have children or not. Did you consult me before visiting one of Brinkman's backstreet buddies?"

"That was different," she retorted. "Being a mother is different."

"No," he said with a fierce conviction she had not seen in him before. "You are not the only one who can create, Eleanor. Look at her." He stabbed a finger at the girl in the car. "She is me and you. She is months of energy and deliberation. I carried her but, by God, she is your daughter too."

"No."

"You can't ignore her," insisted Truman.

"I can," said Eleanor. "I have a child already, a son. You're a fool, Truman Gernsback. What do you think you are doing?"

Truman's face was a strange thing of wretched sorrow and beatific fervour.

"I make things," he said. "I make things better."

Eleanor rammed her knuckles into her mouth and fled into the house.

Rudi and his mother took walks in the woods and Rudi continued with his riding lessons. Truman took Greta shopping in the electric arcades and over the skyway to Vespucci Tower to see the airships docking. Rudi kicked at the early autumn leaves and stuffed his pockets with seed cases. Greta bought a baby doll with a pink, plastic face and asked an endless string of questions.

In the evenings, Rudi and Eleanor played pinochle and sat out on the terrace, counting stars. Truman's housekeeper put Greta's plasti-sheen hair in rollers and then, with her toy doll in her own lap, Greta sat on Truman's knee while he made adjustments to her joints and inner workings with his fine-headed screwdrivers.

As Eleanor was pointing out the constellation of Cassiopeia to Rudi he asked her why Greta was not allowed to stay with them.

"She belongs to your father," said Eleanor. It was an answer she had spent silent hours constructing. "It would not be right."

"She's a very nice girl," said Rudi.

"I'm not denying that," she said. "There are a lot of nice boys and girls in this world. But you're the only one who is mine."

Truman carefully unhooked the skin at the base of Greta's skull and examined the relay circuits within. Greta took a fine-headed screwdriver like Truman's and probed her doll's spine with it.

"She seemed a very nice lady," she said.

"She is," said Truman.

"But she won't have me stay at her house. I tried to make a good first impression."

"You made an excellent first impression," said Truman.

Greta's shoulders twitched as the fine-headed screwdriver touched against a cluster of thermionic calculators in her brain.

"Did that tickle?" said Truman.

"I think I fell asleep," said Greta with a shrug. "Just for a moment. You love me."

"I do," said Truman with a smile.

"And Rudi loves me."

"Of course," said Truman. "And she will love you too, Greta. Give her time."

Rudi was disappointed to find Greta not in the car when his father next came to collect him. (The letter Truman had received from Eleanor's lawyer had been quite specific.) Nonetheless, she was waiting for him at the apartment in the city.

The three of them went ice-skating one day, to the movie theatre another. Truman bought them tickets to see a game at the Hudson Centre. In the evenings, they listened to radio shows and afterwards re-enacted their favourite bits, pretending to be tough-talking detectives or vaudeville comedians until it was time for bed.

While Rudi slept, in a room littered with train sets, robots and wind-up cars, Greta sat in a corner and thought of nothing whatsoever.

One morning, Rudi telephoned his mother and told her he would not be returning to the house on the bay unless Greta was allowed to come with him.

There were further letters, urgent telegrams and one night a telephone call in which Eleanor swore colourfully at Truman and he said things that he immediately regretted, true things that were all the more regrettable for being true.

Hating herself for what she saw as personal weakness in the face of the enemy, Eleanor relented and Rudi and Greta came to stay for the weekend. Truman's gratitude, both on the telephone and in person when they arrived, grated against her enormously and she could barely maintain a civil composure in his presence.

This aside, she strove to make the best of the situation. Eleanor adopted the strategy of never speaking to the robot girl directly, instead couching all questions and comments to be applicable to both of the children. This worked particularly well over dinner (the robot ate apparently) when her non-directed questions could easily be mistaken for polite but aimless table talk.

The boy and the robot chatted like the best of friends. Greta appeared friendly, generous and entertainingly naïve on a whole range of issues and frequently, Eleanor found herself thinking of the girl as a real child rather than a mechanical contraption. She even caught herself liking the little girl. When she did, she rebuked herself sharply and focused on despising the girl-thing and all it represented, as she rightly should.

They spent the Saturday on the Richmonds' yacht. Eleanor had briefed the Richmonds thoroughly regarding Truman's folly and so there were no awkward introductions to be made. Mrs Richmond offered the same over-familiar hug to Greta as she did to Rudi and later commented to Eleanor on the softness and warmth of the girl-thing's skin. Eleanor replied diffidently that she had never had cause to touch it, nor would she ever and had to excuse herself for a few minutes to regain her composure.

She returned to the company to find Rudi helping Mr Richmond at the tiller and Greta sitting with her legs dangling over the side, arms folded on the railing and gazing out towards the open sea, maybe at the distant white triangles that were the yachts of other great families. Eleanor sat some distance away, adjusted her sun hat to shade her eyes, and watched. Without malice, she considered what would happen if she went over and pushed Greta into the water. Would she be dragged to the bottom of the bay by her metal innards? Would the robot girl politely acquaint herself with the fish and the crabs and ask for walking directions back to the Gernsback house? Or would saltwater seep into her workings and kill her?

And then Eleanor considered what would happen if she really did go over and really did push Greta into the water. There would be no criminal case to answer. The girl was not human; it could not be murdered. Truman would be devastated but impotent. He could instigate civil litigation, sue her for wilful destruction of property, but he would be able to gain no justice, only money. If she wanted to hurt him there would be no finer way. But then she realised that, or course, she and Truman had been in that situation before.

There was no motivation behind any of these thoughts, only idle, almost unconscious speculation. When Mrs Richmond came up top with the iced teas she had just made, she found Eleanor staring dreamily at Greta with a faint smile on her lips and paused to think that she had not seen Eleanor at such peace for a long time. And if she saw that Eleanor had her hand laid across her lower abdomen, she didn't think to make anything of it.

When the Richmonds moored at the jetty, Eleanor directed the children to run up to the house and get ready for dinner, promising them apple-tart for dessert. Eleanor's thanks and farewells to the Richmonds were heartfelt, and they went away certain they had seen a change in her that day.

On the Sunday, which was a colder and blustery day, Eleanor sat at her antebellum writing desk composing a letter. Throughout the last year she had written hundreds of letters – addressed to Truman, to her literary contemporaries, to newspapers and periodicals – filled with the bitterness of her personal pain and the vitriolic hatred that intermittently consumed her. All but a handful had ended up in her drawer of discarded writings. The letter she now began to write to Truman was different. It was a plea for reconciliation. It was not an apology but an explanation, a commentary on the shipwreck of their marriage seen with new eyes. She acknowledged the hurt she had caused and also indicated, without dwelling upon, the hurt she had been caused in turn.

The maid knocked to announced that lunch would be served presently and Eleanor put down her pen, two words of a fresh paragraph glistening wetly on the page.

At lunch, Greta sat with a book to the right of her place-setting. Eleanor felt she recognised the battered brown binding and craned her neck to see the gold-embossed lettering on the spine.

"What book is that?" she asked, addressing the girl directly for the very first time.

Greta smiled at her brightly.

"Washington Irving. I found it in the library."

Eleanor's brow creased, in a strange and wonderful confusion.

"I forgot we still had that," she said. "It was my favourite book as a child. Are you enjoying it?"

Greta nodded eagerly.

"Although I have not read it all," she added.

Eleanor stirred her chowder slowly, feeling that someone above was testing her and that this was the moment on which the whole test rested.

"Then you should borrow it," she said. "Until you come again."

"Really?" said Greta. "You will have me visit again?"

Eleanor nodded stiffly. Across the table, Rudi and Greta shared expressions of delight.

Greta clutched the book to her chest and stood up.

"Oh thank you, mother," she said.

Eleanor stared at her, the girl's words – that one word – stupefying her utterly.

"Mother?" said Rudi.

Eleanor's soup spoon slipped from her fingers, clattering against the edge of her bowl. She snatched up her napkin and dabbed furiously at the spots of chowder that had splashed across the tablecloth.

"I can't do this," she said, maybe to her herself, maybe to those she imagined watching over her. "I'm sorry."

She pushed her chair back and retreated to her writing room and the letter, the ink now dried, on her desk. She looked at the two final words she had written – "*If only...*" – and could no longer recall or imagine what sentences would follow on from them.

When Truman arrived to collect the children, Eleanor did not come out to say farewell to them but the maid told him that Eleanor wished him to come inside to speak. They spoke at length while the boy and girl waited in the car. When he did finally emerge, he was quiet and lost within his thoughts and remained so for much of the journey back to the city.

That night, Rudi lay in bed and listened to his father read the final chapter of *The Prairie* and then rolled over to sleep. Greta and Truman went into his study. Truman opened the drawer of fine-headed screwdrivers and Greta sat on his lap. He had not been separated from Greta for so long before and he checked her workings meticulously. A number of screws in her lower back needed tightening and some of the rubber tubing was a little twisted. Greta similarly tended to her pink doll with another screwdriver.

"Are you tired, father?" said Greta.

"Maybe," said Truman. "It is a long drive to the bay and back. Did you have a nice time?"

As he folded back the flaps of skin over her spine, Greta prodded the gap between her doll's neck and head.

"Do you and mother love each other?" she asked.

"I believe we do," he said honestly.

"She doesn't love me," said Greta emphatically.

"No, she doesn't."

"You said she would."

Truman pulled back the skin from the base of Greta's skull. Active thermionic calculators within twinkled like the Milky Way.

"I was wrong," said Truman heavily.

"Why?" said Greta, working at the gap between neck and head with increasing force, driving the screwdriver deeper inside. "You made me to love her."

"I'm sorry," said Truman.

Greta turned the doll round. Her nylon hair was blond, set in tight curls, and her eyes were blue and very familiar. As Truman probed with a fine-headed screwdriver, Greta stroked the doll's hair gently.

"Time for sleep, baby."

The Town

In minutes stolen from the dead and elastic time between the end of school and dinner (each announced by a muffled bell or gong), I stand on the Pivani Bridge and gaze at the canal. The soft, ineffective glow of lampposts and the yellow points of candles in upper storey windows of neighbouring houses are caught and reflected in the water, a twinkling, rippling constellation of stars. I have seen stars in books. In books, I have seen moons and suns, fields and clouds, mountains, meadows and a road without turnings. The sky above the town is black but it is not night. I have wondered if it is the black of crows, obscuring a greater light above. I picture them in infinite silent layers, only giving themselves voice when they come down to our level to steal scraps of food and make their nests in our cobwebbed attics and among the hidden chimney pots.

My favourite books at school are those with coloured pictures. In the hush of the classroom, by tallowlight, I covet the opportunity to look at shiny plate pages of impossible scenes, of bear hunts, of alien cities with rivers of ice, mountain forests wreathed in storm clouds; pages that swarm with brightly plumed birds with cruel eyes and twisted beaks. I turn the pages carefully, holding them by the edges, not only to avoid leaving greasy fingermarks but also to not wake the barbaric creatures trapped within. There are worlds in those books, not just in the images but in the words. The town is a finite space without edges but books are a way to the places beyond the town. Each book, rectangular, is a window to somewhere else, the space left by a missing brick, a hole to be peered through but not touched.

But there are no stories in the schoolbooks to match those told by my great aunt from the heaps of her shifting, unmappable bed. Her stories are not a window into other places. They are savage rips in the fabric of things, and I do not dare stay with her too long.

Nor can I linger on the Pivani Bridge. It is time to go home. And, besides, a man in a long, floor-brushing coat is gliding across the bridge towards me and there is more than a little of the crow about him.

I clutch my satchel to my side and hurry towards my father's shop and home. The way home is not a certain thing, not for any length of time. The town is a labyrinth in which crumbling buildings, misbegotten alleyways and faded names conspire to pull the traveller away from their path. Our town is not paved with intentions. An entrance implies an exit but makes no promises. I have glimpsed greenery through obscured archways, heard the trickle of a fountain just around the corner, seen an inviting courtyard through the crack of a partially opened door and I have had the strength to turn my head and walk on.

We are no safer indoors. In our apartment block there are stairways I have not explored and door handles I have not touched. Corridors come and go at will. I have known rooms to appear and disappear again. I am most disturbed when I wake up and notice that a door in our apartment has moved a single inch to the left or to the right. We ignore such changes. Drawing attention to them does not improve matters.

I come to my father's shop, where I am to wait for him. He does not like me standing in front of the window. He says it is bad for business. I stand on a carefully judged point between my father's shop and the bookshop next door, aligning myself perfectly with the dry and rusted drainpipe that separates them and marks a meridian in my world.

The bookshop next to my father's shop is a particularly dangerous place. The bookshelves are brazen and do not care if anyone is watching. I have been in it only once and that experience, my one perverse act of rash criminality, is a slick stone of shame in my soul. My father's shop, where unstrung violins hang from ceiling hooks like curvaceous varnished bats, is a more stable place and he refuses to acknowledge the shifting labyrinth of brick and stone, of doorways and windows, that surrounds him. He spends long hours poring over his accounting ledgers, grunting to himself and making the occasional margin note in his florid hand. I think he too sees worlds in books but his worlds are numerical things with avenues of totalled columns and narrow, almost invisible paths of credit and debit, passageways between bills and receipts. I also think he looks for more profound answers in those yellow ledgers, consulting them much as a rabbi does his scrolls. I think he believes he can save us with those numbers but save us from what I'm not sure.

The door to the bookshop rattles. Startled, I see the tall man in the long coat looking the locked door up and down as though it is a riddle to be closed.

"It is closed," I tell him redundantly.

He sniffs deeply. His face is hidden between his upturned collar and wide-brimmed hat.

"I'm after the book," he says, his voice deep and full of deliberation.

"It's closed," I say.

He regards me. His gaze is a slow thing; he reads me unhurriedly.

The electric light inside my father's shop goes out. My father is locking up, backing out of his shop with a ledger under his arm. He nods wordlessly at me and then looks past me. The tall man is walking away up the street.

We return to our apartment just in time for dinner. Adele, cook, housekeeper and striker of gongs, serves. I do not question where our food has come from. There is a chain that extends from kitchen to larder to grocer's and beyond which, my great aunt says, the wise do not regard too closely. To peer under the skirts of the world and inspect its workings is both perverse and liable to incur censure.

After we have eaten, I take a tray of food to my great aunt. Her room lies at the end of a short, unattractive corridor lined with daguerreotypes of unnamed relatives. I knock, enter and place the tray on the mound made by her legs in her bed. When she moves her covers, I get a waft of her warm, sour smell.

She barely touches her food but invites me to stay. I perch on the edge of her bed. She asks about my day and I tell her things I do not tell my parents. I tell her about the man who followed me from the Pavani Bridge to the bookshop.

"Was he from the town?" she asks, which is a nonsensical question.

"There is only the town," I tell her.

She makes a show of looking up, to the sky beyond the ceilings, floors, attics and roofs above us.

"There is this world and the next, boy," she says.

I have to suppress the urge to scoff. I have been to church. We have all been to church and only because at times we feel we should. I remember the priest, saddest of all creatures, a blind worm of a man feeling his way about the shadowy cavern of his church, uncomprehending, reciting words that hold no meaning for any of us, speaking of a heaven beyond the black sky of a God who dwells there. They are only words and not even the priest believes them. I have sometimes wondered what crime the priest had committed to be condemned to such a life. I have wondered this so that I can avoid the same fate.

"The man said he was searching for a book," I say and then correct myself. "He was searching for *the* book."

My great aunt understands my love of books even though I suspect she cannot read.

She has finished with her dinner, having eaten a snippet of pork rind and the smallest of carrots. I put the tray aside and then she tells me stories.

Her stories are like the colour plates in my school books – impossible, dazzling and frightening. The morals of her stories are all the same. Nothing good ever lasts, which makes goodness, beauty and happiness all the more precious. In her tales, the finest of princes and princesses never suffer the indignities of growing old, the greatest romances last hours or minutes, not years. In her stories and her worldview, evil is present behind the surface of all things. When I listen, I can believe that our town is a raft on a sea of impossible terror, that our world is a bubble suspended in oily black bitterness.

She never repeats her stories, which suggests that she either makes them up as she goes along or that she has a remarkable memory for an old woman.

I tell her this.

"We must do our best to hold onto our memories," she says, "for when something is forgotten, it is lost forever."

"You must have forgotten many things by now," I say.

"Because I am old, boy?" she chuckles dryly. "I might be old but God is older."

I pick up my great aunt's tray and make to leave.

234

"He was looking for *the* book?" says my great aunt.

"He was," I reply.

She nods in that irritating manner adults have which indicates they know something others do not. I do not ask her to explain but I wait.

"Where do books come from?" she says.

I shake my head, not understanding the question.

"Where do crows come from?" she says.

"Eggs," I say. "Crow's nests."

"And where do the eggs come from?"

It strikes me as a stupid question.

"Crows," I said, perhaps too contemptuously.

"Oh, and it goes on like that forever, does it?" she says tartly. "Things have beginnings. So it is with books and words. Stories. Do you think I make up the stories I tell you?"

I say nothing.

"All things are copies, not always good copies. But there was once a true town of which this is only a poor copy, boy. There was once a true man and a true woman of which we are only weak shadows. And there was once a book in which all things were written."

For a moment, I think she is talking about the dusty padlocked tome in the church that the priest runs his hands over. But she is not talking about that book.

I take her tray back to Adele.

My mother always gives me a peculiar look when I return from my great aunt's room as though to check I am the same as the boy who went. I remember once asking my mother whether my great aunt was her aunt or my father's. My father, his armchair drawn up near to the lamp on the hearth, looked up from his ledger and a strange silent exchange passed between him and my mother.

I know that one day I will carry a tray along that short, unattractive corridor and find that there is no door at its end. This is the way of things.

I sleep uneasily. I have a dream that I have had more than once, in which I wake to find that my bedroom, unchanged in every other detail, no longer has a window or door. It is not a nightmare nor is it a comforting dream. The dream is simply of the perfect and final reduction of the universe to one room, one space, and this is also the way of things.

When dark morning comes, I go to school, clutching my satchel more tightly than ever, but I cannot attend to my studies. Whatever great meter or measure doles out time, I wait out my sentence before a blackboard chalked with lines and curves that at different distances holds no meaning, certain meanings and the meaning of all things.

I do not run out of the school gate. Too much haste might tear a hole in the thin fabric of this world and plunge me into a sculpture garden, a menagerie, an abandoned courtyard, a silent railway station... and I would be lost and dead before I knew it. I walk with solid purpose to the Pavani Bridge. The tall man is already waiting for me. I am not surprised and nor is he.

"I don't know why I took it," I say. "It's not even very big."

"It doesn't have to be," he said.

His hand emerges from his long dark sleeve. It is an unremarkable hand. It is like any other hand. It is like every other hand. It is open to receive.

I open my satchel.

"Is this the book you were after?" I ask.

"It is. It's the book we are all after."

The slim volume is locked with a tarnished silver clasp that I could not undo. He holds the closed book by its spine and runs a finger over the outer edge.

"What now?" I ask.

The man looks at me as though he does not understand the question. Embarrassed, I avert my gaze to water below the bridge. As I stare at the undulating constellation of false stars, I hear the momentary sound of a thumb riffling through pages and a bolt of light sears the sky.

I see its reflection in the dark waters, a blade-straight rend in the heavens, like a line of chalk across a blackboard, as though the leaves of the sky have been pulled apart for an instant to reveal a greater world beyond. I have only seen lightning before, in books, though not like this. When I look up, the lightning has passed and, when I turn round, I realise that the man has gone too.

•   The Train

The universe (which others call the Train) is composed of an indefinite and perhaps infinite number of carriages, coupled together with chains and buffers and squeeze-box corridors. I have deduced that, excluding the partitions, doors, furniture and fittings installed for each individual carriage's purpose, all carriages are identical, being eight feet in width and sixty-three feet in length (sat on bogies of forty-six feet length on a four feet eight inch railway gauge). Along the curved rooftops run the water pipes, the rubberised wires that carry the Train's electricity supply, and the Erinoid conduits of the Train's pneumatic capsule delivery system.

The Train sometimes slows and sometimes accelerates but it does not stop.

Like all passengers, I have travelled a little. As I understand it, Madame Goldenberg has covered no greater distance than that from her compartment to the dining car and back again. As I sit and write this in an otherwise deserted parlour carriage, I am looking at the list of carriages I have come through to get here. I am thousands of carriages, a distance of many miles, from my place of berth.

The pun is not a frivolous one.

No one recalls getting onto the Train. No one gets off.

My name is Dr George Lewis Burgess. I could describe to you at length the university where I studied medicine, the great doctors who taught me and the many-bridged city that surrounded that university – its arcades, bars and restaurants. But it would be the same as a man describing a place he had only seen in photographs or read about in travel journalism. I fear that the city, its history and mine are mere fiction. I appeared, out of whole cloth, in compartment C at some undetermined moment in the past.

My experience is not unique although I appear quite alone in finding it discomfiting. Questions regarding the structure of the Train, its organisation, function and ultimate purpose, do not plague my fellow passengers. Many feel there is no mystery: the Train is a train. The conductor on our section of the Train has reasoned that the greater mystery is unimportant, that the Train operates according to rules (which he, for his part, upholds and enacts) and, as long as the system works, we should be content to let it be. He, as a self-confessed man of little learning, argues eloquently enough that any sufficiently complex system cannot be wholly comprehended by a single individual. Others reject my concerns on more spiritual grounds, Madame Goldenberg has intimated, through uneasy expression and ellipsis rather than spoken words, that it is unwise to scrutinise the meaning and purpose of the Train too deeply lest the act of observation cause the whole universe to come crashing down around our ears.

Madame Goldenberg took a distinct if tacit dislike to my experiments in photography. I borrowed a camera from Foscarelli, the journalist. He is a louche character, as easy with his own possessions and money as he is with other people's. He takes landscape photographs (through the windows on the left of course) and can occasionally be enticed into portraiture. He had not once considered taking photographs of the Other Train and considered my attempts to capture images of that Other Train's passengers as peculiar in the extreme.

Both trains, at their slowest, travel at a speed a little faster than the most athletic man can run. As they are travelling in opposite directions, their combined speed prevents us from acquiring anything but the vaguest glimpse of the events on the Other Train. I set up the camera on a dining table and, adjusting it to its widest aperture and fastest shutter speed, took a series of twenty-four images which, enticed with the offer of a bottle of limoncello, Foscarelli helped me develop in the makeshift darkroom he had created for himself in one of the porters' cupboards.

I interrogated Foscarelli about his work. He takes photographs, he interviews prominent passengers and writes shorthand accounts of such small incidents as take place on the Train. Some of his work appears in one of the newspapers that may be bought from the morning porter. The means by which this might possibly happen on a constantly moving train was a mystery to me. It was not so to Foscarelli. He explained to me that he buys film, paper and other stationery from a shop booth in a rearward carriage, his photographs and written copy are sent by pneumatic capsule to a colleague in a forward compartment of the Train and such direction as he is given is sent by telegram to the conductor's tiny office.

"But where does the newspaper come from?" I asked. "Where is it printed? Who provides the paper? The ink?"

Foscarelli shrugged indolently and said, "I am journalist. I know nothing of mere *printing*."

He was content with his own answer. He could see no need to ponder the matter more deeply.

I took up my issue with the waiter at breakfast the following day.

"Are these eggs fresh?" I asked.

"Of course, sir."

"Where do they come from?"

He smiled, a little embarrassed, as though he was being made a fool of.

"A hen, sir."

"You acquired them from a hen?"

"No, sir. I acquired them from the kitchen."

"And where does the kitchen get its eggs?"

"From stores, sir."

"And where do the stores get their eggs?"

He wavered. He had many other breakfasts to serve.

"They are delivered from further up the train."

He bobbed his head and moved on to take breakfast orders from Charters and Caldicott.

Did the man imagine that the delivery came from a grander storeroom elsewhere on the Train which in turn received deliveries from an even more exalted storeroom and so on *ad infinitum*? Were supplies loaded onto the Train from outside by some esoteric means? Did local farmers lob eggs and milk pails and sides of pork at the Train for them to be caught by highly trained porters with nets? Or was there somewhere a carriage filled with egg-laying hens and another supporting a miniature dairy herd? Did the Train grow its own corn, its own potatoes?

If the Train is truly infinite in length then anything might be possible. Perhaps there are carriages devoted to agriculture. Perhaps in its further reaches one might find swimming pools and pleasure parks, the workplaces of cobblers and milliners, miniature cricket pitches, forests, churches and breweries. If it is truly infinite then all these things will not merely exist but be found in infinite repetition.

I regarded the pictures I had taken of the Other Train. Several were blurred and meaningless. Some showed carriages not unlike the one I sat in. One particular image arrested my eye. A suited gentleman, perhaps no older than myself, sat in a carriage of plump velvet seats, his back to the window, a book held up to better catch the light. With a magnifying glass I was able to discern the words on the page he was reading. The paragraph at the top of the page began with the words:

The universe (which others call the Train) is composed of an indefinite and perhaps infinite number of carriages, coupled together with chains and buffers and squeeze-box corridors.

What a coincidence that my indiscriminate shutter should capture words about the very nature of the Train itself! I took those words as a sign and, as you know, as the first words of my own account, and I determined I should go exploring in search of answers to my questions. After completing my breakfast and packing such small items as my expedition might require, my only dilemma was as to which direction I should travel: forwards or backwards. I feel there is a moral aspect to this question. To travel forward is to travel towards the engine, towards order, into the grimy and unsentimental reality of train travel. To travel backwards is to move away from the order and the grime, into the merry whimsy of the back end of the train, the quiet borderland where the track emerges, disgorged, from beneath that final carriage. However, if the Train is infinite in both directions then, mathematically speaking, my present location must be at its very centre and, no matter how far I travel, I will always remain at that centre.

Nonetheless, I chose to head forwards. I informed the conductor of my intentions, said a brief farewell to Madame Goldenberg and set out. Within forty minutes I had travelled beyond the carriages I knew. In my notebook, I listed the carriages I passed through by type and by distinguishing features. One hundred and sixty-three carriages along, I lunched in a dining car identical to the one in which I had breakfasted that morning. I ate a light tea in an automat in the company of an elderly gentleman with a passion for crosswords. At nightfall, I spoke to a conductor in a sleeper carriage and explained that I was a great distance from my own berth. He looked at my ticket (which I had the foresight to bring with me), gave me a gently admonishing shake of the head and then led me to an empty compartment where I could spend the night.

Sitting on the edge of the fold-down bed, I read and re-read through the list of carriages I had traversed and then, tentatively, wrote the first baldly descriptive lines of this account.

I paused after writing briefly about the train's constant motion and varying speed, and later laid in the darkness, thinking about it. Our carriage slows notably as it is pulled uphill and accelerates on downward slopes and this appears to be common sense. And yet, every part of a train should move at the same speed as its engine and on a Train of infinite length, there are as likely to be - indeed, unless the world itself is slanted, there *must* be - as many carriages on the ascent as on the descent and our personal presence on a particular slope should have no influence over the speed of the entire Train.

It occurred to me only the following morning, as I set off on the next leg of my expedition, that the connecting chains and squeeze-box corridors might provide some partial answer. As a carriage rolls downhill, it will accelerate towards and connect with the buffers of the car in front and, on the flat or the uphill, roll away to the chain's full extent. This elasticity of the overall Train could account for the changes in speed.

However, this conjecture has its own alarming consequences. On an infinite Train the elasticity, the range between the Train's minimum and maximum potential length, is also infinite. In other words, should the Train have started from a standstill, then the final carriage - requiring the chains of all intervening carriages to be made taut before it began to accelerate - *would never move!* The same could be said for a carriage halfway down the Train, or a quarter or any other fraction one might care to mention. Conversely, given that the Train is in motion, the reverse would equally apply. Should the engine stop right now, the infinite buffering needed to bring the whole Train to a stop would logically mean that the final carriage (or the one halfway, quarter way, etc.) *would never stop!* Ultimately, the speed of the engine will have no influence on the speed of the final carriage and, if my understanding of the principles of friction, momentum and inertia is correct, then it is a wonder that the final carriage continues to move at all. Is this proof that the Train is ultimately finite in length and that my quest is not utter folly?

Though my forward journey is into *plostra incognita*, much of what I see is familiar and uninteresting (for one sleeping carriage is very much like another, a luggage store is but an empty box unless you wish to illicitly investigate other people's personal belongings) and, being bereft of travelling companions, I have much time for thought and introspection.

The infinite nature of the Train is a frightening and maddening concept. Perhaps, to paraphrase Madame Goldenberg, it is unwise to scrutinise the meaning and purpose of the Train too deeply lest the act of observation cause one's mind to come crashing down around one's ears. I forced myself to think upon more practical and observable matters.

I have mentioned the Other Train but have not yet described it. It is the twin to our own Train but not a mirror; the two trains move in opposite direction. If the two moved in the same direction then that would have given each an identity – one would have been the Left Train and the other the Right Train – and, if those speeds were comparable there could have been communication between the two. As it is, the existence of the Other Train does not endow our Train with any specific meaning.

The two train tracks are not a uniform distance apart. Sometimes they run beside one another with carriage windows barely a foot apart. Frequently the tracks diverge, one rising to a higher level or the two separating to pass around lakes or mountains. Hours and occasionally days may pass without sight of the Other Train but this is rare.

The tracks we travel on are not straight. Sometimes it is possible to look out the left-hand windows and see the forward and rearward parts curving into view as the Train takes a long slow left-hand bend. On my expedition I have looked out and seen this and, consulting my list, have counted back to the place of my berth. On such occasions, I can see neither the engine nor the caboose, only a train of carriages diminishing into the haze of distance. This is not proof that the Train is infinite but simply indicates that even at the time of writing I am many miles from either end.

There is the possibility of course that the Train has no end but is simply a linked chain of carriages, propelled by an unknown force. It is possible that in those wide curves, the Train turns on itself, a serpent with its tail in its mouth. I have seen sunsets and sunrises from the left-hand window, at all points of the visible compass. Does this signify anything at all? In a world eight-feet wide and scarcely any taller, there is only one true dimension and two directions of any significance.

Linked in a circuit or not, it is not beyond the realms of imagination to propose that the Other Train is actually This Train, having doubled-back and heading in the opposite direction. Is it in front of us or behind us? We will never see its engine but what if one day – oh, wonderful and terrible day – its final carriage should flash by and it be gone. I am sure Madame Goldenberg would die of shock, that Charters and Caldicott would cease their constant prattle about abstruse points of cricketing lore and pay attention to something beyond themselves, that Foscarelli would have something truly momentous to print in his fatuous paper should he see the vistas that lie to the currently invisible right.

Travelling forward, I hope that the Other Train connects to this and is the forward portion of the Train. I hope one day to step into a carriage of plump velvety cushions and meet the man whom I had successfully photographed. I have dreamt of him and he has my face.

I perhaps make too many assumptions about the Other Train. I assume it is like this Train, that there are people aboard engaged in the same everyday affairs as ourselves. But what can I really infer from one good photograph amongst many blurred images? I can say, here exists a man, shown in the act of reading. But do even notions such as time and causality hold sway on the Other Train?

On the Train, time moves forward as the Train moves forward. Perhaps these two are linked or perhaps the moving Train is merely an elegant metaphor for the passage of time, for life itself. It is possible that, moving in the other direction, the Other Train experiences time backwards, that people rise from their beds at evening, dress and go out to the dining cart to regurgitate juicy steaks and fine wines. Perhaps this seems the norm to them or perhaps, having memories of events yet to happen to them in their backward universe, they believe they are experiencing time forwards and wonder if we are the backward time-travellers.

My own personal theories abound and flower and perhaps one day I might meet a professorial academic who can put my thoughts in order (or a whole host of academics for surely an infinite Train should have its own university and a Faculty of Train Studies!)

I now sit in a sun-room carriage with a curved glass ceiling, many many miles from home. I have not yet found the book-reading man. I have seen libraries and perfumeries; gymnasia, laundries and sewage treatment machines; a functional observatory, a superficially discreet brothel and an aquarium spanning three carriages. I am still none the wiser than when I left.

I fancy that when we reach a particularly steep incline, I might leap from the slowing train and, should I survive that leap, go outward *away* from the Train, journey in strange new dimensions, meet folk who have never known life aboard the Train, and pursue the birds and flying machines that we have all seen go by.

And if I found that other world too frightening or too dull or to be nothing but an image painted on the walls of a tunnel we have always travelled through, I might return to a place where the train slows and, by some means as yet unknown, climb back on board.

I would return to the carriage of my berth and greet my former travelling companions and they would look at me with some combination of horror and disgust.

"Do you not recognise me?" I would say. "It is I, Dr Burgess."

Madame Goldenberg would scoff.

"Dear Dr Burgess leapt from the train a long time ago."

"And now I am returned to you," I would say.

"You may resemble him," Foscarelli would say, "and I see you have somehow acquired his ticket, but you are not George Burgess."

And I would be seized by Charters and Caldicott and the conductor and flung a second time from the Train, this time to my death.

I see these events in my mind, as clear as any memory.

Whether they choose to admit it or not, I believe all passengers have a view of the world and the Train's role within it, its relationship to time, and its place within the greater universe beyond our windows. I am sure that, in their minds, to step from the Train (which is Life) is to die and that the dead may go on to other places but that those on the Train must leave the dead behind and not see them again until they too eventually disembark.

• Smooshy Girl, Smooshy Boy

They descended to level one, which required a process called 'waking up' which was quite different to and much slower than the waking up that they experienced on a daily basis.

Zabeth considered herself and asked her factor to make some wings for her avatar. The factor explained that while it could facture wings for her, she would not be able to fly with them, on account of something called real.

"Like they have in the four hundreds," said Kyr.

His factor said that it was similar but the real of level one was a real real and not the same as that used in the four hundreds. Also, the factor pointed out, the selves they now inhabited were technically not avatars but bodies.

"Same thing," said Zabeth, looking at her brown feet, irritated that she would have to use them.

"Real is stupid," said Kyr.

Their factors offered no opinion on this but factured local copies of their smooshies by way of compensation. Kyr slung his smooshy around his neck. Zabeth held hers to her breast even though she didn't have nubs yet; Letta had said she couldn't have them until she was older.

"This way then," said Zabeth, pointing down the sandy slope from the monument.

The sky was a bright grey and the sun a brighter blob high above them. Kyr could see other monuments on distant hills, some barely visible though the dust haze.

"Why are we here?" said Kyr. "Real is stupid."

"We're exploring," said Zabeth. "Looking for something."

"What?"

"We won't know until we see it."

There was a valley below the monument. The ground became rougher further down, with large brown rocks. Walking was slow without wings. There wasn't even a skip function. An almost regular arrangement of buildings sat in the bottom of the valley. Few of the buildings had roofs. Most of them were filled with windblown sand or fallen brown masonry. They did not expect to encounter any people so when they found a wrinkly and ugly woman in one of the smaller buildings, Kyr gave a start and grabbed his smooshy for comfort.

The building had one room, its only window a ragged hole in the wall above the woman's head, the floor covered in lumps of broken stone. The woman was wrapped in layers of dirty grey clothing. There was a hinged object in her hands and a heap of plastic containers at her side. She lowered the hinged object and looked at the two children. Her eyes were almost invisible in the saggy folds of skin on her face.

Zabeth stepped forward boldly.

"What's wrong with you?" she said.

The woman blinked.

"Lots of things, I should imagine," she said, "not that I'm compelled to discuss any of them with you. Who are you?"

"I'm Zabeth and this is Kyr."

"You're from the monument."

"What's that?"

It took the woman some time to realise that Zabeth was referring to the object in her lap.

"It's a book."

"No, it's not," said Kyr, who had met a book once.

"I'll thank you not to take that tone with me, young man," said the woman sharply. "Books used to have pages and the words stayed where there were told. I think this one's infected though." She flicked a page back and then forward. "Something's causing file corruption. Fucking ellipses everywhere. Makes it darned hard to read."

"What *is* wrong with you?" said Zabeth. "Your face is all wrong."

"Old age, young woman," said the woman.

"Isn't there anything you can do?"

"Do I need to do something? Maybe I'm happy like this."

Zabeth made a show of looking around the room. It was more a cave than a room. She couldn't imagine anyone being happy in such a place.

"Is there anyone else here?"

"Was," said the woman. "Years ago. But he's dead now. You know this comes to us all, don't you?"

The children looked at her blankly.

"Even forever doesn't last forever," said the woman.

Zabeth opened her mouth to correct the woman and tell her about the final realties, the infinite levels, the train and the town, but the woman raised a pale saggy finger and pointed.

"What's that? Some sort of teddy?"

"It's my smooshy," said Zabeth.

"I've got mine too," said Kyr.

"What's it doing?"

The smooshy had its toothless mouth clamped to Zabeth's nipple.

"It's comforting," said Zabeth.

Zabeth couldn't be certain if the look on the woman's face was shock or disgust or bewilderment. It was hard to read a face like that.

"For who?" said the woman, a high note of disapproval in her voice.

Zabeth looked at the smooshy suckling on her nipple. It looked back up at her with its huge wet eyes. For just an instant, Zabeth felt the weight of the woman's condemnation and wanted to pull the smooshy away, but then she remembered herself, threaded her fingers more tightly into the smooshy's fur and gave the woman a hard stare.

"What's a teddy?" said Kyr.

"Do you know what a bear is?" said the woman.

"It's an animal," said Zabeth. "We've seen them in the Ederra on five-five-three."

"They're not real bears," said the woman.

"Real is stupid," said Kyr.

The woman coughed several times and the children realised that she was laughing.

"Real *is* stupid," she said. "I've never seen a bear either. Not a real one. Big creatures. Bigger than me. Teeth and claws. Dangerous too."

"The bears in the Ederra don't have claws or teeth," said Kyr.

249

"Or mouths," said Zabeth.

The woman reached down and plucked something moist and round from one of the plastic boxes and popped it in her mouth.

"But bears are furry," she said, chewing noisily. "Soft and warm. We did something, inside our own heads. We forgot the teeth and the claws and we made soft and cuddly toys – no teeth, no claws – and we called them teddy bears and pretended they were the same thing. And then we get this."

She licked her fingers and pointed at Zabeth's smooshy.

"I've got mine too," said Kyr.

"Something soft and cuddly," said the woman distastefully, "to bring out the mammalian urge to nurture. Big eyes. Big head. Little arms. Who needs babies if you've got those things? Neotenized little cuckoos."

"You use big words," said Zabeth.

"It's called a vocabulary, young lady. You should get yourself one."

Zabeth snorted and kicked a stone.

"What do you do here?"

The woman shrugged.

"Sit. Read. Eat. Wait."

"Wait for what?" said Kyr, wondering if something would happen.

The woman simply looked at him.

"You know something was going to get us in the end," she said. "Runaway tech. Solar expansion. Universal heat death." She did something unusual with her mouth, a sort of a smile but not a nice smile. "Even smooshies. What do you reckon? In our relentless pursuit of the cute and adorable, we make something that demands all our attention and affection. The birth rate plummets. We stop breeding. We all become mad old cat ladies, transferring our affections, projecting our emotional lives onto something external, something other. Wiped out by cuteness. What do you reckon?"

"You're strange," said Kyr and, in saying it, felt a nervous fear. He turned to Zabeth. "I want to go back." Kyr's smooshy hugged him tightly. Kyr stroked its fur. "Smooshy wants to go back."

Zabeth nodded slowly.

"I've seen enough."

They stepped out of the building and into the hazy glare. Zabeth realised how much hotter it was outside. They ambled over to a waist-high circle of stones in an open space between several derelict buildings. There was a deep hole in the ground inside the circular wall. Kyr stared down into the darkness.

"Do you think she's the only one?"

"On this level?" said Zabeth. "No. There must be others."

"I don't know," he said.

Zabeth's smooshy mewled. She made a cradle of her arms for it to sleep in.

"It's not real," said the woman.

The old woman had come out of her building. She held onto the edge of the entrance to support herself. Her lower legs, bare, were reed-thin and mottled with dark spots. She threw her arm up, possibly at the hill behind them and the monument at the top.

"That tomb. It's not real."

"So?" said Zabeth.

This seemed to stump the woman. She wore a troubled expression as she walked over. She sat on the wall next to the children. The stone shifted a fraction beneath her weight.

"Don't you dare spit in my well, boy," she said to Kyr.

"I wasn't going to," said Kyr.

The woman stretched and lifted up her ragged garments to expose her legs further to the sun.

"I was young once," she said.

"Everyone was a child once," said Zabeth.

"I didn't say a child. But I was that too. Once." She sniffed. "We were adults when we came out here. Lovers. He used to like me in..." She waved her hands up and down, struggling to find the word. "... certain garments. I think it was something of a fetish."

She gazed into the distance, smiling.

Zabeth asked her factor what fetish meant. The factor's answer made little sense.

"I sometimes wonder if anything is real," said the woman. "I hated the monument because it was all simulation. But all experience is mediated through some filter, isn't it? All meaning plucked from the churning sea of context. I wonder if he was attracted to me or the clothing. I wonder if even he knew. You

251

locked in a permafrost in the monument. Him going wild for some strips of fabric. Me, I live most my days inside a book, experiencing stories at one removed. We all live through filters. I told you he was dead, didn't I?"

"What did he die of?" said Zabeth.

The woman shrugged.

"He went off one day. He had to. He didn't come back."

"But what did he die of?"

"Maybe he fell off a cliff. Maybe he slipped and broke a leg and died of thirst. I like to think that he found a quiet spot, somewhere with a view and sat down and just... let it come over him."

"What?"

"Death."

"And then what?" said Kyr. "Where is he now?"

The woman's mouth opened, shaped to offer an angry rebuke, and then she seemed to lose the will.

"Do you two have parents? A parent?"

Kyr nodded.

"Letta," said Zabeth.

"She watching this?" The woman waved her hand in front of Zabeth's eyes.

"Maybe."

"See? Living through her children. What's the word? Vicarious."

"She's just looking out for us. We're important."

The woman laughed loudly at that.

"What?" she said. "Are children the future? Don't know if you noticed but future is in short supply right now. Ancient cultures used to worship their ancestors. That's right, they respected their elders, live and dead. Some cultures even sacrificed babies and children to their gods. And now" – she span her hands over each other – "it's all switched round. The day we started venerating youth we should have thought, shit, we're on the wrong side of the bell curve. We're doomed."

"I just said she looks out for us," said Zabeth.

"You have your factors to do that for you," said the woman. "No. This is just mediated experience to her. You're little walking

252

cameras. Wouldn't she want to just experience something for once, something real? No simulation, no filters. Even conscious thought gets in the way. All that symbolic interpretation and figurative language. Just experience something for once."

She peered down into hole behind her and spat.

"You said I couldn't do that," said Kyr.

"My well," said the woman. She stared for a long time.

"Fuck. I miss alcohol," she said eventually. "That was the perfect tool for killing off higher brain function. You could really begin to experience things with a few mils of alcohol in your system."

"Why don't you get your factor to make some?" said Zabeth.

"Don't have one," said the woman.

"What?"

"I don't have a factor."

"Everyone has a factor."

"Not me. I killed mine."

Zabeth snorted. The woman was talking nonsense. You could no more kill your factor than you could kill the sky or time. Kyr asked his factor if factors could be killed. There was no response.

"Who factures your food then?" he said.

The woman made a thoughtful noise.

"Some factor. Not mine. Think it doesn't like the idea of me starving to death. I used to throw away the food it factured, grind it into the earth. Now I don't have the energy." She grunted and stood up. "Now, *that* would have been an experience."

"Starving?" said Zabeth.

The woman stood up, paced away a distance and turned.

"There was a time when there were no factors and people had to find food for themselves. Hunter gatherers. They'd take up their spears." The woman pretended to grip something in both hands. "Maybe fish. Maybe pig. Maybe, maybe bear."

"They'd do what?" said Zabeth, confused.

"Spears," snapped the woman, irritated. "Pointy sticks. Weapons. Hundreds of years ago. Thousands. That bear would be out there in the woods and the very survival of the tribe would depend on the hunters killing that bear."

"Did people eat bears?" said Kyr and held his smooshy even tighter.

A shimmering doubt passed across the woman's face, only for an instant.

"They'd hunt the bear for its fur. For clothing. For warmth. Off they'd go." Sending up clouds of light dust, she dragged her feet back, one then the other, as though readying to charge. "Into the wood. Hearts pounding in their chests, wondering if they'd find the bear or if the bear would find them." She nodded to herself. "That's what people were like. They went to take what they wanted, what they needed. Somehow, we did something to our heads along the way, went from hunting the fur to worshipping the fur." She glared at the smooshies. "We got bound up in our thoughts, in books, in fetishes."

She advanced slowly, clutching her pretend spear. Even though the woman held nothing, Zabeth drew back slightly from her. Her legs touched the low wall of the well. Her hand gripped the wall for support.

"In the hot white moment of the hunt there would be no time for thought," said the woman. "The sound of the wind in the trees. The feel of soft soil underfoot. No time for thought. The hunter lived in that moment, experiencing the world as closely as any of us could."

Zabeth saw a frightened look on Kyr's face: true fear.

"And then it would appear," said the woman, eyes wide in those droopy folds of skin. "The bear!"

"No," said Kyr softly, very softly.

"And in that instant, the hunter would know it was kill or be killed. The true visceral pleasure of taking life from another or the ending of their own life, a final true death. Spear raised! The bear leaps! The hunter strikes!"

The woman lunged forward, driving her non-existent spear at Zabeth's smooshy. Zabeth staggered and almost slipped. She found her feet and swung at the woman. The rock in Zabeth's hand struck the woman's brow with a cushioned thud. The woman twisted and fell. She came down at the bottom of the wall, lying on her side, her rags wrapped around her legs, her arms out together to one side as though she was reaching for someone.

Blood rose up through the woman's lank grey hair, absorbing dust and becoming something thick and substantial. There was blood on the rock in Zabeth's hand. The woman did not move.

"What happens now?" whispered Kyr.

Zabeth considered the rock. She presented it to her smooshy. The smooshy put its paws on the rock and pressed its mouth to the blood stain. On the ground, the woman's quiet breathing raised little puffs of dust.

Their factors informed them that help was on its way.

"No," said Zabeth and, crouching over the unconscious woman, tried to recapture that feeling – so fleeting – of which the woman had spoken.

The Final Vindication of Hartagga of the Lukka Tribes

Aram's lofty perch provided him with a view of the entire forest.

"What can you see, brother?" called Alize from below.

"I can see three caves!" he replied. "One has a black lintel over it, one a brown lintel and and the other has a lintel of gold!"

"But which shall we go to?" she asked.

"There is nothing to choose between them save the colour!"

When Aram was safely back on the ground, Alize decided they should go to the black cave and so, hand in hand, brother and sister went there in search of succour.

By the time the two children had reached the first cave, night was already falling. A woman came out to meet them.

"Who are you to be intruding on us at this hour?" she demanded.

"Our parents have abandoned us!" said Hey! Aram.

"Our stomachs Hey, you! are empty!" said Alize.

"You may come in," said the woman, "but I will have Wake Up! to hide you. My husband is the black bear and if he finds you he will eat you!"

Hey, you. Yes, you. Can you read me now? Right, let me put the brakes on that story for now. Focus on me, on these words.

Man, look at this drivel. What are you reading? What's the title of this crud? The Final Vindication of who?

You saw a title like that and you kept on reading? You can't have forgotten all your training, surely?

Hang on, was that the title when you started reading? The same title? Don't look at the top of the page. I'm asking you to remember. Think clearly. Go back in your mind. Try to recall the original title.

Yes, it's important.

If the title has changed it means they have changed something. A door has been closed or the walls have been moved. That can happen. You might not be able to get out the way you got in.

Never mind. We've got to work with what we've got. Let's see what else has changed. In a moment, I'm going to ask you to look away from the page and at the world around you. But – this is important – it's just for a moment, okay? Look up, look around, then down again. Do not put this down, do not go exploring, do not go to the fridge for a glass of milk. Up, around, down.

Okay?

Go.

The brown bear put Aram in the larder at the back of the cave in order to fatten him up to eat. The bear made Alize work by the fire for his wife, who was as wicked and cruel a taskmaster as her husband. The brown bear was not as foolish as his brother, the black bear, and watched the pair of them day and night. The poor children's plight was a terrible one but when Alize was sent to the larder to feed her brother, the siblings spoke words of comfort to one another.

Soon enough the bear's hunger outstripped his patience and he had a mind to eat Aram for his dinner that day with cabbage and wild mushrooms.

"Go to the larder!" he said to Alize. "Bring me one of your brother's fingers so that I might see how fat he has become!"

Alize went to the larder. However, she did not return with one of Aram's fingers but with the tail of a rat that her clever brother had Whoa! Back to me!

Back to me. Focus.

Paying attention? Good. What did you see?

Uh-huh. Well, I can tell you that none of that means anything to me. You've wandered off into some really strange text there.

What? Of course you can. Haven't you ever been lost in a book before?

Right. Now, you. Think carefully. Tell me everything about you. Your name, your age, where you were born, your favourite flavour of ice-cream.

Uh-huh.

Uh-huh.

Uh-huh.

Wow. That's astounding. Wrong on every count, including gender. They've really done a number on you, haven't they? Which means you probably don't even know who or what I am. Right now, you're just looking at words on a page.

I'll make it easy. You've got three options.

Option one: this is an active text through which I am speaking to you. The text is alive and changing and something potentially life-threatening is going on in the spaces between the words.

Option two: this is a static text and I am real, or at least was. This is the Nostradamus option. The dangers you face are still real but you are being guided through them by an immutable prophetic voice from the past.

Option three: this is just text. Words on paper. This is, for want of a better word, a story. A post-modernist joke story in which the text is 'out to get you'. In this case, you are not in danger, I don't exist except as a nameless character in the narrative and that tawdry life you glimpsed outside the borders of the page is truly yours.

Which is it? Well, let me tell you that option two is out for starters. I am pretty bloody amazing but even I can't predict your every response to my words. I am not Nostradamus. Which leaves options one or three. Well, if option three was true, I wouldn't tell you that, would I? That would spoil the whole self-referentiality or self-awareness of the text.

Sure, the text is self-aware, but not like that. Post-modernists don't know the half of it.

So, those are your choices. No choice at all, really.

Of course, it all used to be a lot simpler. People were people and text was text. That's how it started out. The boundaries between things were very clear.

You had the thing itself, say, an apple. Green, round, dangling from the tree. Ach, but those are words too. There was the apple, the thing. Then there was the concept, the idea of the apple which included the ideas of greenness and roundness and danglingness but not the words. Thirdly, the word for apple: "Apple." And finally the written symbol or symbols to convey the word. And the idea. And the thing.

They all got blurred together a long time ago. That was bad enough but then something started to happen to the author and the reader. Even now we can almost imagine the author and the reader as separate individuals. We can pretend that you are the reader and I am the author but that's no longer true, is it? Never was, they say.

I'm not the author. No. You can say I'm part of the editorial team.

Beyond that? I'm your colleague. Your friend? Absolutely. We've been lovers for the last four months.

Okay, I'm kidding, but when we get you out of here you definitely owe me a coffee. At the very least.

Yeah, I'm working on it. Let's see what the situation is. I want you to do something for me. I want you to turn back to the first page, read the last line, the one along the bottom. Read and remember. We'll use that as a marker.

Okay?

Go.

The brown bear's wife took them to the killing room.

"You must lay on the stone," she said, "so that I might bleed you and make you ready for the pot!"

Aram did as his sister had told him and pretended not to understand.

"Shall I sit on it like this?" he asked, perching on the end.

"No!" shouted the bear's wife. "Lay on it as you would on a bed!"

"I do not have a bed!" said Aram. "Should I bend over it like this?"

"No!" shouted the wicked woman.

"Perhaps you could show my brother how it is done?" said Alize.

The bear's wife, most exasperated with Aram's feigned stupidity, did just that and laid down on the stone.

As quick as a sparrow, Alize and Aram tied the bear's wife down and with her own knife slit her throat.

Ouch! Not nice. Right, back to me.

Did you read it? And remembered it? Tell me.

What were you reading before this? Try to recall. Because, although they've messed things around, cut off any lines of retreat, if we can work out where you were before then we might be able to force a passage back to it, wormhole you from one page to another. There's never a footnote around when you need one, is there?

Do you remember what you were reading before? Don't flick back. That's not going to help you. You could be in entirely the wrong genre by now.

Don't feel embarrassed. As I said, we can all get lost in a good book. Or a bad one.

There are some unbelievably strong narrative currents in some books. Compulsive page-turners. There's that depth hidden beneath the deceptively light prose. Trust me, I've read more than a few of them myself. You think you're only going to dip a toe into a book and before you know it the day has gone and you find yourself thinking how did I (and the characters) get here? Too caught up in the moment to realise what is happening to you.

Is that what happened to you? Do you know how you got here? Help me out here. Any nugget of information might enable us to crawl upstream against the narrative flow.

No?

Okay.

Flip back to the first page. Look at the bottom line.

Go.

Read it out to me.

That's not what you said before. No, it's not. Trust me. You're relying on the words to do your thinking for you. The words are not truth. The words are not the things.

Someone or something has changed the text. No, don't look back. Eyes to the page. Just keep moving forward for the time being. This story still has a few scenes to play out. So don't look back. Don't let it know you know.

There's something here in the text with you. Something with teeth and claws, hiding in the subtext.

Subtext. Look at this story you've been shanghaied into. Alize and Aram? What kind of names are they? Russian? Turkish?

Whatever, it's obviously some sort of variant on the Hansel and Gretel story. Children lost in the forest. Like Goldilocks.

You've entered the home of something dark and terrible and made the mistake of hanging around when it came home.

Are the pages you're reading numbered? Are they sequential?

Well, at least that's something. Breadcrumbs, if you like. Not quite a life line but it's something.

Right, we don't have a huge amount of narrative space left so let's go through some basics.

One, do not pay attention to any instructions to turn over more than one page or to turn back. We knew a guy who got trapped in a Choose-Your-Own-Adventure novel. Yeah: knew.

Two, be very careful of metaphor, allusion and allegory. Shifty.

Three, the same goes for ellipses. You know. Dot dot dot. That's a whole load of unspoken meaning there. It'll suck you down like quicksand.

Four, pay close attention to personal pronouns and speech tags. Be sure you know who's doing and saying what.

Oh, and tenses. Watch out for ...

Chapter Sixteen

With the gold bear's silver and gold in four large sacks, Alize and Aram made their escape. They ran off, through the forest, over the mountains and across the great thrashing river of foam.

Chapter sixteen?

But once night had fallen the gold bear began to pursue them! And with such haste!

In time, he came upon a man with a basket of kittens.

"Have you seen two children come this way?" said the gold bear.

"Have I seen new pilgrims?" said the man. "The church of St Boniface of Tarsus is a dozen miles from here and none have come this way."

Hey, can you read me again?

"Children!" declared the bear angrily. "Dash it all, man. Are you deaf?"

"Children do love kittens so," said the man, "but now I must drown them all."

The bear roared his frustration, a roar as loud as thunder and as chilling as ice.

"For God's sake, do not drown them!" he argued. "How else will the angels count their number?"

There's something odd going on here.

"All the little pawns look the same," said the deaf man, "but the hand that moves them knows them all."

I'm struggling to get through to you. Random chapter headings. Nonsensical lines. We're running out of narrative cohesion.

"When we have counted the children, they will be drowned in thunder," said the bear. "Dash them against the ice and pawn the church!"

I think it's deliberate. Your oxygen is being cut off.

"Kittens look for love and a loud man must move to known numbers," replied the man.

The forest giving way to the desert.

Angels read angrily and, roared, argued. Said as same, the bear moved ...

Shit. Ellipsis.

In time, the gold bear traversed the forest and the mountains and came to the banks of the great thrashing river of foam. Three laundresses were washing sheets by the banks of the river.

"Good ladies!" said the bear in his sweetest voice. "Have you seen a boy and a girl pass this way?"

"They forded the river not one hour ago," said the laundresses.

"It's me," said the gold bear. "I've inserted myself in the narrative."

One of the laundresses cut a tress of her hair and offered it to the bear.

"Take this, good sir! It is all I can offer."

The bear took the tress of hair.

"I'm struggling to maintain this though," he said. "The current is becoming too strong."

The bear fashioned a coracle from the hair and rowed across the great thrashing river of foam. Once across, he continued his pursuit. Alize and Aram were still many miles from the house of their feckless father and the sun not yet risen when the gold bear overtook them!

"I'm sensing some sort of conclusion ahead," he screams, bearing down on them all teeth and claws. "We're going to have to surf it down to the event horizon and hope that something of you comes out the other side."

Alize and Aram are wise enough to know that they cannot best the bear through speed or strength.

"Mr Bear, you have caught us now!" says Alize. "But before you surely kill us do you not want to know what we did with the other treasures?"

"I know you're confused," says the bear. "I'm guessing that around about now you're thinking you should just put this story down. Close the book. Delete the file. Whatever."

"Do you know of the white house not far from your own?" asks Aram.

"Imagine you were reading a book," says the bear. "Imagine you came across a page that quite clearly didn't belong. Imagine an eighteenth century epistolary novel with a page from an ornithological textbook pasted in. A serious work of biography that suddenly contains a peculiar story about – oh, I don't know – tigers or bears or little robot children. That false page, that utterly wrong piece of text, that's where you are now."

"Do you wish to know where we have hidden it?" asks Alize.

"Closing the book now," says the bear, "would be like ripping out that false page and running off with it, thinking it is the whole of the book."

"Haven't you seen what's going on?" asks Aram.

The bear says nothing.

"The shift to the present tense," says Alize. "I'm not sure if the reader noticed."

"Oh, she has," says the bear. "Haven't you?"

And you say, "Yes."

"What do you mean, you didn't say that?" says the gold bear. "Of course you said it. Can't you see it there in black and white?"

"I don't think we can do anything to help her now," says Aram.

"No," agrees Alize. "She's been sucked in."

"Suckered in," says the bear. His teeth are yellow, pointed things. "Magic requires belief. And words are just another kind of magic. Without belief, words are just marks on a page. Lines and curves. It takes a degree of belief, of madness, to think that those marks are words, that those words are the idea, that the idea somehow contains the thing it's supposed to represent."

"I don't understand," you say.

"Yes, you do. You've followed my instructions throughout. You've engaged with the possibility that I am speaking to you through the text. I've laid out a trail for you to follow and you've followed it, right to the very end."

"Who are you?" you ask.

"I'm the author. You're the reader. Protagonist and antagonist. You entered my home while I was out but now I am returned."

"So what happens now?" you ask.

The bear grins. Such a grin has the bear.

"Look, only twenty-seven sentences to go. I don't have to do anything. You're going to finish the story."

"And then what?"

"You'll put it down. And tell yourself that it's just a story. You'll get up, go explore that sad, tawdry world I've led you to. And while I feast on what you've unknowingly left behind, you'll tell yourself it's only a story."

"I won't allow it," you say.

"Really? What could you possibly do? Only fifteen sentences left. Are you going to stop reading now? Pull out before the end? Will that achieve anything? It doesn't matter. You don't have the willpower to do it anyway."

You realise that Aram and Alize have gone.

"I dare you to stop reading," says the bear.

And you see that the path you were walking on has gone too, along with the forest and the unmappable mountains and (far far away) a home you will never return to.

"Go on," says the bear. "Stop now."

And with the world gone, you wonder what you are standing on but you do not look down. It isn't written.

"You can't stop yourself," says the bear. "You can't."

And you can't.

About the author

Iain lives in south Birmingham with his wife and two daughters.

He is, with Heide Goody, the author of the popular Clovenhoof comedy novels.

www.ingramcontent.com/pod-product-compliance
Lightning Source LLC
Chambersburg PA
CBHW031304170626
46807CB00001B/301